Books by T.J. Mindancer

Tales of Emoria

Jame and Tigh Saga
Book 1: Future Dreams
Book 2: Present Paths
Book 3: Past Echoes
Book 4: Fall Time

Hekolatis' Promise

Emoran Campfire Tales

Other Books

The Queen's Sister

Novellas

Bountiful Glen

Tales of Emoria
Book 4

Fall Time

T.J. Mindancer

Mindancer Press
Bedazzled Ink Publishing Company • Fairfield, California

978-0-9886061-5-9 paperback

Cover Design
by

Mindancer Press
a division of
Bedazzled Ink Publishing, LLC
Fairfield, California
http://www.bedazzledink.com

The Saga of Jame and Tigh, Book 4

Note on Pronunciation

Jame is one syllable with a long "a." Rhymes with "fame." Tigh is pronounced "Tig." Rhymes with "twig." The spelling of her name follows the Ingoran rules of grammar where the "h" indicates the eldest daughter of the House of Tigis.

Chapter 1

"YOU CALL THIS person a challenge? I've seen bigger and stronger weeds in my grandma's garden."

"You bet I'm challenging you, you daughter of a Yitsian snow monster."

Jame looked up from inspecting a wad of wool on display and frowned. She arched her neck to look around the maze of animal pens and vendors, not to mention all the people. She spotted the black hilt of Tigh's sword and scooted through the narrow gaps between pens and people to the sheep shearing demonstration.

Tigh saw her and waded through the spectators away from the demonstration to an open space outside the pens.

"Did you hear it?" Jame asked as she approached Tigh.

"Hard not to." Tigh squinted into the dusty late afternoon sun. "She has to be close." She turned in the direction of a large and raucous crowd. "Isn't that the wrestling pit?"

"I don't believe it," Jame muttered. "We'd better see what's going on."

They ignored the calls from vendors hawking trinkets and food as they hurried, as best they could around loitering groups of people. Jame had to admit she enjoyed harvest fairs. The villagers were usually at their best, and it was fascinating to see what they had pride in. Came in handy when arbiting cases.

They winnowed to the front of the jeering and yelling crowd surrounding the wrestling pit.

"There." Jame squeezed around several rapt spectators to a thin woman with pale hair and wearing a loose archivist tunic and leggings.

The woman was wringing her hands and watching the challengers in the pit with shaking anxiety.

"Seeran," Jame said.

Seeran turned, gasped in surprise, and almost collapsed into Jame's arms. "Jame. Thank Bal you're here. Can you stop her from getting herself killed?"

Tigh came up next to Jame and gazed at the sparring pit. She shook her head in disbelief.

Jame looked over Seeran's shoulder and winced as Tas hurled colorful insults at a woman with bulging muscles upon muscles who towered a good two heads over her.

"If this is an insult calling contest, Tas is the sure winner," Tigh said.

Seeran sniffed and wiped her eyes. "It's a wrestling match."

Tigh shrugged. "Tas still shouldn't have much of a problem."

Seeran stared at her in disbelief. "But that woman is huge."

"You forget she now has the skills of a Guard," Tigh said.

Seeran blinked at her and then gazed at Tas.

The woman refereeing the match sighed at Tas and glanced at the healers who were looking on with interest from the edge of the pit. "The first woman who pins the other wins." She sprinted out of the ring of dirt.

The large woman, wearing the loose undershirt of a federation soldier, flexed her muscles as she looked down at Tas. "I'll try not to do too much damage."

The soldier dove forward, and Tas launched into a graceful flip over her. The soldier hit the ground with a thud in a cloud of dust. Tas bounced and sat down hard on the soldier's shoulders, slamming them into the dirt.

The crowd was still for only a few heartbeats. Jame's ears popped from the explosive roar of approval followed by excited twitters.

Jame and Seeran stared speechless at Tas who was already standing and helping the soldier to her feet.

"What do they feed you up there in the mountains?" the soldier asked as she rubbed her shoulder.

Tas straightened and thumped her chest. "We feast on the spirits of the best warriors in the world."

The referee, now smiling, strode into the ring. "Who wants to challenge the warrior from Emoria?"

Several women pushed and jostled through the crowd to get to the edge of the dirt. "Me."

Seeran sighed. "Now she's going to be here all day."

Jane looked around bewildered. "What are you doing here?"

"We're on our way to see my folks in Glaus and pick up my things in Artocia." Seeran eyed the first challenger—a tall, wiry young woman—stepping into the circle. "We decided to go now so we'll be back in time for the joining."

Jame laughed. "It'd be hard to have a joining without you there."

Seeran shook her head. "Not ours. Argis and Goodemer's."

Jame stared at Seeran. "What?"

Tigh turned to them with a raised eyebrow.

"You didn't know? That must have happened after you left Emoria." Seeran scratched her head.

"Argis. The one who never trusted mind games or magic is being joined with a Wizard?" Jame asked.

Tigh shrugged. "Must be love."

"When are they going to be joined?" Jame asked. "I can't believe we haven't heard about it."

"They just set the date a fortnight ago," Seeran said. "Wintermas Eve."

Jame wrinkled her nose. "Ugh. Emoria in the middle of winter. Why then?"

"They're thinking of children," Seeran said, lowering her voice.

"What?" Tigh and Jame asked together.

Tigh frowned. "What does Wintermas have to do with children?"

Jame ran a hand through her hair. "I'll explain later. It's a rather complicated tradition."

Tigh frowned at her.

"I'm sure an invitation has been sent out to you," Seeran said.

Tigh nodded. "It was probably sent to Ynit. We haven't been home in a while."

The crowd around them burst into a frenzy of noise as they chanted "Emoria, Emoria, Emoria."

Tas bounced around, looking ready for any and all challenges, as her third challenger rubbed her shoulder as she walked out of the pit.

Seeran sighed. "I really don't want her doing this all day."

"Who wants to be the next to challenge this formable warrior from Emoria?" the referee yelled out.

Tigh sighed and strode into the circle of dirt. Jame almost laughed at how sudden the crowd stopped yelling and sucked in their collective breaths.

The referee gazed up at her with a raised eyebrow. "Looks like we might finally have a real challenge."

"Tigh." Tas's voice cracked. She sighed in resignation.

"ARGIS STARTED OUT pretending to protect Goodemer from the attentions of the other warriors," Tas said with enthusiasm as they sat around a table in the town of Letahly's only Inn. The place was overflowing with festivalgoers who had cheered and pounded the tables when Tas and Tigh walked in. The tale of their challenge was sure to be told for festivals to come.

"Pretending." Tigh, as always, latched on to the important word.

Tas grinned. "She put up a good front but we could tell she was a goner."

"I'm glad Argis has finally found someone." Jame stared into her mug of spiced tea.

Tas reached across the table and laid a hand on top of Jame's. "She's always known you two weren't really meant for each other. But her feelings and her stubborn pride were too deep to let it go. She respects Tigh and knows the depth of your feelings for each other."

Jame nodded and gazed up at her old friend. "I still haven't been able to stop feeling guilty about it."

"That's because you have a good and gentle heart." Tigh wrapped an arm around Jame's shoulder and pulled her close.

Tas grinned. "I have to admit, Argis was never the sweet talker you are, Tigh."

"Tigh never had to worry about defending her big bad warrior image against her peers." Jame playfully nudged Tigh.

"Argis always seemed to take our good-natured ribbing a little more seriously than most." Tas clinked her tankard with a soldier passing the table. All night, soldiers had been going out of their way to congratulate her for taking down their undefeated comrade.

"I hope she's loosened up a bit for Goodemer," Jame said as a pair of young men put steaming plates of food in front of them.

Seeran and Tas looked at each other and fought to keep from laughing.

"I take that as a no," Jame said.

"Fortunately, Goodemer doesn't seem to mind," Seeran said.

"So when are you two planning to head back to Emoria?" Tas asked.

Jame shrugged. "Haven't really thought about it. We're headed home for Tigh's annual evaluation."

Tas scrunched her face. "You still have to do that?"

"For the rest of my life," Tigh said. "It's a small price to pay for my freedom."

"Besides, it's always good to get together with old friends," Jame said. "Not to mention air out the house."

"I can't believe you've been living there for, what, seven years now," Tas said. "And to think I was at your house warming."

Tigh raised an amused eyebrow. "If I remember correctly, you fought one of the soldiers over a certain healer's assistant in our front yard."

"Uh, yes," Tas cleared her throat as she glanced at Seeran, "but that was when I was young and didn't know what love was."

Jame smiled in amusement. "It seems the warriors of Emoria have been taking lessons in sweet talk."

Tas straightened. "We try to learn from the best."

Seeran looked Tas up and down. "For a warrior she's not bad at it."

Tas whipped her head around but stopped at the affectionate glimmer in Seeran's eyes and grinned.

"Fortunately, Tas can take being teased better than Argis," Jame said.

"Goodemer has a way of teasing Argis without Argis realizing it," Seeran said. "It's so cute to see."

Jame grinned. "Can't wait to witness all this."

"Everyone wants to see you again," Tas said. "Panilope has been wondering when you'll be coming back."

"Panilope?" Jame frowned. "That's odd."

"She's probably wondering if you've successfully converted Tigh to the way of the waterfall." Tas laughed at Tigh's expression.

"Tigh and I have an agreement," Jame said. "I don't try to turn her into a follower of Laur, and she won't make me memorize the names of all the Children of Bal."

Tas stared at Tigh, shocked. "And I thought Tigh the Terrible's cruel ruthlessness was gone. How dare you threaten our princess with such torture?"

"I didn't threaten," Tigh said with an innocent look. "I simply put forth the best cultural swap possible."

Seeran laughed. "I doubt the theologians would agree with you."

"I'll do anything that's required of me as consort to your princess," Tigh said.

Jame squeezed Tigh's hand, and they exchanged affectionate looks.

"I'm enjoying learning about Laur," Seeran said. "I'd never imagined Emoran children were a gift of Laur. There's nothing about it in the scrolls in Artocia."

"We treasure Laur's gifts and protect them from others who may not understand them," Jame said.

"I was happy to hear an outsider can participate in these ceremonies." Seeran smiled at Tas. "That an outsider can be the one to carry the child."

"Really?" Tigh asked.

"Laur usually selects the woman best suited to be the birth mother," Jame said.

"You mean there isn't any choice?" Tigh worked to digest this new piece of information.

"We don't even know who the birth mother is until Laur has bestowed the gift," Jame said.

Tigh struggled to keep down an unbidden panic. She'd never even contemplated she'd be the one carrying the heir to the Emoran throne.

Tas grinned. "And Goodemer and Argis want children. Argis would never live it down if she were chosen to be the birth mother."

THE WATER SPLASHING into the pool from the falls looked as icy as the mountains in the distance. Jame stuck a tentative hand into the pool and was as shocked from the warmth as she would have been from it being cold. The warmth seemed to go straight to her soul, and she pulled off her leathers and slipped into the water.

She sighed in the aqueous embrace, surrounding her with an aura of love she felt only in the arms of her warrior.

A throaty laugh reached her ears, and she smiled before she even turned toward the falls where the warrior in question stood. Water cascaded down the long muscular body, sending new sensations of warmth through Jame's body. Never had the warrior looked more magnificent, even with the impish twinkle in her eyes.

"What has you in such a good mood?" Jame asked as she half-swam, half-floated to Tigh.

Tigh's impish grin broadened. "You."

"Me?" Jame laughed as she pulled on Tigh's leg. Tigh lost her balance on the slick uneven stone and tumbled into the water next to Jame.

"Yes, you." Tigh swam away from Jame.

"Hey, where are you going?" Jame splashed into a swimming stroke and chased after the playful warrior.

"Wherever you go," came the contented response.

JAME BLINKED HER eyes open and stared into the dark as her mind tried to grip the dream before it slipped away. Waterfalls, warm pools . . . them happy and content. It was, she concluded, the most peaceful, wonderful dream she had ever had.

She turned her head to the slumbering Tigh curled up next to her. Six years. It was hard to believe. Time was passing quickly for them with their lives so full of what they did for a living. Strange, she dreamed about a waterfall.

TIGH STIFLED ANOTHER yawn. How could two people argue for three sandmarks over the ownership of a cow? Her Ingoran sensibilities made her unsympathetic to both parties since they wanted the cow for meat rather than for milk. She could settle this dispute fast enough—if the killing of animals for food wasn't against her heritage.

She sighed and tried to amuse herself by watching Jame struggle to maintain an interested expression. In that respect, she had the easier job. Jame actually had to stay alert and pay attention to the monotonous expounding of the local arbiters on the reasons why their clients should be in possession of the cow.

The intense interest of most of the villagers, who not only filled the seats but were crammed shoulder to shoulder along the walls, seemed a little extreme, telling Tigh there was more to this situation than an errant bovine. That was the reason for the endless impassioned arguments over something that was so simple to resolve. The arbiters couldn't argue what was really going on between the disputing parties.

Local politics. Tigh knew she was going to endure several days of ranting from Jame about swords never being completely buried about some minor altercation from years before. Any little excuse for a dispute was enough to open up all the unhealed wounds.

The arbiters finally tired of nit picking every letter of every word uttered in their arguments, and the small hall grew silent as the spectators turned their attention to Jame.

Jame had the ability to muster a confident command over a situation just by straightening and casting her intelligent green eyes around the chamber. Tigh knew her verdict for this case had been settled in her mind within the first quarter sandmark of arguments, but she knew better than to rush the defendants before they had a chance to develop a false sense of victory over each other.

"I would like to thank arbiters Hejla and Tinbac for their *thorough* arguments in this case," Jame said.

Tigh rolled her eyes.

"I'd like to clarify a few things." Jame made a show of finding something on one of the documents in front of her. "The defendants are members of the most prominent families in Wenter. Is this correct."

"Correct," both arbiters said.

"And both defendants are active citizens in the community and are known for their generous contributions to community projects and to the Temple of Bal," Jame continued.

"Yes." The arbiters looked a little wary.

"Then why are they arguing about who owns a cow?"

Tigh stifled a laugh. She was glad they hadn't bothered to find a room in the local inn. Jame's sense of logic and fairness at any cost might require a rather quick departure from the village.

"How dare you imply this suit is not a serious matter," Tinbac sputtered.

Jame leveled a calm gaze at her. "I didn't say anything about this suit not being a serious matter. I'm just wondering why you're arguing about a cow and not about what's really behind the animosity between the defendants."

The spectators gasped and stared at Jame in shocked silence. Tigh was certain the arbiters weren't getting paid enough to touch that bowl of eels.

"So," Jame glanced around the chamber, "this is my verdict on this case. Will the defendants stand?"

The two older well-dressed women, who wore the arrogance and entitlement of their standing in the community throughout the hearing, stood with their confident bearing and expressions. Tigh was impressed by their unflappable merchant demeanor.

"Since I'm not convinced either party has greater claim over the cow," Jame linked her fingers together and rested her hands on the table, "and since neither party depends on the cow for their livelihood or survival, I declare the cow property of the acolytes of Bal to be used to provide milk to the orphans of Wenter Park Orphanage."

Jame waited for the noise from the spectators and the indignant sputters of the defendants to die away.

"Being such devoted followers of Bal, I'm sure the defendants will agree to this simple resolution to their dispute and will welcome the effort to help the orphans."

Tigh grinned. Jame was going to make a great queen someday.

"We're going to appeal," Hejla said.

"That is your privilege." Jame stood and stretched. "In the meantime, the cow serves Bal and the orphans."

Tigh strode down the middle aisle before the stunned spectators got to their feet and blocked the way. She planted herself by Jame's side and gazed at the arbiters who looked like they were about to badger Jame about appeals.

"Shall we go secure the cow?" Tigh raised an eyebrow.

"With pleasure," Jame muttered as Tigh guided her through a small side door into the deliberation chamber. "Sometimes I wonder why I keep doing this."

Tigh stopped and closed the door behind her. "So you can ensure orphans get enough milk to drink."

Jame blinked up at Tigh and nodded. "As long as I can pull some good from this kind of nonsense. It still doesn't ease my disappointment in the pettiness and greed of some people."

"There will always be pettiness and greed," Tigh said. "That's why there are arbiters like yourself to divert it into good deeds every once in a while."

Jame sighed as she dropped the case documents on a simple wooden table and sat down. "How can I have dreams of utter contentment and happiness, and have to put up with this kind of stuff every day?"

Tigh knelt next to Jame and pulled an ink jar and pen to her. She took the stopper off the jar. "Because what counts is on the inside."

Jame smiled as she picked up the pen, dipped it into the ink, and signed her official ruling in the case. "And what's on the inside is you."

"THE COW HAD more sense than those arbiters," Jame muttered as she kicked a stone, sending it scuttling down the hill they were climbing. The patches of white over the light brown of harvested fields foretold of an early winter.

Tigh sighed and shifted Gessen's reins to her other hand.

"They should have had enough sense to convince their clients not to waste everyone's time with such a case." Jame stomped moodily on a tiny clump of snow.

Tigh exchanged a long-suffering look with Gessen.

"Do you think I'll be granted a leave of absence?"

Tigh blinked at Jame. "I don't see why not."

"It's just I've never even thought about taking a leave of absence before." Jame knelt down and picked up a long thin twig. "It's such short notice. Maybe they won't be able to find a replacement that quickly."

"It'll just be for a moon at most," Tigh said.

"I only got away with it the last we were in Emoria because I arbitrated Kylara's case to Jyac." Jame twisted the twig into sinewy strands.

Tigh gazed at the sky. "The fact we saved them from a mad Wizard trying to take over the world had nothing to do with it."

"That may have helped at bit." Jame wrapped her hands around Tigh's arm. "I'm being a little silly, aren't I?"

Tigh shrugged. "It's natural to worry about things."

"I guess I spent so many years not thinking about Emoria as a place where I could just drop in and visit, that it feels kind of strange," Jame said.

They took the last few steps to the top of the hill. Tigh stopped and stared with a frown. Before them was the southernmost edge of the desert plain and Ynit sprawled in the distance.

"Wow," Jame said. "That's incredible looking. Have you ever seen it covered in snow?"

"Once. Eleven or twelve seasons ago," Tigh said. "They doubled our field training time to get us used to maneuvering in snow."

"Ugh." Jame made a face as they tromped down the hill.

Tigh cocked her head at Jame. "We loved every minute of it. We only felt alive when we were being warriors."

"I think that's the hardest part to understand about the whole enhancement thing," Jame said. "They took away your own life, yet you loved the life they gave you."

Tigh shrugged. "For their purposes, I would say the enhancements worked perfectly."

"It still doesn't make it right."

They followed the farm trail down the hill to the main road of smooth stone blocks. Jame stood in a mixture of churned up snow and sand next to the road and studied the glistening moisture through melting snow on the stone slabs.

"I think I'm going to follow the trail made by the other travelers," Jame said. "Messier, but less treacherous."

"Wise choice." Tigh lead Gessen onto the cleanest narrow rut tamped down by travelers.

Jame trudged along her in a matching rut. "I hope this isn't a sign of a nasty winter."

Tigh gazed at the expanse of snowy sand. "It snowed a couple more times, last time."

Jame sighed as she resettled her bag on her shoulder. "Glad we're not on the road. It's like glass now."

"We used to practice walking on slick surfaces when the roads got like this," Tigh said.

"Practice falling more like it," Jame muttered as she eyed the watery layer of ice over flat stone.

Tigh shrugged. "We got pretty good at it."

"Are you trying to tell me that you can walk on that without slipping?" Jame asked.

Tigh shrugged. "I used to be able to."

"Maybe really slow."

"Pretty normally, as I recall." Tigh gazed at the road as she remembered lines of black clad warriors marching down it as if it were as dry as the summer desert.

Jame walked up to the edge of the stone and slid her boot around on it. "Too slick."

Tigh gave her an impish sidelong look. She handed Gessen's reins to Jame, jumped up, and landed solidly in the middle of a stone slab.

"If you break your leg, I'm not carrying you all the way to Emoria," Jame said.

Tigh grinned. "If I break my leg, your warriors would never let me live it down."

"They have enough sense not to walk on ice covered with water." Jame crossed her arms.

"And they call themselves warriors." Tigh tuned in to all the little slippery signals shooting through her feet and then balanced her body so it reacted to those signals. Two full years of Guard training involved learning how to read the body until reactions were second nature.

"You haven't taken a step yet," Jame said.

Tigh took several steps forward. She twisted around and lifted an eyebrow at a stunned Jame.

"How did you do that?" Jame asked.

"It just takes altering how you walk," Tigh said. "Keeping the center of gravity over the feet so the body falls into itself rather than outward."

Jame frowned as she walked up next to where Tigh stood and studied her feet. "I guess it takes a little practice to do that."

Tigh laughed.

They looked up at the sound of galloping horses crunching on snow from up ahead. The eastern gate of Ynit had opened and a group of soldiers on horseback were charging toward them in the snowy sand next to the road.

"What the—?" Tigh concentrated a moment on what the riders were shouting and thudded onto the hard ice and stone.

Chapter 2

PENDON STOOD AT the top of the steps of the fortress, raised a bony hand to his crinkled brow, and couldn't keep the amused grin from his ancient face. The fortress had erupted in chaos the moment word had spread that Jame and Tigh were on the road. Endless footfalls echoed through the corridors as every soldier rushed to the main doors and raced to the wall gate.

A quarter sandmark later the soldiers swarming the gate were pushed back as their comrades charged through with a confused and embarrassed looking Tigh and Jame clinging to their shoulders.

"They just can't help being heroes, can they?" Ingel asked as she sauntered up to Pendon.

"Reluctant heroes," Pendon said.

The joyous shouting changed to uproarious shock and then laughter as the soldiers supporting Tigh and Jame hit a slick spot in the slush on the adobe brick. Tigh and Jame tumbled off of the shoulders as the soldiers lost their footing.

"Come on. Let's go rescue them." Ingel pushed through the grinning knots of people who had come out to see what all the noise was about with Pendon behind her.

The soldiers parted for them as they approached Tigh and Jame, who sat in the slushy ice with bemused expressions. The soldiers around them were laughing so hard they kept slipping as they tried to stand up.

"Welcome home. As you can see, everyone's been looking forward to your return," Pendon said.

"If we'd known that, we'd have stayed away longer," Tigh muttered as she climbed to her feet and put a hand out to Jame.

"Interesting weather you're having." Jame took the hand, and Tigh pulled her up.

"Sign of a bad winter." Pendon shook his head. "It's just as well you made it home before the worst of it."

Tigh and Jame exchanged glances.

"I'm sure any pending case can wait until spring," Ingel said.

Jame shook her head. "That's not it. We have to return to Emoria for a joining ceremony."

"Surely they would understand," Ingel said as she and Pendon led Jame and Tigh away from the grinning soldiers.

Tigh looked around.

"I'll make sure Gessen is taken care of." A young soldier held Gessen's reins.

Tigh nodded. "Thanks."

Jame grinned. "A little snow and ice isn't enough to keep us from this particular joining."

"So, I take it, you've resolved your differences with Emoria," Ingel said.

"Not only have we reconciled our differences but Tigh and I have been joined in an Emoran ceremony," Jame said.

Ingel clasped her hands in delight. "That is good news."

Jame eyed a heavyset man in Tribunal robes standing at the bottom of the steps of the fortress. His arms were crossed, and he wore a stern expression on his rather florid face. She didn't remember any news about a Tribune retiring.

Jame and Tigh strode to within a few paces of the steps, and the man shuffled to stand in front of them.

Ingel groaned.

"So the heroes finally return," the man said with barely concealed contempt.

"Jame, Tigh, this is the Tribune Iksoc, he's filling in for Ewan while she's on leave to visit her family," Ingel said with a sigh.

"Glad to meet you, Tribune." Jame smiled at the scowling man.

"Don't try that Emoran smooth talking with me," Iksoc said. "You may have pulled the sheep's wool over everyone's eyes around here but you haven't fooled me. You two have a lot of explaining to do about that so-called uprising in the mountains."

"You didn't see my report?" Jame asked with a frown.

"An entertaining document," Iksoc said. "Reads enough like fiction to be fiction."

Tigh stepped up to Iksoc, cold menace glinting in her eyes. "I suggest you take that back."

"Or you'll do what?" Iksoc crossed his arms.

"I'll step aside and let Jame argue the veracity of her report with you," Tigh said with a wicked glint in her eyes. "Here in public. In front of all these witnesses."

Iksoc leveled a cold gaze at Jame. "There's a time and place for everything. You'll be receiving a summons before the Tribunal soon enough."

"If the Federation had a problem with my report wouldn't they have let me know?" Jame asked. "It's not like we've been out of sight for the past year."

Iksoc straightened. "All this will be covered when you appear before the Tribunal." He lifted his chin, turned around, and climbed the fortress steps.

Jame turned to Ingel. "What's that all about?"

"Why don't you get settled in and join me for the evening meal," Ingel said. "It's a long story."

"GREETINGS FELLOW WIZARD slayer."

Tigh turned from brushing out Gessen's mane. A grinning small soldier trailed by a dark-haired woman walked toward her in the streams of late sunlight filtering through the upper openings of the stable. Tigh nodded at the greeting and the soldier.

"Of course, you got your Wizard on the first try," Tigh said.

"But I had help from another Wizard." Claudi grinned and turned to her friend who was looking up at Tigh with unconcealed awe. "This is my friend, Fant. She's writing a history of Ynit."

Tigh looked into the bright blue eyes of the young woman, seeing the unasked question. *Uh, oh. She's going to want to interview me.*

"Speaking of Wizards," Claudi said, glancing around the stables. "There's this new Tribunal who thinks you're trying to take over the world."

Tigh rolled her eyes. "We've already met, and Ingel filled us in on what he's up to."

"For the record, everyone here has told him he's wrong," Claudi said. "He's got some crazy theory that all the wars you've been able to stop were really your own plans gone wrong and to cover up for your failure, you contrived to make yourself the hero."

"He's just setting himself up to be target practice for Jame's well-aimed counter arguments." Tigh put Gessen's brush into the saddlebag draped over a wooden slat. "She's the one he should be worried about if he's looking for someone capable of taking over the world."

Claudi laughed, and Fant's eyes widened.

"I wouldn't mind being ruled by an Emoran princess." Claudi feinted a few fancy thrusts with an imaginary sword. "Especially if we can wear those leathers. It's amazing how they can reveal so much and still protect the body in a fight."

"You'd be bashing yourselves in the head all the time if you wore those leathers." Tigh pulled their bags of provisions and Jame's scrolls from the bulging saddlebag. "The Emorans are used to seeing each other more scantily clad."

"We're flexible. We could adapt," Claudi said.

"Perhaps you could suggest that to Tribune Scowl-and-Snarl," Fant said in a low voice. "Then he can expand his theories of world domination to include the Emorans."

"What makes you think he hasn't already?"

They turned as a handsome woman with thick gray hair and a striking scar across her face approached them from a small side door.

"Commander." Claudi straightened.

Commander Maure nodded at Claudi then turned her attention to Tigh. "Glad you could finally make it home."

Tigh shrugged. "Yearly meeting with Pendon."

"Let me give you a friendly warning about Iksoc," Maure said as she patted Gessen. "He may be more vocal about his theories about you and your involvement in stopping several potential wars, but he's been studying Jame's involvement just as closely."

"What does he think he's going to prove with these theories?" Tigh asked, running a hand through her hair. "Besides being proven wrong and most likely wrecking his career."

"Rumor has it he's ambitious." Maure walked to the stall next to Gessen's and gave the dark horse there an affectionate rub on the nose. "And he doesn't want to take the time to realize that ambition the old fashion way. Like developing a reputation as a good arbiter and Tribune and working up the ranks to the Federation Council."

"So he wants to become a hero by taking down our heroes," Claudi said.

"Jame's the hero, not me," Tigh muttered.

Maure crossed her arms and put herself in front of Tigh. "Whatever you want to call yourself, you're a hero to the rest of us and that's certainly how Iksoc sees it."

"If he's so certain Jame and I are trying to take over the world, why hasn't he called us back?" Tigh arched a brow.

"Sometimes it's easier to brag about beating an opponent when the opponent isn't around," Maure said with a grin.

"I have the feeling he's not going to know what hit him when he takes Jame on," Claudi said.

THE FALLS WERE higher than any she had ever seen before. High and wide and thunderous as they splashed against a tumble of smoothed boulders. Beautiful and terrifying at the same time. Luring her in to feel their danger firsthand.

She wasn't surprised to see Tigh standing at the top of the falls. Tigh's sturdy legs diverted the rushing water into separate streams but the water didn't seem to be strong enough to budge the powerful warrior.

"Is the water warm or cold?" she called out.

Tigh looked down and smiled at Jame. "It is warm. Very inviting."

Jame didn't hesitate in slipping out of her leathers and diving into the deep pool that spread out from the bottom of the falls.

She sputtered and gave the grinning Tigh an accusing look. "It's freezing. I thought you said it was warm."

Tigh bounced a few times on her toes and dove smoothly into the pool. Waves of warm water pulsed away from her and brushed against Jame's chilled body like gentle caresses.

"Ah, that's better." Jame sighed, and Tigh floated up to her and pulled her close.

"You know I'd never leave you out in the cold," Tigh breathed in Jame's ear, sending a different kind of chill through her body.

JAME SAT UP with a start. Cold air hit her, and she pulled the blanket up around her.

Another strange dream. Different from the other one, yet in many ways the same. At least the lingering feeling from the dream was the same. Why was she dreaming of waterfalls all of a sudden? Maybe it was meeting with Tas and Seeran and being reminded of home. At least reminded of some of the more special traditions at home.

She sighed and lowered herself back down and curled around the warm body of her sleeping warrior. Funny how she was thinking of Emoria as being home again.

"YOU DON'T THINK it's strange that I'm dreaming about waterfalls?" Jame asked as they trudged around the patches of ice. The crews of soldiers shoveling ice onto the back of wagons were still on the other side of the courtyard in front of the fortress.

"They're a part of your traditions and the symbol of your patron deity." Tigh shrugged. "They sound like nice dreams. Most people worry about disturbing dreams."

"But I've never dreamed about them before." Jame hopped over a puddle of slush. "Why now?"

"Maybe meeting up with Tas and Seeran and talking about Emoran traditions with them tapped into something deep within you." Tigh broke up a slick of ice with the heel of her boot.

Jame sighed. She'd spent so many years trying not to think of Emoria she still hadn't completely accepted it was once again her home. A part of her still retained that youthful resentment of the hold the country had on her. Maybe that's what was bothering her about these dreams.

"I think I'm not quite used to the idea I'm actually welcomed in Emoria now." Jame scuffed her boot on a bit of ice. "It's strange what our subconscious latches onto when it's dealing with things scraping against the back of our minds."

Tigh grinned. "I wouldn't worry too much about it. Sounds like you're conjuring up nice warm images, so whatever it is your subconscious is dealing with must be a pleasant thing."

Jame stopped walking. Tigh stopped, turned, and gave her a questioning look. "You're right. I dream about wonderful waterfalls and warm pools and you, and here I am worried about it."

"Maybe you're hinting you want me to find a nice waterfall we can play in." Tigh raised an impish eyebrow.

Jame stepped forward and grabbed Tigh's arm as they resumed their trek across the slick adobe bricks. "Hmmm. Let's just work on it being a conscious hint."

"I'll pursue it with diligence." Tigh laughed.

"Laugh while you can, warrior."

Tigh and Jame stopped walking and turned in the direction of the sneering voice.

Iksoc sauntered up to them . . . as best he could without slipping on the ice. "I have entered a request for a hearing concerning your involvement in the so-called Battle of Balderon. No one else is suspicious of why you stayed away from Ynit for so long and only returned when you had to meet your terms of freedom. Everyone here are blind fools. But I'll open their eyes soon enough."

Jame gazed at Iksoc and slowly nodded. "I think you may be right."

"What?" Iksoc blinked at Jame.

"You'll open people's eyes all right." She gifted him with a charming smile as she led an amused-looking Tigh away.

PENDON POURED MORE tea into Tigh's cup as Tigh stared out the window of the tiny parlor—a parlor that shared a door with her old office from when she was the supreme commander of the Southern Territories. A life so vivid, yet was as if she had lived it in a dream many would consider a nightmare. Snowflakes drifted in a swirling breeze betraying a cold day for the desert community.

Tigh sighed and turned her attention to the cup on the low table in front of her. "Thanks," she murmured as she picked it up and took a sip of the spicy tea. "I guess my problem is, I don't feel anything one way or another about it, and I should."

Pendon sat forward and selected a piece of cheese from the tray of cheese and fruit. "Why do you think you should?"

Tigh looked at him, startled. "I turned into Tigh the Terrible for two days. I should be feeling something about that."

"Did you do anything horrible while you were Tigh the Terrible?" Pendon gazed at Tigh as he picked up his cup.

"No. I mean, I was rude to Jame and I wanted to kill Meah—"

"But you didn't actually do anything." Pendon sipped his tea, eyes still resting on Tigh.

"No." Tigh turned her attention to the snowflakes. "I did feel bad about letting Jame see that cold, ruthless person."

Pendon nodded. "That's only natural. Has she been disturbed or distressed from lingering memories of it?"

Tigh snapped her attention back to Pendon.

"You never talked about it?" Pendon asked.

Tigh frowned. "We talked about it right after it happened. We talked it through pretty thoroughly, I think."

"And Jame hasn't shown any unexpected reactions when you had to fight or aggressively confront someone?" Pendon asked.

Tigh grinned. "Jame's in charge of aggressive confrontations."

"Ah, yes." Pendon cleared his throat. "Which brings us to the point I'm trying to make. Although you must have been horrifying to Jame as Tigh the Terrible, she only saw you like that for a few heartbeats. She comes from a warrior society. she's seen her share of insane rage and even ruthlessness as a part of her people's ongoing defense of Emoria's borders. Also, I happen to know from the reports, Jame saw the cleansed Tigh briefly after your transformation and that left her with hope you could be captured and cleansed again. Even though it was horrific for her, she kept it from overtaking her because she knew whatever had been done could be undone."

"So"—Tigh rubbed her finger around the rim of her cup—"you think I shouldn't be worried about it?"

Pendon's wrinkled face creased in amusement. "I think you've grasped the essentials."

"And you don't think there will be any lingering effects?" Tigh asked.

"Have you felt any?"

Tigh shook her head. "No."

"I don't think you're at any more risk of turning back into Tigh the Terrible than you were before you were given that potion," Pendon said. "Any more than any cleansed Guard has of turning back into a Guard. None of us know how long the cleansing may last or if unpleasant side effects will develop at some point. That's why we have these yearly meetings with all of you. So we can monitor you and possibly stop any ill effects before they become too bad."

"What about Iksoc?" Tigh asked. "He seems convinced I've been trying to take over the world for the last six years."

"Through a series of bungled efforts?" Pendon chortled. "That in itself is enough to ridicule his claims. You've never lost a campaign, and Jame has never lost a case. That makes both of you a moving target for ambitious people with delusions of grandeur like Iksoc."

"Great." Tigh sighed. "Another thing to have to put up with."

"I'm rather glad you'll be wintering in Emoria," Pendon said in a thoughtful tone. "Give things time to settle after Jame wipes that arrogant scowl off of Iksoc's face."

"You really think she can beat him?" Tigh asked.

Pendon looked surprised. "You of all people should know she can."

"I have no doubt that Jame could beat him while half asleep and underwater, but only if everything else was equal," Tigh said.

"Ah, still not quite trusting the Military Tribunal or the Federation Council." Pendon nodded. "Even though they've always been fair with the both of you."

Tigh hung her head a bit sheepishly. "I guess it takes a while to shake off old distrusts."

"You're both heroes who saved the Southern Territories from going to war—several times," Pendon said. "The Federation Council is ever grateful."

"But according to Iksoc, those were my failed attempts to take over."

"And he's got to prove it beyond a doubt," Pendon said. "Think he can do that? Against Jame?"

Tigh finally relaxed. "She'll feed him to Bal's dog as an appetizer."

"ARGIS WANTS ME to stand up for her." A strange mixture of emotions flowed through Jame as she stared at the words, written in Argis's strong bold handwriting.

"She stood up for me." Tigh looked up from polishing her armor. They were seated on Tigh's workbench next to the fire giving off a welcomed warmth in the chilly evening.

Jame sighed. "I know. It just feels a little strange. I guess I'd be a little more settled if I'd been living in Emoria all this time."

"Argis has truly moved on," Tigh said as she put her armor down and slid closer to Jame. "I think both of you will always hold that special place in your hearts for your first love."

Jame looked up into soft, affectionate blue eyes.

Tigh put a gentle finger to Jame's cheek. "But you've been blessed with the gift of everlasting true friendship. Don't question it just cherish it."

"I've been blessed she cherishes your friendship also." Jame rested her head on Tigh's shoulder. "I've just been having this strange feeling ever since we met up with Seeran and Tas."

"I think you're just nervous."

Jame lifted her head and looked at Tigh. "Nervous? About what? Emoria's my home."

"This is the first time since you left Emoria to go to school that you're returning without having to fight their expectations of you and the life you've chosen to live." Tigh put her arm around Jame's shoulder and pulled her close. "You've been treated like a child and you've been treated like an outcast by them. For the first time, you'll be treated like a grown-up royal heir."

"You're right." Jame snaked her arms around Tigh's waist and sighed at the wonderful warm comfort she felt in her arms even after being together for almost seven years. "I'm so lucky to have found you."

I'm the lucky one," Tigh murmured into Jame's hair.

The sound of their knocker hitting the door disturbed the peaceful calm.

"Who could that be?" Jame muttered as she stood with a stretch and padded to the door. She peeked through the eyehole and frowned. Now what? She pulled the door open.

Iksoc, gleefully smug with arms crossed, was flanked by a pair of sad-faced soldiers who looked as if they wanted to be doing anything other than whatever Iksoc was ordering them to do.

Jame kept her arbiter face firmly in place. "Tribune Iksoc, please come in."

"This is not a social call." Iksoc sneered as he lifted a superior nose.

He pushed inside, barely giving Jame time to step out of the way. His hulking presence made the tiny front room too cramped for Jame's comfort. He thrust a scroll with an official Tribunal seal on it into her hand.

Jame gave Tigh, who stood in front of the fire on the back wall, a puzzled look and broke the seal. She unrolled the scroll and read the incredulous words. "I can't believe the Tribunal agreed to this without any evidence to back up your claims."

"What makes you think I don't have any evidence?" Iksoc asked. "You think your partner is so perfect she can attempt such crimes against the Southern Territories without leaving behind crumbs of her actions?"

"No," Jame said. "I mean there isn't any evidence because she's done nothing wrong."

"Of course you'll assert her innocence." Iksoc looked her up and down with a malicious grin. "It'll only make my victory sweeter."

Jame leveled her best Emoran princess gaze at him. "Or your loss greater."

Iksoc's grin turned to stone as he tried to bore into Jame with an angry stare. Jame, who had faced much scarier things, simply crossed her arms and gave him her I-can-see-right-through-you arbiter look.

"I was going to have this place searched but I don't trust the local soldiers to be impartial in this case." Iksoc glanced around with disdain. "Besides, I don't think she'd be stupid enough to keep incriminating evidence here in Ynit. So my only course of action is to take the honorable Paldar Tigis into custody to ensure you don't play any tricks between now and the hearing."

"What?" Tigh stepped up next to Jame. "I've done nothing to merit this."

Iksoc looked as if he was trying not to take a step back as Tigh made the cramped space even tinier. "Tribunal law allows a person who is under suspicion of bringing great harm to the Territories to be put into custody until the person's case is heard."

Jame frowned as she stepped in front of Tigh. "That's only when the case has been put on the docket."

"The case went on the docket this evening," Iksoc said.

"Then I hope to Bal you've scheduled it for tomorrow because I'm not going to allow my client to suffer any longer in custody than she has to." Jame fought to control her growing anger.

Iksoc straightened. "I've scheduled the hearing for next moon."

"With hope you'll be able to scrape together your non-existent evidence by then?" Jame squinted at him as if he were a first-year arbiter student.

Iksoc glared down at her. "You will not speak to me that way. Take the suspect into custody."

The soldiers glanced at each other and then at Tigh with uncertain looks. Tigh sighed and smoothed down her cloth tunic. She removed the knife from her boot and placed it on the workbench.

Jame met Tigh halfway across the room and wrapped her arms around her, shocked into disbelief. "I'll have you out as soon as I can."

Tigh nodded against the top of Jame's head. "I know. I'll be fine."

Jame looked up, and their eyes met for a long sad moment before their lips met in a gentle kiss.

"As her arbiter, it's my right to accompany her." Jame turned to Iksoc as she stepped aside.

Tigh put herself between the soldiers.

Iksoc nodded, eyeing Tigh. "Put the restraints on her."

Jame, along with Tigh and soldier stared at the Iksoc, the outrage wafting off of them.

"As Tigh's legal advisor," Jame said, "I need to see concrete evidence she is a danger to the people of Ynit or has reason to bolt from custody."

"I don't need—" Iksoc sputtered.

"The first case on the docket tomorrow morning will be you defending your insistence at making Tigh walk across the compound in restraints," Jame said, allowing a confident calm to overtake her. "I'm sure the Military Tribunal will think it important enough to squeeze in first thing."

Iksoc glared at Jame. "It'll be a waste of time, but the pleasure will be all mine to crush that confidence out of you."

Tigh gave Jame a quick glance. Jame raised an eyebrow, conveying that she had a plan. A really good plan. Tigh put her hands out and nodded to the soldier holding the shackles.

"Forgive me, Tigh," the young woman murmured as she clicked the iron restraints around Tigh's wrists.

"A soldier must always obey orders," Tigh said. "You're a good soldier."

The young woman straightened, but didn't look happy about any of this.

Jame put out the flame in the fireplace, then grabbed a leather poncho, pulled it over Tigh's head, and straightened it. Tigh gave her an indulgent look as Jame pulled on her own cold weather poncho.

Iksoc led them through the door and into the frozen night, holding his smug head high and strutting down the lane like a rooster who thinks he has outsmarted the fox.

Chapter 3

INGEL RELAXED WITH a sigh as she sat back in her most comfortable chair and opened her book. This was her favorite time, when she could shut out everything but the warm comfort of her home, surrounded by her plants, and the soothing words of writers of fiction. The only time that was all hers, away from her students and the school.

She sighed again at the gentle rap at her door, tempted to ignore it but knew her conscious wouldn't let her do it.

"Jame," she said as she opened the door. A tense, furious-looking Jame. "What's wrong?"

Ingel stepped back, allowing Jame to stomp through the doorway.

"Tigh's been taken into custody," Jame said as she turned around in the middle of the room.

"What?" Ingel frowned. "For what?"

"For suspicion of making several attempts to conquer the Southern Territories," Jame said in frustration.

"Iksoc can't do that unless the case is on the docket." Ingel indicated a chair in front of the fire for Jame to sit in.

"It is, as of tonight." Jame sighed and plopped down in the chair.

Ingel eased into her own chair as she tried to piece together this strange puzzle. "He could only do that if some evidence has been brought forth."

"He scheduled the hearing for a moon from now." Jame clenched her fist, looking as if she was ready to burst with excess rage. "He's gambling he'll have his evidence by then."

"A moon." Ingel sighed. "Tigh can't remain in custody for a moon. The soldiers won't let it happen. The healers and the Tribunal have spent all their efforts working with rehabilitating the Guards, but they never thought about the impact the Elite Guard had on the common soldiers who served under them. If given a choice, their loyalty is with their former Supreme Commander. Even the young soldiers who never fought in the Grappian Wars have seen and heard enough of Tigh to come to her defense—in any way necessary."

Jame stared at Ingel a moment then barked an ironic laugh. "You mean Tigh wouldn't have to hire a mad Wizard or be in league with invaders from across the sea to put together an army to take over the Southern Territories?"

"If it looked as if she was being treating unjustly, she could have the entire military at her command," Ingel said with confidence.

"So they're not going to be too happy I allowed Iksoc to parade Tigh across the compound in shackles," Jame said.

"You what?" Ingel couldn't have been more shocked.

"As you said, Tigh can't sit in custody for a moon"—Jame shrugged as she relaxed back in the chair—"so I had to think of a way to get a hearing set up for first thing tomorrow morning."

Ingel could only stare speechless at the feisty and clever Jame. She grinned. "You're going to make a great queen someday. And Tigh is the luckiest person in the Southern Territories to have you fighting her battles for her."

"That's why I'm here." Jame leaned forward. "I need your impression of Iksoc. Is he really so driven with ambition he's blind to the trap he just fell into."

"How can I put this?" Ingel put her hand to her chin, pretending to think. "You're the only arbiter I know who is capable of making the kind of connections you have obviously made, in order to trip Iksoc up. You could've stopped Iksoc from putting restraints on Tigh but you didn't. Did he show any suspicion at the fact you didn't resist it?"

"No." Jame shook her head. "In fact he's looking forward to—how did he put it?—crushing the confidence out of me at the hearing tomorrow."

Ingel held up a finger. "He doesn't know you don't make a move without having several more steps—and alternate steps—worked out in advance."

Jame fell back into the seat. "You've figured out what I have in mind."

"You forget I've spent the last several years teaching your arbiting techniques in my advance classes."

Jame grimaced. Poor students.

Ingel laughed. "I'm writing a treatise on your defense technique."

Jame steepled her fingers together. "When was the last time you witnessed a successful use of Kanderal's Rules of Evidence?"

"I was hoping that's what you had in mind." Ingel couldn't hide her delight. "Those Rules have never been successfully applied. But, of course, the occasion to use them rarely comes up. Unless you cleverly allow the circumstances to happen."

Jame shrugged. "Iksoc set up the circumstances, I simply took advantage of them."

"And that's what makes me proud to have been your mentor." Ingel slapped her hands on the chair arms. "I look forward to teaching Jamelin Ketlas' Interpretations of Kanderal's Rules of Evidence."

TIGH WOKE JUST as the darkness outside the small round window lightened into a deep gray. She glanced around the tidy room, noticing the embers in the fireplace still glowed from the late-night fire.

She grinned at the thought of how Iksoc would react if he knew the moment he'd left the holding cells tucked beneath the main fortress, the soldiers removed her from the dank cell she was in and put her in one of the chambers reserved for important or influential people.

The soldiers didn't care about how much trouble they'd be in, if their act of indignant rebellion was discovered. It did take some time for Jame to convince Tigh they wouldn't get into trouble because anyone other than Iksoc would have allowed the former Supreme Commander to be put in the private rooms away from the common holding cells.

Tigh looked down affectionately as Jame snuggled closer to her. They had spent most of the night covering strategy for the hearing. She sighed. How long had it been since Jame had to defend her before a Tribunal? That wonderful heady day when she had been finally released from the Guards and then turned around and pledged her life and sword to Jame.

Best decision she'd ever made.

She sighed at the loud voices from somewhere deeper in the dungeon. A distinctive agitated voice bounced into the corridor outside the door.

"You're sighing," Jame said in a groggy accusing voice.

"Iksoc's continuing his campaign to make our lives miserable," Tigh mumbled.

Jame raised a puzzled head.

"Where's the guard?" a muffled voice demanded. "This door doesn't even have a lock on it."

Jame rolled her eyes and climbed out of bed. She listened to the conviction in the voices of soldiers as they explained they were following protocol for Supreme Commanders in counterpoint to Iksoc's sputtering threats and audibly throwing his weight around. She slipped on her tunic and boots and ran a hand through her hair.

"This wasn't what I wanted to do first thing this morning." She gave Tigh a rakish grin.

Tigh sat up and blinked at Jame and then the door and back to Jame. "I'll take care of him if you want."

Jame laughed and gave Tigh a kiss. "You're in enough trouble with him as it is. Don't go away. This should only take a couple of heartbeats."

"Don't go away," Tigh muttered. "Emoran humor."

JAME GRINNED THEN faced the door and put on her best arbiter expression. She eased the door open, slipped out, and closed it behind her. She blinked in the dim short corridor as she took in Iksoc, in full Tribunal vestments, shaking the gaudiest ceremonial Tribunal stick she'd ever seen at a pair of soldiers, showing more indignation than fear as they stood tall and unbudging in front of him.

Iksoc spun around and glared at Jame. "What are you doing here?"

"Meeting with my client," Jame said. "We do have a hearing first thing this morning."

"You shouldn't be representing her." Iksoc scowled. "Given your relationship."

"We've already set that precedence," Jame said.

"I'll protest your right to represent her." Iksoc straightened and waved the stick around. "Now. Before this hearing."

Jame shrugged. "Fine with me. If you don't care how it'll look."

"You're trying to pull something clever on me. I'm not like all the rest of these blind fools." He pointed the stick at the soldiers, who crossed their arms and looked unimpressed. "You won't be able to lure me into one of your word playing traps."

"I'm not playing with words." Jame turned to the soldier with a mop of blonde hair and a nice scar over her brow. "Why do you think Tribune Iksoc doesn't want me to defend Tigh?"

"He thinks you'll beat him and make him look bad," the soldier said with a smirk.

Jame turned back to Iksoc and raised an eyebrow.

Iksoc glared at the soldiers who shrugged with innocent looks. "Then it just looks like I'll have to change everyone's high opinion of your skills as of defense."

"It looks like you will," Jame said.

Iksoc gazed down at Jame and managed to sneer and grin at the same time. "Enjoy your little antics while you can, before the morning is out, you'll both wish you'd never returned to Ynit." With a final scowl at the unlocked door, he turned and stomped down the short corridor to the steps leading to the upper floors of the fortress.

Jame sighed. "I'm wishing that now. If he gives you any trouble let me know, I'll defend you myself if I have to."

The soldiers grinned and nudged each other.

"It's our pleasure to serve both you and Tigh," the blonde said.

Jame clasped a hand on each of their shoulders. "Thanks. That means a lot to Tigh."

She slipped into the room, considerably grayer as the cloud-covered sun rose higher in the sky. Tigh sat on the bed with her elbows on her knees. Jame had no doubt she heard every word through the thin wood door.

"I think if he was a quarter as good as he thinks he is, he wouldn't be on the Military Tribunal," Tigh said.

"Good point." Jame walked to the bed and sat next to Tigh. "Do you think he could actually have something? I mean, it's not like we played by strict rules of conduct or anything. Even the way I handled Kylara's case was not exactly by the book . . ."

Tigh captured Jame's hand in both of hers. "The only thing that will defeat you is any self-doubt you have in how we battled Misner and in your own abilities to stand up for your actions."

Jame gazed at her and nodded. "I am showing self-doubt aren't I?"

Tigh nodded back. "Not something I've ever witnessed before—at least as far as being an arbiter is concerned."

"Maybe it's just because this hits so close to home," Jame said. "And being here in Ynit brings back all those memories of how each of your hearings affected my future as well as yours. I didn't want to lose you then, and I certainly don't want to lose you now."

"So there isn't any way you're going to let an egotistical sour-faced Federation Council member wannabe separate us, right?" Tigh wrapped her arms around Jame.

"Putting it that way . . ." Jame leaned against Tigh's warm solid body. "I think Iksoc's going to need a sponge to recover all the bits of his ego when I'm through with him."

Tigh laughed. "Spoken like a true Emoran."

IN ALL THE years she had lived in Ynit, Jame had never felt anything like the anger and indignation that snapped the air particles around her. Citizens of both the military compound and of the city of Ynit were crowded so tightly that soldiers struggled to keep a narrow path from the jail. A clear demonstration that no one had forgotten how it was Tigh's strategy that brought the army of the Silver Dragon to a halt outside the gates of Ynit.

Jame, standing on the middle steps of the Tribunal Hall so she had a good view of the courtyard, fought tears as she concentrated on keeping her expression level and professional. She couldn't believe the people of her adopted city stopped their everyday lives to stand in silent support of her right to defend Tigh, so early in the morning, no less.

"Amazing, isn't it," Ingel said.

Jame shook her head. "And this is just for a hearing to see if I can be the one defending her."

The respectful silence erupted into angry shouts from the crowd closest to the fortress. The sea of people shifted and waved as others tried to see what was going on, Jame stretched as tall as possible to see over the roiling people crowding the fortress but only caught glimpses of black. Tigh. In chains. Iksoc had insisted, and Jame had not resisted, knowing it would get this reaction from the people of Ynit.

Ingel stared in disbelief. "Doesn't Iksoc know those chains aren't going to win him any supporters?"

"I haven't gotten the impression he's that perceptive," Jame said.

Ingel choked back a chuckle.

A single screaming voice cut through the shouting crowd. Jame ran down the steps and dashed down the narrow pathway maintained by the soldiers.

"Traitor," the voice cried out.

Jame squinted ahead and caught a glimpse of shiny armor topped by a wild mess of black hair. A sword flashed as the stocky assailant leapt into the cleared path in front of Tigh and her escort of guards.

"You'll not be allowed to betray us or our cause," the stranger's voice rang out as she ran swinging the sword at Tigh. The soldiers lifted their swords too late as the blade crashed down on an astonished Tigh who crouched to use her manacled hands for protection.

Jame watched in horror as Tigh went down in a heap of heavy chain and cursed Iksoc ego for insisting on running a length of chain from Tigh's hands to her manacled feet.

The assailant lifted her sword for another blow to the sprawled Tigh and was swallowed by Tigh's escorts and their nearby comrades. They disarmed the wild eyed woman and held her face down on the slushy cobblestone. She spit out curses and insults at Tigh as she struggled against the hold.

Jame slid on the water slick stone onto her knees next to Tigh. Dazed, unfocused blue eyes blinked up at her as Jame ran her fingers through the dark hair in search of the source of the blood running down Tigh's face.

Several healers joined Jame on the wet stone and gently took over her probing of Tigh's head.

One of the healers' popped up. "Get these shackles off of her."

A soldier dropped to her knees and pushed a key into the lock with shaking hands.

"What are you—?" Iksoc's mouth snapped shut as the crowd parted down to the middle of the courtyard. Tribune Sitas, looking beyond outraged, strode toward him. "I think we can stop this whole farce, once and for all," he said loud enough for Sitas to hear him. "It seems Tigh's allies are not too happy with her being caught."

The crowd shook their fists at him and yelled, "You're the liar! You're the traitor!"

"Tigh would never betray us," a woman shouted.

"Never," came a chorus of indignant voices.

Iksoc raised his chin and crossed his arms. "Then I guess it'll be my job to prove all of you wrong. I proclaim myself the keeper of peace over the Southern Territories by dedicating my life to bringing down the single creature who wants to enslave us into her mad dreams of domination over all of us."

Jame gave Iksoc a look that would have frozen the waterfalls of Laur. She rose to her feet and took deliberate steps, her eyes never leaving Iksoc's, until she was an arms-length away from him.

She held out blood-soaked hands. "I hope, for your sake, this is the only blood of Tigh's you're allowed to shed in your own mad dreams of power. You'd better start thinking fast about whether you really want to pursue this game or not, because if you don't have the backbone for it, I'll crush you until you have to crawl around like the slimy worm you are."

"You dare insult a Tribune," Iksoc sputtered.

"I dare speak the truth," Jame said. "And, unlike you, I have nothing but truth behind me."

Iksoc pointed to the woman. "How do you explain this assailant then?"

Jame stepped up to the woman and took in the stringy black hair and vivid sea green eyes. Her silver armor glinted in the early morning sun as she stood head down with her arms bound behind her back. A pair of soldiers clutched her arms.

"Where are you from?" Jame asked.

"The Land of the Silver Dragon," the woman muttered, giving Jame a dark look. Her accent had an odd lilt to it.

"Where is that?" Jame asked.

The woman darted a look at Iksoc and then glared at Jame. "Across the water."

"Where did you land?" Jame glanced back as Tigh was lifted onto a ragged stretcher by the healers.

The woman shrugged as if it were a spat. "How would I know? I don't know anything about your infernal land."

Jame nodded thoughtfully. "What city did you leave to get here?"

The woman stared at her. "What?"

"Which city or town in the Land of the Silver Dragon did you embark from to come here?" Jame asked.

The woman swallowed and flicked a glance at Iksoc.

"It seems you don't know your own infernal country very well either. Not the kind of person I'd send on such an important mission as this. Especially by as proud of a people as the followers of the Silver Dragon." Jame turned to Iksoc and winced inside at the anger wafting off of him. "Now, if you'll excuse me, I want to see how much damage this Silver Dragon imposter did to Tigh."

Jame rushed past Sitas, half-wishing she could stay for the dressing down Iksoc was about to get and muttered thanks as the crowd made sure she didn't break her stride to the infirmary.

SITAS FOCUSED HER anger into the glare she leveled at Iksoc. The people around her sucked in a collective breath. Glad she still had an arbiter's skill to capture attention.

Iksoc's body was tense like a trapped animal. Coward, Sitas wanted to spat out loud and let her disdain flow off her.

She planted herself in front of Iksoc and looked him up and down. "What makes you think you could pass a first term debate with her, much less something like this?"

"Her cleverness doesn't make her right," Iksoc sputtered.

"No." Sitas glanced around at her rapt audience. "But it doesn't make her wrong, either. Consider the strength and the veracity of your evidence against Tigh very carefully because if there is a speck of lie about it, she'll find it and trounce you with it." She smiled. A wicked, knowing smile she knew would make Iksoc squirm. "That is her gift and that is what makes her the formidable arbiter she is."

BEDE KOMLIC BLINKED up from his meticulous notes at the commotion outside the door. He sighed and stood up. With such a crowd outside it was only a matter of time before someone got hurt . . .

Healers were hovering over a stretcher held by a pair of soldiers in the foyer. Bal's children. Tigh. He frowned and pointed to the corridor with rooms for special patients.

They carried Tigh into the first room.

"Some lunatic went after her with a sword," a young healer said as they lifted Tigh onto a low pallet.

"And she didn't defend herself?" Bede asked.

"She was in shackles and chains," another healer said.

"Shackles?" Bede looked down at the pale Tigh and shook his head. "I'll need this wound cleaned."

The healer nodded and put several white clothes into a basin of water.

Bede went to a small side table and collected the tools for stitching up the bloody wound. "What is all that commotion out there?"

A healer peeked out through the curtained door of the room. "A lot of people, Tribunes, arbiters, soldiers . . ."

Bede hated to have the infirmary disrupted but he knew it was best to give in sometimes—especially when he knew these people were not only showing concern for Tigh but giving her silent support. "Please tell them to keep the noise down."

He watched as the healer cleansed the shallow slice across Tigh's scalp. She had managed to deflect the brunt of the blow.

"Here." He put a small mug to Tigh's lips. "Drink this down."

"Thanks," she muttered. She took the mug with shaky hands and downed the potion.

Bede nodded as he sewed the long cut, using small stitches to minimize the scarring.

"Tigh," came a strained whisper from the doorway, and Jame slipped into the room. She took a deep relieved breath to see Tigh was sitting up and appearing to be all right.

Tigh lifted fuzzy blue eyes to Jame and managed a sheepish grin.

"Looks like you're going to have a bit of a headache," Jame said as she took Tigh's hand.

"What was she doing in shackles anyway?" Bede asked, indignant.

Jame sighed. "Indulging Tribune Iksoc's ego."

"His whole case against Tigh is absurd," Bede muttered as he put a soothing salve over the stitches and wrapped several strips of cloth over the area and around Tigh's head.

"This little incident didn't help him any," Jame said. "It turns out your assailant was hired to pretend to be from the Land of the Silver Dragon."

"You were able to determine that already?" Tigh asked in a groggy voice.

Jame shrugged. "It didn't take much."

"Am I still in custody?" Tigh adjusted the bandage around her head.

Jame grinned. "Let's just say at this point, Iksoc is in more trouble with the Tribunal than you are. I don't think anyone is going to step forward to escort you back to the jail."

Tigh nodded and turned to Bede. "Thank you, Bede."

Bede placed a fatherly hand on Tigh's shoulder. "Just promise the next time you visit it'll be a social call."

"I promise," Tigh said as Bede and Jame helped her up from the cot.

"That mixture I gave you is going to make you groggy for a while so don't move too fast or you'll get dizzy," Bede said.

"Don't worry," Jame said, "I'll make sure she takes it easy."

"Do you still have to defend your right to defend me?" Tigh asked.

"What?" Bede stared at her, shocked. "What kind of absurdity is this?"

"The kind that Iksoc insists on," Jame said.

"He actually thought he could convince the Tribunal you don't have the right to defend Tigh?" Bede chuckled.

"That's what we were supposed to be doing this morning instead of visiting with you," Jame said.

"Sounds to me, then, he got off easy." Bede almost laughed at Jame's expression.

"I think I'll take that as a compliment," Jame said.

"It was a compliment," Bede said. "Now take my patient home and make sure she doesn't tear open those stitches."

"Sounds like the best suggestion I've had all day," Jame said.

TIGH BLINKED AT the people quietly gathered around the beds and in any available free space in the building.

Sitas stepped forward. "Are you all right?"

Tigh stared at her, her mind befuddled as she tried to figure out what all these people were doing in the infirmary. She remembered to nod.

"She'll be fine," Jame answered. "Just a nasty cut to the head."

"That's good to hear," Sitas said. "Iksoc isn't the kind of person who will back down, but we'll try to cut through all the nonsense and give Tigh the proper hearing she deserves in response to any accusations Iksoc has against her."

"Thank you, Tribune," Jame said, squeezing Tigh's hand.

Chapter 4

JAME HATED SWIMMING upstream but it was the only way to get to the stately waterfall ahead of her. She had to get there before it was too late.

The water pushed harder against her as she got close enough to the falls to inhale the mineral odor from the water pounding against the rocks. The splashes roared in her ears as she sought out a dark area behind the falls.

Her strong arms propelled her under the thundering falls. The pressure of the water pushed her down but she struggled against it and emerged behind the curtain of water. After a few heartbeats of catching her breath, she grabbed hold of a ledge of white rock, polished smooth by the cascading water, and pulled herself into a shallow cave.

She stood on shaky legs and focused on the black-clad figure lying on the stone floor.

"It's too late." A wispy voice floated on the mist.

"Too late?" Jame's voice cracked with panic. "It can't be too late, I got here as fast as I could."

"Sometimes your best effort is not good enough," the whispered voice said.

Jame spun around the shallow cavern as anger and frustration built up inside her. "No. You don't understand. When it comes to Tigh my best effort has to be enough."

"Or what?" the soft voice asked.

Jame dropped to her knees and crawled to the still body. "Or I die myself." Her voice faltered into a sob as she threw herself over Tigh's body.

"What about your duty to your country?" the fading voice asked. "Don't let it be too late . . ."

The voice echoed in Jame's head as she sat upright in the bed. Tears streaked down her cheeks as she forced her body and mind to calm down. She turned to the sleeping body next to her and placed her cold hand onto a warm cheek, relieved to see the gentle rising and falling of Tigh's chest.

By the waterfalls of Laur. Jame fought back the terror she felt at the thought of a life without Tigh. There would be no life. Nothing else matter, not Emoria or her people. Only Tigh. She certainly wouldn't be able to rule as queen. Not without Tigh by her side.

Too late. Is it almost too late? She plopped back onto the pillow, rolled over, and wrapped her arms around Tigh, reveling in the solid reality of her presence. She blinked away tears as she lifted her hand and arranged Tigh's hair over the long gash on her head. The action calmed her, and her thoughts focused on the dreams. On why this dream had been so different from the others.

Because Tigh was hurt. Almost too late . . . Jame disentangled herself from Tigh, sat up, and wiped the tears from her face. She gave Tigh's shoulder a shake and allowed a groggy Tigh to wake up on her own.

Tigh blinked her eyes open and focused on the cross-legged Jame next to her. She gingerly sat up.

"What's wrong?" Tigh asked.

"We have to go to Emoria," Jame said.

Tigh frowned a little. "We are. Just as soon as we take care of Iksoc."

"I mean . . ." Jame sucked in a deep breath and took Tigh's hand into both of hers. "It's time to return home."

Tigh scooted around so she faced Jame. "You mean for good?"

Jame nodded. "I had another dream. It wasn't as pleasant as the other ones. I think Laur is calling me home."

"Calling you home."

"Legend has it a princess knows when to return home because Laur calls her back," Jame said. "But this last dream was more than that. It was a warning of some kind, and I'm not going to take a risk and ignore it."

Tigh squeezed Jame's hands, her body tense and on alert. "Something happened?"

"It was warning me to come home before it was too late." Jame lifted their hands and pressed them to her cheek.

"Too late?"

"Too late for us to have a safe and happy life together in Emoria." Jame captured Tigh's eyes.

Tigh relaxed a bit. "They're just dreams."

"Maybe," Jame said, "but I don't want to take the chance. When we return to Emoria, I'll know if Laur has been trying to call me back or not."

Tigh pulled Jame's hands to her lips and kissed them. "Wherever you go, I go. You're my home. You're my world. It makes no difference where my body is as long as my soul is with you."

Jame gazed into Tigh's eyes. "Our souls are one. Laur knows this and is calling for both of us."

JAME GLANCED AT Tigh and mentally shook her head. Tigh's soft blue eyes rested on a spot on the stone floor in front of the defendants' box as she floated in a meditative state. Jame sighed, wishing she could shut out the grating attitude and posturing masquerading as an argument against Tigh spewed from a smug faced Iksoc. Two sandmarks of endless accusations spun out of fantastical speculation. This was not the way Jame had pictured ending her career as an arbiter-at-large.

She was sure the only thing keeping the overflowing audience in place was the anger they felt at Iksoc words and their determination to stand behind Tigh's innocence. Their tense indignation was almost a solid entity in itself.

The only thing that kept Jame from putting them all out of their misery and strangling the man was wanting the satisfaction of witnessing his smug little world deflate.

" . . . and I'm sure you can now understand why we're gathered here today. We've let this threat to our society roam free for too long." Iksoc strutted down the first row of spectators and then strode to a chair opposite the defendants box on the other side of the Tribunal bench.

"Thank you, Tribune Iksoc." Sitas turned to Jame. "Arbiter Jamelin, do you have anything to say in Tigh's defense?"

Finally. Jame watched Tigh come out of her meditative state and turn those thoughtful confident eyes to her. She gave Tigh a private reassuring smile, faced the Tribunal, and stood.

"Yes, Tribune Sitas, I have a few words to say in Tigh's defense," she said.

The spectators twittered in amusement and anticipation.

"I'm sure I'm not the only one wondering what we're all doing here," Jame began as the spectators settled back with knowing grins. "Just off the top of my head I can think of two reasons why these charges Iksoc has brought against Tigh are not only false but ridiculous. The first is, we all know Tigh has never said or done anything to indicate she's interested in leading an army, much less one that conquers the Southern Territories. Second, we all know if she had an interest in conquering the Southern Territories, she'd had done it by now because she wouldn't have failed."

Murmurs of agreement rose up from the spectators.

"But the fact we know all this doesn't make my job today any easier." Jame stepped out of the defendants' box and strode up to Iksoc. "Because truth is much harder to prove in a case that is crafted out of lies than one based on facts."

Iksoc glared at Jame. "Prove to me that what I've laid out before this court are lies."

Jame nodded and strolled in front of the Tribunal bench. "I think I'd prefer for you to prove to me what you've laid out before this court aren't lies."

Iksoc crossed his arms with a condescending look. "That means we'll have to postpone this hearing until all my evidence has been gathered."

"That's not what I mean," Jame said.

Iksoc turned to the spectators with a smug expression that clearly questioned Jame's reputation as a cunning arbiter. "It's either one or the other."

"What I mean is, you misunderstood what I said," Jame said. "I'm not interested in proving what you've presented to the Tribunal is true. I'm only interested in you proving to me your statements are not lies."

Iksoc narrowed his eyes. "I don't see the difference."

"I don't want this hearing to be drawn out as you gather your evidence," Jame said. "Tigh and I are expected in Emoria this winter, and I'm anxious to return home. Because of this, I'm willing to take the risk and give you the opportunity to argue your case without evidence according to Kanderal's Rules of Evidence."

Iksoc opened his mouth and then closed it. He gave Jame a wary look. "You're willing to let me argue my case without evidence according to Kanderal's Rules of Evidence? You have no chance of winning."

Jame shrugged. "Attempts to use Kanderal's Rules have never been successful, so you have no precedence to believe you'll be able to win the case."

"But the Rules stack everything into my corner," Iksoc said.

"That's true." Jame nodded. "I'm willing to take that risk, if you're willing to accept the Tribunal's final decisions on each step of the procedure."

Iksoc stood and studied Jame, as if looking for a trick. "I accept the use of Kanderal's Rules and the Tribunal's final decisions."

Sitas turned to the Tribune on either side of her, and they all nodded their agreement. "Very well. We'll adjourn until the afternoon session to allow Tribune Iksoc to prepare his case according to Kanderal's Rules of Evidence."

Iksoc turned to Sitas with a puzzled look. "My case has been presented."

Sitas leveled at steady gaze at him. "Then take the time to review Kanderal's Rules so we can proceed smoothly through the hearing."

"All right. If you insist." Iksoc scowled. "I guess a few more sandmarks won't make a difference."

"YOU TRICKED ME!"

Jame rolled her eyes and sighed before turning around. The main square was covered with pockets of people getting some air before the afternoon Tribunal session. She turned in time to dodge Iksoc lunging his considerable bulk at her.

Iksoc stumbled forward and ungracefully regained his balance. He spun around to Jame, who stood with arms crossed, and swung his arm out. Jame took two steps back, and he met air instead of her face.

Tigh grabbed Iksoc's still suspended arm.

"Let go of me," he said.

"You're threatening an arbiter, it's my job to protect her." Tigh raked cool calm eyes over the angry Iksoc.

"She doesn't deserve the title of arbiter," Iksoc said as he shook his arm free from Tigh's loosened grip. "I'm sure the only reason she was allowed in this school in the first place was her queen made a sizable monetary donation."

The sound of a dozen swords being unsheathed filled the air. Soldiers stepped out from the groups around them, glaring at Iksoc and casually displaying their weapons.

"Who's being threatened now?" Iksoc asked.

The soldiers' action calmed Jame's initial indignation at the accusation, and she sauntered up to Iksoc. "Are you sure you want to accuse the Queen of Emoria of bribing the school for allowing me to be a student? Are you sure you want to add one more lie you'll have to defend in a hearing following Kanderal's Rules?"

"Kanderal's Rules," Iksoc said. "You tricked me into agreeing to them."

"I tricked you?" Jame asked. "How did I trick you? Did I prevent you from taking a recess to review the Rules? You gave the impression you had a clear understanding of them."

"What I have a clear understanding of," Iksoc shook a finger at Jame, "is your kind should never have been allowed into our society. Much less in a position to judge others."

"My kind . . ."

"You know what I mean." Iksoc sneered. "How can you stand there and pretend to be one of us. All Emorans are unnatural creatures conceived without male assistance. I wouldn't want one of you passing legal judgment on me."

Jame and Tigh, along with everyone within earshot stared dumbfounded at the red-faced Iksoc.

"You don't like Emorans because we have a different kind of parentage?" Jame asked.

"An unnatural parentage," Iksoc said. "Anyone born of two women is not a whole person."

Tigh raised an eyebrow and stepped up to Iksoc until they were breathing the same air. "Are you suggesting Jame's unnatural and not a whole person?"

"I'm suggesting Emorans aren't like the rest of us," Iksoc said.

"No," Tigh put a finger under Iksoc's chin and forced eye contact with him, "you're suggesting there's something inferior about Emorans based simply on the way they reproduce."

Iksoc shook away from Tigh's eye lock and took a step back from her. "Of course it's inferior. Anyone can see that. Without the male presence, something very fundamental is missing from their human make-up. I mean look at them. The only important things to them are being warriors and fighting—dominant female traits without any male traits to balance this violent way of life."

"And you've met enough Emorans to prove this?" Jame stepped around Tigh and poked Iksoc's ample stomach. "You've visited Emor and know everything about everyday life there?"

The people around them went deathly quiet.

"I think you're a dangerous race waiting for the perfect opportunity to quench your need for war and conquest," Iksoc said. "This alliance between yourself and the former Supreme Commander is that perfect opportunity."

"What's the matter, Tribune?" Claudi called from a handful of soldiers. "Did an Emoran turn down your advances?"

Iksoc's face grew redder if that was possible as he shook an angry finger at Claudi. "I'll have you thrown out of the army for speaking to a Tribune that way."

Jame and Tigh exchanged looks.

"If all of this is revenge for being spurned by an Emoran, I'm not going to be a happy warrior," Tigh murmured.

"As outrageous as it sounds, it does help all this make sense," Jame whispered back.

"I'd like to see you try." Claudi crossed her arms.

"Time to break this up," Commander Maure said as she and Sitas stepped in between Iksoc and Claudi.

Sitas looked around and sighed. "The afternoon session is about to begin. Unless you want to settle it out here instead."

"I refuse to be a part of a common brawl," Iksoc said.

Tigh sputtered out a laugh. "Who was attacking who when you tried to squash Jame."

"Squash?" Iksoc squeaked.

"Who bribed the school to let you in?" someone cried from the crowd.

"You dare let these people treat me this way?" Iksoc, tense with rage, turned to Sitas. "I am a Tribune."

"Then act like one," Sitas said in a voice that conveyed her deep disappointment in Iksoc. "You forget your presence on the Tribunal is probationary."

Iksoc straightened. "Fortunately for me, I plan to make this job a short steppingstone in my career."

"First true thing he's said all day," Jame muttered as she and Tigh walked to the Tribunal Hall.

"THE MOST OBVIOUS mistake Tigh made showed her desperation at having her dreams of conquering the Southern Territories continually hindered." Iksoc clasped his hands behind his back and leisurely paced in front of the overcrowded chamber. "She made the mistake of joining forces with a mad wizard from the Northern Territories. This wizard had been called upon by the Northern Territories during the war to create enhanced Guards much like our own. Several Guards were sent one by one to destroy this wizard and all were killed. All except Tigh the Terrible. She claimed she had killed the wizard but she could never properly answer questions about how she had succeeded in doing it. And, as we found out, the wizard survived."

Iksoc paused long enough to center himself in front of his audience.

"The wizard survived because Tigh made some kind of deal with her," he said. "The wizard didn't help the Northern Territories because Tigh the Terrible offered her a much more ambitious project to work on. This project was to create an invincible army that would take over both Territories once the war was over."

Iksoc stole a look at Jame and Tigh, who watched him with bland expressions. His lip twitched and his eyes sparked with frustration.

"It was hoped that the Guard enhancements were enough to defeat a wizard but that belief turned out to be false. Because of this, I present as irrefutable evidence that Tigh couldn't have killed the Wizard Misner when so many Guards before her failed in the task," Iksoc said.

"Thank you, Iksoc." Sitas nodded as Iksoc sat in the chair facing the defendants' box. He cast an arrogant sneer at Tigh and Jame.

Sitas gave Jame a nod.

Jame stood and stepped out of the defendants' box. She ran her eyes over the spectators ending with Tigh. Unwavering confidence gleamed from Tigh's eyes, and Jame smiled.

"You're right. Guard enhancements aren't enough to stop a wizard," Jame said.

The audience, silent during Iksoc's speech, came to life in a twittering reaction.

"And you're right. Tigh's answers during the inquiry after she thought she had killed Misner never truly satisfied the Military."

Jame looked out a side window and returned calm eyes to the spectators.

"It's also true none of the magic used during the cleansing process worked on her. That may be one of the reasons why she had a more successful cleansing than the other Guards."

"What are you saying?" Iksoc asked.

Jame turned to him and raised an eyebrow. "I'm stating known fact that's available in the archives for anyone to read. These strange mysteries surrounding Tigh and magic were finally solved when Minchof, the wizard who removed our abilities to enhance other people, sent Goodemer to stop Misner from raising her army and conquering the Southern Territories. Goodemer revealed to us that Tigh is immune to magic. A correspondence with Pendon Larke confirmed they suspected Tigh didn't feel the magic directed at her during her rehabilitation and used alternative methods for her cleansing. Tigh had indeed disabled Misner to the point the wizard used every bit of magic left in her to render Tigh unconscious and create an illusion of her decapitated self so she could get away from Tigh. As it was, it took years for Misner to recover from her confrontation with her."

"Can you prove that?" Iksoc asked.

Jame smiled. "Yes. But according to Kanderal's Rules I don't have to."

Iksoc jumped to his feet, or it would have been a jump if his bulk hadn't made it more like climbing to his feet. "You and your arbiter tricks."

"I merely suggested using them, I didn't force you to accept them," Jame said.

"I refuse and I look like a fool." Iksoc scowled.

Jame bit off her first response and kept her calm professional demeanor in place. "So you'd rather take the chance of looking like a fool if you lose after all your boasting that you'd win?"

"I will win," Iksoc said, the change in his voice revealing his barely concealed frustration at not being able to meet his own high expectations of himself. "I won't let you beat me. I'll prove you're not unbeatable." He whipped his hand up, and a streak of silver passed over his shoulder from behind.

In a split heartbeat, Jame found herself on the floor with Tigh clutching her legs in a tackle. A second silver streak came at them and Tigh pulled herself over Jame and rolled them out of the way.

TIGH LOOKED UP and saw the surprised-looking knife thrower in the gallery stopped in mid-throw of another knife as an arrow penetrated his heart. The knife clattered to the wood floor, and he crumpled against the balcony.

She looked in the crowd of spectators. Claudi slung her bow over her shoulder.

Tigh untangled herself from Jame and caught an odor coming from one of the knives on the floor. She crawled to the knife, picked it up, and sniffed it. She scrambled to her feet and glared at him with as much hatred as she had ever felt for another person.

Iksoc took a stumbling step backward only to be stopped by a pair of soldiers grabbing each arm.

Tigh held his frightened gaze for a heartbeat longer then turned to the spectators and raised the knife above her head. "This blade is coated with a lethal poison. One scratch would have killed Jame."

The spectators gasped and stared at the knife in stunned silence.

Tigh turned to Iksoc and walked to within a pace of him. "Who do you think you are that you think you can control other people to fit your demented view of what the world should be like? Who are you to think you can walk outside the legal and moral ethics of this land to get what you want? And what exactly do you want? Control? Power? To rule the Southern Territories?"

She pressed the knife blade against his ample throat, letting him splutter in fear for several heartbeats.

"I think you want me out of the way so you can pursue your ambitions to conquer the Southern Territories yourself," Tigh said. "I can't imagine you going to all this trouble to beat an unbeaten arbiter just to forward your career. A seat on the Federation Council wouldn't be good enough for someone who thinks he's better than everyone else."

"We're in a hearing," Iksoc sputtered, careful of the blade at his throat. "This defendant is armed and threatening me." He glanced at the Tribunal who sat watching with their hands folded on the table. "I'll report all of you for this insubordinate behavior. It'll cost you your positions."

Sitas gave Tigh a weary look. "Are you through playing with him?"

Tigh shrugged, removed the blade from Iksoc's throat, and stepped back. She laid the knife on the Tribunal bench.

Jame wrapped an arm around her and gave her a squeeze.

"Iksoc," Sitas said. "Tigh is exactly who she appears to be. No other Guard has been monitored or studied to the extent that she has, and there has never been any indication she is nothing more than a peaceful soul with a warrior heart. We're not the blind fools you have painted us to be, but we know how to face the truth and treat Tigh as the decent, law-abiding citizen of the Southern Territories she is."

"You can act high and mighty now," Iksoc said. "I'm sure the Federation Council will be interested in this travesty you dare call a hearing."

"You have a very selective memory." Sitas stood with a grim smile. "You seem to remember what everyone else does but never what you do. It's something I'd work on before you tell your story to the Federation Council when you are defending yourself against charges of trying to kill a peace arbiter and a peace warrior. You also might want to polish up that story when you face the Emoran Council for attempting to assassinate their princess."

Iksoc indignant response was hampered by a gag placed over his mouth.

"I think you've said quite enough for today, Tribune." Sitas nodded to the soldiers behind Iksoc. "Please take the Tribune to his new accommodations."

The soldiers grinned and dragged a struggling Iksoc out the side Tribunal door.

"The Tribunal apologizes that you were subjected to this travesty as Iksoc called it," Sitas said to Jame and Tigh. "It seems the times are growing unstable again, and perhaps your decision to return to Emoria is best. We'd hoped your career would last until you became queen but that was only because you've been an invaluable member of our team of arbiters and a cherished member of our community. Your skills as an arbiter rank with the best the Southern Territories has ever produced, and we hope you'll accept the position of arbiter for the Territories of Emoria and Lukria until you take over your duties as Queen of Emoria."

Jame choked on a surge of emotion as the full impact of what she was about to do crashed down on her. She was leaving this world—Ynit, her friends, her career as an arbiter-at-large behind forever. She swallowed down a lump in her throat and willed the tears to stay back, then straightened and faced the Tribunal. Tigh took her place a step behind Jame.

"I thank you for your kind words, and I accept the position of arbiter for Emoria and Lukria," Jame said in a voice thick with emotion.

Sitas smiled and nodded as the chamber erupted in cheering and stamping.

Chapter 5

"DO YOU REALLY think that's necessary?" Jame watched Tigh roam around their bedroom, her body as unsettled as her thoughts.

Tigh stopped and turned to Jame. "Maybe not, but I'd feel better about it."

"But Iksoc's in custody," Jame said.

Tigh slipped her hands under her belt and stared out the window at the grim mixture of snow and rain penetrating the gloom draped sand and adobe.

Jame got up from her little corner desk and walked to Tigh. "What?"

Tigh sucked in a breath and gave Jame an affectionate sheepish look. "Something doesn't ring true about Iksoc."

"Maybe because everything he says is a lie," Jame said.

"That's just it," Tigh said. "Even his lies were lies."

"Of course they were." Jame frowned. "What do you mean?"

Tigh sighed and gazed at the gray-soaked garden. "Have you ever wondered how Iksoc got to be a Military Tribune in the first place? His career as an arbiter was short and undistinguished."

Jame shrugged. "He was nominated and passed the Tribunal exam."

"Yet he didn't know the details of Kanderal's Rules of Evidence," Tigh said. "You learned it in school eight or nine years ago, and you remembered the details of it. The other members of the Tribunal seemed to understand it. Iksoc is not smart enough to pass the Tribunal exam."

Jame rubbed her chin as she ran the idea through her mind. It was true, Iksoc didn't seem to have a sound grasp of the tomes of legal concepts the other Tribunes have demonstrated. "So you think someone's behind his Tribunalship and behind his attempts to bring you and, by association, me down."

"Yeah." Tigh nodded as the rain slanted into sheets of water. "Miserable weather."

"So you think this person is dangerous enough to merit an Emoran escort back to Emoria?" Jame wrapped her arms around Tigh's waist, seeking her warmth from the rapidly chilling air.

Tigh cast affectionate eyes down at Jame. "Yeah."

"Now let me try to understand this." Jame looked up into blinking blue eyes. "You've been able to protect me from invading armies, mad wizards, power hungry scroll sellers, irate defendants, and hero worshipping girls but you don't think you can give me enough protection from here to Emoria?"

"Uh. Yeah." Tigh turned her attention back to the rain.

Jame had obviously missed something important going on with Tigh. Had she been too caught up in her own soul-searching, while Tigh struggled with issues of her own? "Why?"

Tigh sighed. "Whoever's behind this is powerful enough to buy a Tribunalship, which means this person is a respected member of our society. Someone we may trust without thinking."

"So, a group of Emoran warriors with Guard enhancements might deter anyone from trying anything," Jame said, "even though they may be in the perfect position to because we have no reason not to trust them."

Tigh blinked at Jame a moment. "Right."

Jame caught the uncharacteristic hesitation and the momentary confusion in Tigh's eyes. Perhaps the delay in leaving Ynit wasn't such a bad idea. It would give Tigh a chance to recover from her wound and give Jame a chance to talk to Bede about it.

In a way, Jame was relieved Tigh's self-doubt seemed to come from her dealing with something she rarely had to deal with—a wound bad enough to require time to heal. Tigh wasn't used to having her body not be able to respond quickly or gracefully to potentially dangerous situations.

"If it makes you feel better, we'll send for a patrol of warriors to escort us back to Emoria," Jame said.

Tigh answered with a thankful smile.

Jame loved that smile and couldn't stop her own in return. "Let's put together a simple meal and turn in early."

Tigh's smile became a happy grin. "Good plan." She turned in Jame's arms and captured her lips in an unexpected tender kiss.

"What was that for?" Jame asked a little breathless.

"Because I can't ever tell you enough how lucky I am you're in my life," Tigh breathed in her ear. "I'm glad you made the decision to return to Emoria."

"Really?" Jame pulled back to study the soft blue eyes.

"Really," Tigh said. "I think we're ready."

Jame gazed into Tigh's eyes and tried to swallow but her throat was suddenly too dry. "You really do?"

Tigh pulled Jame in for another kiss. Answering the question in the best way she knew how.

"LAUR'S WATERFALLS. HOW can a place change so much in seven years," Argis muttered as she nudged her horse around and around where several roads converged in the middle of Ynit.

"You said you know where the safe house is." Olet gave Argis a sidelong look.

"I do," Argis said, "once I find it."

"Let's just ask these soldiers." Wolfie nodded to three young women in Federation uniforms who had stopped in mid-stride to stare in awe at the gathering of fifteen mounted Emoran warriors in the road's intersection. Fifteen Emoran warriors who were suddenly looking at them. "Where's the Sword and Bow?"

"Uh," one of the soldiers managed to stammer out.

"You know where the safe house is, don't you?" Wolfie asked.

"Uh, yes." The soldier straightened. "You're Emoran warriors."

Wolfie grinned. "Last time I checked."

"Wow," the three soldiers said in unison.

Argis rolled her eyes. "The Emoran safe house."

A tall soldier with wispy blonde hair took a step forward. "We'll show you."

Argis looked back at her warriors and noted more than a few were eyeing the soldiers with curious interest. She sighed and turned back to them. "Show us."

The trio of soldiers grinned and led the group of mounted Emorans down the narrow streets of Ynit, receiving surprised and then envious looks from other soldiers.

"What do you think you're doing?" Argis asked a pair of young warriors who were pushing their horses past her.

"We, uh, we were just wondering if they were interested in, uh, doing a bit of sparring," Mara said with her best innocent look.

"Sparring?" Argis leveled a knowing look at them. "With or without weapons?"

Mara straightened in mock indignation. "We're enhanced. We wouldn't think of engaging in any kind of sparring they couldn't handle."

Olet sputtered a laugh. "So you think they can handle an Emoran?"

Mara grinned. "Life is full of new discoveries."

"Just remember we're representatives of Emoria," Argis said. "In other words, try to stay out of trouble."

"Trouble? Us?" Mara and her friend laughed as they nudged their horses alongside the trio of soldiers.

"WILL YOU NOW take it easy a bit?" Jame asked as she and Tigh stepped out of the infirmary into the first sunny day in a week. "Wounds take time to heal."

Tigh looked down at her boots and whispered, "I promise."

Jame sighed and wrapped her hands around Tigh's arm. "I know you hate feeling out of sorts."

"I hate upsetting you," Tigh said. "And my getting wounded has upset you."

Jame was about to protest but caught the sad, earnest expression in Tigh's eyes. Tigh would know she was lying anyway. "I don't know why, but seeing you get hit in the head like that really got to me. It made me think about how we're not getting any younger."

Tigh laid her hand upon Jame's. "A year ago I could have avoided that blow."

Jame looked up at Tigh. "You don't know that. Your hands were in shackles and chained to your feet."

"I saw it coming," Tigh said. "I had plenty of time to avoid getting hit."

Jame knew Tigh was very attuned to what her body could and could not do. "You saved me from the knives."

"That was child's play," Tigh said.

"But that's the kind of situation you usually have to deal with," Jame said. "How often are you going to be in chains and shackles with a crazy person with a sword coming at you?"

Tigh stared at her.

"There they are!" came shouts from across the courtyard.

"We'll talk about this," Jame said. "But I think you're overreacting in this case."

Tigh nodded. "Maybe."

Jame grinned and gave Tigh a quick kiss on the cheek before turning to the group of Emorans walking across the courtyard toward them. "How many did Jyac send?"

"It looks like I'm not the only one who is overprotective," Tigh said.

Twenty paces from Tigh and Jame, the Emorans stopped and fell into three lines of five, with Argis standing to the side of the group.

"Dear Laur, they're going to entertain the locals," Jame murmured.

As if hearing her words, people from all over the courtyard stopped whatever they were doing and walked toward the Emorans. Knots of soldiers, who had been following the warriors, loosely gathered around. Excitement and anticipation crackled in the air.

Argis unsheathed her sword with a hiss, and the warriors snapped into a rigid stance. She spun around, whipping the sword over her head before resting the tip on the adobe brick ground. The precise hiss of fifteen swords flowing out of scabbards cut through the sun-soaked air.

They performed in a display of swords whipping and slashing, blurring in the overhead sunlight, on the edge of abandonment while still in complete control. They compounded their intricate blade patterns with tosses sending the swords airborne and combat maneuvers bordering on the impossible. The gathering spectators held their breaths at the wondrous combination of Guard enhancements and traditional Emoran sword work.

Argis snapped her sword into a salute followed a heartbeat later by fifteen swords raised in honor of their princess.

"Hail, Jame, princess of Emoria," Argis called out.

"Hail, Jame, princess of Emoria," the warriors echoed in strong proud voices.

Jame sighed and walked to Argis followed by a beaming Tigh.

The warriors sheathed their swords in unison and grinned.

"Argis." Jame pulled her into her arms. "Thank you for the impressive greeting. Maybe a bit overdone but nice."

"We've been working all year on it, and I couldn't talk them out of doing it when we saw you," Argis said.

Tigh snorted a laugh and held out her arm. "Well met, Argis."

"Well met, Tigh." Argis grasped Tigh's forearm. "What happened to you?"

Tigh lifted a hand to the bandage around her head. "A part of a long story."

"A story I'm anxious to hear, since we're here because of it," Argis said. "We've made arrangements at the safe house for a special evening meal honoring our princess."

Jame studied the group of expectant warriors, the proud expressions in their eyes touching something deep within her she had kept buried during her time away from Emoria. Tigh always told her the Emoran princess was present in everything she did, and she only half believed it. But seeing herself through these warriors' eyes, she felt that princess surface too quickly to be buried too deep.

"It would be my honor to join you, Master Warrior, and your brave warriors." Her grin was reflected in the relaxed faces of the Emorans. The realization they were there to take her home for good settled over her like a warm blanket.

"WHAT WAS JYAC'S reaction?" Argis took a sip of the potent Emoran Ale and stared into the lively chamber filled with Emoran warriors and soldiers who had been only too happy to accept the quick invitations to attend the evening meal. "She was alarmed. And she has a right to be by what you've told me."

"I hate to say it, but I'm glad to be getting home." Jame gazed at Tigh, who was demonstrating her favorite knife trick to a table full of attentive Emorans and soldiers. "Tigh getting injured reminded me we're not getting any younger."

"I hate seeing warriors grow old," Argis grumbled into her mug of ale.

"Tigh can still beat any one of you blindfolded," Jame said, a little alarmed at Argis's serious despondency. Was she already feeling her age? "Not a year has passed since she beat sixteen Emoran warriors barefoot and without weapons."

Argis sighed. "I can only hope I'm in her kind of shape when I'm her age."

Jame faced Argis. Something was really bothering her. "Are you getting cold feet about your joining?"

Argis looked at her startled then shook her head. "It may sound funny, but that's the only thing I'm really sure about right now."

"Is it like an unsettled feeling? Like something uncertain is going to happen?" Jame asked.

"Yeah." Argis frowned. "An unexplainable something menacing my thoughts."

"I've been getting the same feelings," Jame said.

"Really?" Argis sat up and gave Jame her full attention. "Do you think it could be related in some way?"

"I don't know." Jame shook her head. "I do know this feeling has something do with Emoria because I've also been having dreams."

"Dreams?"

"Like Laur was calling me back," Jame said.

"Oh. Those dreams." Argis bit her lip.

"I always thought they were myths or legends," Jame said. "But I now know they're very real. The only difference is this undercurrent of menace, as you call it."

"I hate things I can't see," Argis muttered.

Jame smiled, happy to see the old Argis peeking through. "Maybe once we're all in Emoria, these feelings will go away."

"So you're really coming back for good?" Argis looked across the tavern. "Tigh doesn't have any problem with it?"

"Tigh has never had a problem with settling in Emoria," Jame said.

"I would never have made you happy." Argis looked down into her mug. "You were right. We would have been miserable together. I'm just glad one of us had the sense to see that at the time."

"I'm just glad that it all worked out," Jame said. "Your friendship is important to me and to Tigh."

"I'm glad." Argis raised her head. "I look forward to getting to know Tigh better."

"Claudi here can beat any one of your archers in the fog with crooked arrows," a challenging voice rose up from a table in the far corner.

"Hah. Peacetime soldiers can't even spit straight on a breezeless day," came the inevitable retort.

"Lon's not going to be happy if they start an all-out brawl in here," Jame said.

Argis shrugged. "Warriors will be warriors."

"Might I suggest setting up a formal competition?" Jame smiled at Tigh's rolled eyes as she stood to monitor the rowdy challenges flying back and forth.

A body clad in Emoran leathers dove across the table at an Ynitian soldier, sending food and ale in every direction. The others at the table turned over chairs and mugs in their haste to back away.

"Looks more like an Emoran mating ritual than a challenge from here," Argis said.

Jame shook her head in amusement and gave Tigh an imperceptible nod. Tigh walked over to the rowdy table and stood, arms crossed, over the Emoran and Ynitian who were rolling on the floor in a drunken wrestling match.

The room quieted as everyone's attention focused on Tigh. The brawlers stopped in mid move and looked up. Their eyes widened at Tigh standing over them.

"Why don't the two of you get a room or something," Tigh said.

The tension in the room shattered in hoots of laughter. The Emoran warrior and Ynitian soldier rather sheepishly disentangled themselves and helped each other to their feet.

"Why don't we straighten up this table so Lon will consider letting you all in here again." Tigh raised a wry eyebrow.

"I like the idea of a competition," Argis said. "We should be thinking about our place in the Southern Territories more."

Jame turned to Argis in surprise. "What happened to Emoria's desire to be isolated?"

Argis took a deep sip of ale and wiped the foam off of her lip with her arm. "You and Tigh happened."

THE EXCUSE WAS to give homage to the celebrated Emoran warriors. Argis knew the soldiers of Ynit just wanted to remain in the presence of her warriors for as long as possible. Before they slipped behind their curtain of secrecy high in the Phytian Mountains.

Of course, Argis didn't know who was more surprised, the Emorans upon seeing the two neat lines of soldiers mounted on horseback waiting for them to cross the courtyard to Jame's house, or the soldiers when they saw Emorans on horseback in full battle gear complete with menacing masks partially covering their faces.

Argis lifted her hand and the band of Emorans stopped behind her as Commander Maure rode down the line of mounted soldiers to them.

"Greetings, Master Warrior Argis." Maure lifted her sword in a salute that was precisely echoed by the rest of the soldiers.

"Greetings, Commander Maure." Argis returned the salute with her sword, her warriors not echoing but performing a simultaneous salute.

Eyes widened on the motionless soldiers, swords held at attention. Argis knew the rumors that Emoran warriors were magic soaked were common in Ynit.

Maure snapped her sword down and then sheathed it—her soldiers mimicking her movements with precision.

The Emorans whipped their swords in an intricate presentation before sheathing. The soldiers of Ynit stared in awe at the effortless display performed without a signal from Argis.

"Allow us the honor of escorting you as far as Rihnon," Maure said.

Argis ran puzzled eyes over the line of proud soldiers of the Southern Territories. She then turned to gauge the reaction of her warriors to the request, catching herself from rolling her eyes at their grins. She wasn't sure if a collaboration between the soldiers of Ynit and the warriors of Emoria would turn out to be a good idea but, at the moment, it wouldn't hurt her warriors to expand their horizons in more than one way.

Argis faced Maure. "The honor is ours."

Maure bowed her head and then grinned. Argis grinned back as she nudged her horse along the line of soldiers with her warriors following behind to the lane that went to Jame and Tigh's house.

"Stay here." Argis gave her warriors a knowing look. "And don't do too much flirting."

The Emorans grinned unrepentant at her. Argis shook her head and led a horse draped in full battle gear. The narrow lane echoed with the clip clop of the Emoran war horses. She mused on the first time she ventured down that lane in search of Jame. That was when she met Goodemer, although she had been astonished when Goodemer had told her she was the gangly girl who led her to Jame's house. Strange how their paths had crossed so early.

THE SPIT OF road that pretended to be a lane was crowded with two large wagons filled with seven years in the life of Jame and Tigh. Gessen burdened with saddlebags grazed along the side of the lane.

"Oh, for Laur's sake." Jame stood with her hands on her hips in her yard, not believing Argis would insist on full Emoran ceremony.

Argis rode up to the tiny adobe house and slipped off the horse. "What?" She frowned at Jame's look of dismay.

"Why can't we just ride out of town without causing a spectacle?"

Argis looked down at her boots and then raised thoughtful serious eyes.

"We want the world to see you the way we see you, this last time you'll be among them as a citizen of the Southern Territories rather than visiting Emoran royalty."

Jame held Argis's earnest gaze for a few seconds. She then sighed and looked at their belongings on the carts. Her choice had been made. She could no longer have it both ways. She had to learn to be a princess again.

Tigh stepped through the front doorway and took in Argis's formal dress and the war horses. She nodded and approached Jame and Argis.

"The horse matches your leather," Tigh said.

Jame sighed. "You don't have to convince me. I've already accepted my fate." She arched an eyebrow. "What about you?"

Tigh blinked at her. "What about me what?"

"Don't you think you should wear your Emoran leathers?"

Argis's eyes widened.

Tigh bit her lip and looked down into Jame's inscrutable eyes.

Jame snaked her arms around Tigh's waist and gazed patiently into the pale blue eyes. \

A smile tugged at Tigh's mouth. "I think they're in a saddle bag."

Chapter 6

JAME WASN'T QUITE sure what she was feeling as her escort spread out across a field of dried brittle grasses in the rolling hills halfway between Ynit and Rihnon. She knew she should be feeling some kind of sadness to be moving from a place she had lived since she was fifteen. But it wasn't as if they were never going back. Tigh had to return for her yearly evaluation with a healer, and she had to renew her arbiter's permit, now she was no longer an arbiter-at-large but a simple provincial arbiter.

"How about in the middle?" Remnants of a conversation reached her ears.

"Leave a circle free in the middle," another voice shouted to the warriors setting up tents.

Tents. Not an Emoran tradition except when escorting members of the royal family outside Emoria's borders. She wondered why Jyac wanted such a display of ceremony.

"How big a circle?"

The warriors had ridden all day, and all they could think about was finding a way to make good on all the good-natured boasting and challenges that had been casually tossed between troops. If nothing else, the exchanges kept Tigh grinning during the journey. Seeing Tigh in a good mood lifted Jame's spirits.

"I'm not sure about this. Except for Balderon, we've never gone against anyone who hasn't been enhanced." Argis's voice reached Jame, and she spun around.

Tigh and Argis were strolling in her direction oblivious to the jaw dropping stares Tigh received. Jame almost regretted insisting Tigh wear the Emoran leathers. On the other hand, she kind of liked showing off her partner's magnificent body.

"We haven't even sparred with the Lukrians," Argis said.

"Didn't you talk to Goodemer about it?" Tigh asked.

Argis shrugged. "She said she didn't give us the ruthless need to fight that you had. But . . . I don't know. Our skills are so strong, I'm afraid we could hurt someone even when we're being careful."

"Hmm." Tigh rubbed her chin. "I think you should have been sparring with the Lukrians."

"Perhaps."

Tigh grinned as she wrapped Jame in her arms and gave her an affectionate hug.

"What do you think about these challenges between the soldiers and our warriors?" Argis asked Jame.

"I think it's a wonderful idea," Jame said. "And I also think our warriors will be able to meet the challenges without harming the soldiers."

Argis cocked her head. "How can you be so sure?"

Jame shrugged. "Just look at how Tigh fights. Have you ever seen her hurt anyone beyond a simple flesh wound to end a challenge or enough to knock them out? Have you ever seen her kill anyone?"

Argis gazed at Tigh with a speculative look. "I've been wanting to ask you about that."

"I've only killed once since the end of the Wars," Tigh said. "That was Misner."

"Why?"

"As long as I can stop the enemy I'm not compelled to kill," Tigh said.

"She has so much control over her skills she can stop an adversary without killing," Jame said. "You and your warriors have the same gift."

Argis didn't look convinced.

"If I were you, the challenges would be the least of my worries," Jame said.

Argis frowned. "What do you mean?"

Jame scuffed a few rocks out of the dirt. "I'd be worry that some of your warriors might lose to an adversary that even your enhancements can't withstand."

Tigh snorted an amused laugh.

"Oh, you think some of my warriors are going to get all moony eyed over these somewhat adequate soldiers?" Argis crossed her arms.

Jame scanned the tent raising activity around them, noticing quite few exchanges of glances amidst the good-natured ribbing between the two groups. "I think some of our warriors are going to make fools of themselves they'll be so moony eyed."

"Emorans aren't like Tigh," Argis said.

"That's true." Jame nodded thoughtfully. "But traveling to new places and meeting up with new people brings out the unexpected."

Argis opened her mouth. Shouts cut through the general din of the camp. They turned as the young warrior and soldier who had fought in the Emoran safe house the night before stood face to face in the middle of the camp hurling colorful insults at each other.

"I predict a late summer joining," Tigh said, grinning at Argis' look of disdain as she stomped off to stop the warrior and soldier before the words turned into blows.

"HOW ARE YOU doing?" Tigh sat down on one of the many boulders around the camp.

Jame was perched cross-legged on an end of the rock, watching the preparation of the challenge pit.

Jame looked up and smiled. "I'm doing all right. Surprisingly enough."

Tigh nodded as her attention drifted to the activity in the center of the camp. "Uh . . . have you been thinking about the reason you're returning to Emoria?"

"Have you?" Jame cocked her head.

Tigh shifted and gazed at the ground. "Yeah."

"Good thoughts, I hope," Jame said.

Tigh nodded, scuffing her boot in the loose dirt. "Uh . . . should we . . . uh . . . do we need to do anything to prepare?"

Jame uncrossed her legs and scooted next to Tigh. "You mean like practice?"

Tigh blinked up startled before catching Jame's playful expression. "Do we need to practice?"

"I don't know if we need to, but it couldn't hurt." Jame pressed her arm against Tigh's. "And we know it'll be fun."

"So, you're not worried or nervous or anything?" Tigh focused on the feel of Jame's arm against hers. The patchwork of holes in the Emoran leathers had some advantages.

"Not worried, maybe a little nervous," Jame said.

"I'm a lot nervous," Tigh said.

"You didn't grow up in the Emoran tradition."

"I just hope I can . . . contribute . . . everything that's needed." Tigh mentally kicked herself for being so tongue-tied.

"Hmmm." Jame wrapped her arms around Tigh. "You have everything I need and that's what counts."

Tigh took a deep breath and relaxed as she held Jame in her arms. She blissfully ignored the puzzled and even envious looks from the Emorans. Perhaps the next generation of Emoran warriors will have a different attitude toward displays of affection in public.

The next generation. Tigh sighed as Jame cuddled closer and wondered what her place will be in Emoria's future.

THE LIGHT SPRINKLING of new snow only added to the history being made that night as Emoran warriors learned to temper their enhancements so they could fight without doing harm. Shouts and clashes of weapons filled the winter-touched air in the torchlit sparring circle.

"I don't believe it." Argis scratched the back of her head as one of her best warriors whipped and slashed her staff with blazing speed without even nicking her opponent.

Tigh turned to her with a quizzical look. "You mean you haven't figured out the skill it takes to strike an opponent is the same skill it takes to not strike?"

Argis blinked at Tigh. "It's not that easy."

"Sure it is," Tigh said. "The warrior just has to be as focused on not causing pain as she is on causing pain."

Argis gave Tigh a sidelong look as she tried to digest this almost alien concept.

"Your warriors are doing it without even thinking." Tigh swept her hand at the sparring circle. "All they know is they don't want to harm their opponents, so they're not."

Argis scowled. "They're all too enamored of these soldiers, just because they're new and different to them."

Tigh rolled her eyes. "Why don't you just give it try and find out for yourself?"

Argis felt unexplainably trapped by the idea. Like she didn't want to let go of the idea of being able to use lethal skills for something other than causing injury. "I don't . . ." She shook her head in frustration.

"Someday when you're ready," Tigh said. "You'll know when."

Argis nodded, remembering Tigh went through a period of having to relearn how to fight. Any kind of uncertainty wasn't good for the mental well-being of a warrior.

"So, how is Jame really reacting to coming home?" Argis crossed her arms and scuffed her boot in the powdery snow. "The truth."

Tigh sighed and watched a new pair of opponents flash their swords at each other for several heartbeats. "She's ready but it'll still be a difficult adjustment for her."

"She's really ready to come home?" Argis asked.

"Yes."

"She's ready to settle down and start a family?" Argis pressed. "Jyac is starting to worry about an heir."

"She's ready," Tigh said.

Argis studied Tigh as Tigh watched the swordplay. "Are you having a problem with this?"

Tigh sighed and ran her hand through her hair. "I didn't grow up around it like you. I'm a little nervous that I won't . . . uh, get it right."

Argis blinked at Tigh and barked a laugh. "I don't believe it. You'll face down a foreign army with little more than a sword and you're afraid that you can't perform a simple ceremony?"

"What if Laur chooses not to give us a child?" Tigh asked. "I wasn't born Emoran and I have it in me to be a ruthless, uncaring killer. She may not think me worthy."

Argis stared at Tigh. "You're kidding?"

Tigh turned to her with sad, earnest eyes.

"You're not kidding," Argis said. "How can you even doubt if you're worthy of Jame or your child? If it weren't for you, our warriors wouldn't be the best in the world, as we were many generations ago. You're a hero, and we're honored your blood will become a part of future generations of Emorans."

Tigh stared at Argis as if she didn't believe her.

"Why aren't you out there showing these pups how to swing a sword?" Argis asked.

"I'm supposed to take it easy for a while." Tigh lifted her hand to the bandage still wrapped around head.

"Getting whacked in the head by a sword really scrambles things up there for a while," Argis said.

"Yeah." Tigh sighed.

They squinted in the direction of shouts coming from the other side of the fighting circle.

"Now what?" Argis said as she and Tigh quickly strode around the circle of cheering warriors and soldiers.

Maure crunched and slipped on the night hardened snow as she hurried into the camp past the outer torches.

"Our scouts met up with some travelers from the north," Maure said as she slid to a stop on the snow-slick ground. "They said a big snowstorm is blowing this way."

"A snowstorm? This far south?" Tigh wrinkled her brow. "This has been a strange season for weather."

"As ever, the master of understatement," Maure said. "I don't know about you, but I'd be happier if we found some shelter. There aren't any natural wind breaks on these hills, and we're not prepared for a storm of that kind."

"Any ideas?" Argis turned to Tigh.

"There's a town on the coast not far from here." Tigh pointed to the south. "They have high bluffs overlooking the ocean, and the high tide doesn't engulf the beach."

"Will they let a small army stay there?" Argis stared into the gray filled with snowflakes.

"Oh yeah." Tigh grinned. "We saved their town from the army of the Silver Dragon many years back. I think they still have a yearly celebration."

Argis barked a laugh. "You see. Being a hero isn't such a bad thing sometimes. We can move the camp tonight."

Maure nodded and ran off toward her seconds in command.

Argis looked around and signaled to Olet. "This'll give us the practice of breaking down and setting up the tents." She turned to Tigh, who had the strangest look on her face. "Tigh?"

Tigh's blue eyes stared blankly at her, before she slumped to the ground.

SHE COULDN'T THINK of a sight that completed her soul more than the endless sprawl of campfires spread across the frozen valley that stretched to Lake Operal in the far distance. Fifty thousand enemy troops. Her blood warmed at the thought of sinking her sword into every one of them.

She didn't have to turn at the footfalls behind her. She knew who it was.

"I know that look." Ardhat, the Council's chancellor always had a smugness in her voice that grated on Tigh. "You can't wait to rid the earth of all traces that army ever existed."

Tigh allowed a feral grin as she saw the valley in her mind's eye with the snow littered with bodies and red with blood.

"They stand between us and the city of Operal," Ardhat almost purred.

Tigh turned, keeping, as always the scornful expression from her face at Ardhat's obvious enjoyment of the finer things their society had to offer. The clothing, bright and expensive, was wholly inappropriate for a military camp. The complexion and unhealthy roundness of body told of a lack of discipline that was as necessary as breathing for a soldier. All these would have made Ardhat insignificant to Tigh except for one small thing. Ardhat was the Council's voice that controlled the Elite Guard.

"There's a storm coming," Ardhat said. "We need to get into position around Operal before we're waist high in snow."

"At dawn," Tigh said

"We need the road cleared for Patch to move the siege engines to the city," Ardhat said.

Tigh returned her gaze to the camp, nostrils flaring a bit at the aroma of stew wafting up from the fire cauldrons where lines of soldiers snaked in between the tents. "My pleasure."

"Ah, yes," Ardhat stammered. "We're all thankful for your dedication."

Tigh did nothing to hide the disdainful sneer as she glanced at Ardhat before mentally dismissing her and studying the camp of the enemy.

Scraping. Something was scraping against . . . something. Tigh opened her eyes and saw dark gray skies thickened by a brewing storm and nightfall. She was moving. She tried to turn her head and winced at a sharp pain that pierced deep inside her skull.

"Tigh." The voice came from far above her. She tried to focus her eyes on the pale beast crunching through the snow beside her makeshift litter. "Don't try to move. We're getting you to a healer."

She nodded as she shut her eyes. Funny. She didn't remember getting wounded during the battle.

"HOW'S SHE DOING?" Argis waited for Olet to pull up next to the healer's door, as the rest of the troops filtered through the streets of the village down to the expansive beach. Townspeople had lit extra door and window lamps to illuminate the way through the storm-darkened streets.

"Restless." Olet looked back at a bundled up Tigh on the litter attached to her horse.

"She woke up briefly," Jame said as she dismounted and handed Gessen's reins to Olet. "She seems to be having dreams or something." She put a hand on Tigh's forehead. "Fever. I don't get it. The wound should be healing by now."

"Maybe it's just a minor complication," Olet said.

Jame raised worried eyes to her old friend. "I hope that's all it is."

The healer's door opened, and a short round woman bustled outside. She spotted Tigh on the litter and crunched through the quickly accumulating snow and knelt by her. "What happened?"

"She got hit in the head with a sword several days ago," Jame said. "Healer Bede at Ynit has checked her over twice and said for her to take it easy for a while. Which she was doing but out of the blue she passed out two sandmarks ago."

"Older wound," the healer muttered as she put her hand on Tigh's forehead. "Fever. Restless?" She raised her eyes to Jame.

"She seems to be having dreams or something," Jame said.

"Bede didn't detect anything unusual?" The healer stood up.

"He just said that it was a tricky wound and would take quite a while to completely heal." Jame stared down at Tigh.

"If Bede could have done more for it, he would have," the healer said. "I trained under him. He's the best in the Southern Territories. But he always told us skill won't always catch everything. Especially when complications are slow to manifest themselves and—"

"I know. Head wounds can be tricky." Jame tried to push down the apprehension about this element of the unknown.

Blue eyes fluttered open and then blinked away the falling snowflakes. "How did we get here?"

"You passed out, so we put you on a litter." Jame helped Tigh sit up.

"Passed out."

"The storm was coming, and we had to get moving."

"Storm." Tigh nodded as she tried to get up.

Jame and the healer helped her to her feet.

"We need to get your wound checked. You're running a fever." Jame stepped over the litter without letting go of Tigh's arm and led her through the door.

"WOUND." TIGH WORKED through the images and impressions crowding her fuzzy mind. She was leading a battle up north. But that wasn't possible because Jame was with her. She didn't know Jame then . . . She didn't remember knowing Jame then. But she remembered a snowstorm—like this one. But if she was remembering then, it wasn't happening now. Her mind wrapped itself around that idea to try to overcome the strength of the images of the battlefield of Operal.

"As talkative as ever." The healer chuckled as Jame helped Tigh sit down on a pallet.

"She's much better than she used to be," Jame said. "Sometimes she reverts when she's tired or working through a problem."

The healer held a candle flame in front of Tigh's eyes, going from one to the other. "Or when her thoughts are scrambled. The fever can do that but . . ." She carefully removed the bandage on Tigh's head revealing the neat clean stitches. "Hmmm. Good job but not good enough."

Jame looked at Tigh's wound in puzzlement. "What?"

"It's still very faint but the wizard's trace is finally coming through." The healer parted the dark hair on the edge of the wound to reveal a very faint outline of a twisted design.

"You mean the sword had a spell on it?" Jame and Tigh exchanged alarmed looks.

"I'm being stalked by another crazy wizard?" Tigh rolled her eyes to the ceiling. Her demented deity was at it again.

"It could have been me this time," Jame said.

"You always do like to share." Tigh gave Jame a wane smile.

"It takes a powerful wizard to cast a spell that delays their mark being visible for several days," the healer said as she held the candle flame before Tigh's eyes again. "You were having restless dreams?"

Tigh blinked at the dancing flame. "I thought I was on the battlefield at Operal."

"Why would you be dreaming about that?" Jame sat down and slipped her arms around Tigh's waist.

"The snowstorm, I think." Tigh frowned. "Strange I would think of that after all these years."

"This kind of magic plays with the mind." The healer sat back on her heels. "Unfortunately I can't help you. This needs a wizard more powerful than the one who cast the spell to get rid of it."

"Lucky for us we know just the wizard," Jame said.

"You don't understand. The wizard who did this is very powerful," the healer said. "It's very rare for a wizard to cast a delaying spell as strong as this one."

"Do you think the wizard who outsmarted Misner would be strong enough?" Jame asked.

The healer turned to Tigh. "I thought you stopped Misner."

Tigh grinned. "I wouldn't have been able to do it without some magical intervention."

"This wizard also enhanced the warriors of Emoria," Jame added.

The healer looked impressed. "I suggest you go to this wizard as soon as possible."

"No problem there," Jame said. "We just happen to be on the way to her joining."

TOWNSPEOPLE CLEARED THE way through the mounds of snow to the stables at the several inns for the horses. The warriors and soldiers used their swords and bodies to make a path down the main road past buildings partially hidden by snow with drifts almost to some rooftops. Wind pelted them with swirls of ice as they pooled onto the beach. Argis and Maure stared at the wall of white against the high bluffs edging the beach.

Argis signaled for several warriors to follow her. She led them to a section of the wall with snow that had a blueish tint. She unsheathed her sword and plunged it into the middle and felt it go completely through.

"Carefully, clear a hole here." She outlined an area with her sword. "Try not to bring the whole wall down on top of us."

The soldiers dug out an opening big enough for Argis to walk through, followed by Maure.

Argis stopped a few paces inside a sizable shelter cave. Maure walked around with a torch and illuminated several fire pits with sizable pots and metal grills that were popular on the southern coast. The inner wall sloped far enough into the cliff to accommodate everyone.

Maure walked back to Argis. "I think it's doable."

Argis nodded. "Time to get out of the weather."

"THIS CORNER WILL be good for Jame. Protected, far enough away from the entrance." Argis put Tigh's and Jame's packs on the sandy floor in front of the sloping back wall.

"I didn't think they got storms like this on the coast." Olet scratched her head as she watched a handful of soldiers work to keep a path open through the wall of snow.

"I have the feeling this is going to be a bad winter," Argis muttered as the soldiers backed away from their task, and Jame entered, followed by a pair of warriors supporting Tigh. "Over here."

Jame glanced around, spotted Argis, and nodded.

Argis didn't like Jame's grim expression as she made her way around the cook pots and makeshift sleeping areas. Olet took one look in Jame and Tigh's direction and pulled their furs from their packs and spread them out on the ground.

"Thanks, Olet," Jame said, as she and Argis eased Tigh down onto the furs.

"Why aren't you covered in snow?" Argis felt Tigh's dry leathers.

"The mayor insisted we take her carriage." Jame gave Argis a wry look.

"Could the healer figure out what's wrong?" Argis asked as Jame tugged off Tigh's boots.

"The sword was touched by magic," Tigh mumbled.

"Magic?" Argis frowned. "I thought magic didn't affect you."

"That's what we thought." Tigh sighed. "But I've never been whacked in the head with a spell-bound sword before."

"Goodemer will know the answers," Argis said with confidence.

"But who cast the spell?" Olet took Tigh's boots from Jame and put them against the wall, out of the way.

Jame shook her head. "Maybe Goodemer has some idea about that, too."

"Jame." Tigh's voice was heavy with grogginess. "Warn them about the flashbacks," she managed to get out before drifting to sleep.

"Flashbacks?" Argis turned to Jame.

Jame sighed and placed a gentle kiss on Tigh's forehead. "On the way here, she had vivid dreams of being on the battlefield of Operal during a snowstorm."

"You mean while she was—?"

"Yes." Jame climbed to her feet and stretched. "We don't know if it has to do with the magic or if the snowstorm set off the memory in her feverish state."

"Has she ever, uh, had dreams about being a Guard before?" Argis asked.

"Never," Jame said. "The cleansing spares the Guards of flashbacks and nightmares from the Wars."

"So, for her to dream about that time—"

"Doesn't mean the cleansing is wearing off." Jame flashed a look of irritation. "It means something out of the ordinary has happened to cause it. Like the magic the healer detected."

Argis silently studied the warriors preparing the thick stew in the pots over the fires. Just the year before, she had witnessed what Tigh was like when she had been enhanced. She had seen the harsh coldness in her eyes and heard the ruthless tone in her voice. She also remembered the desperate need in Tigh's eyes when she dropped to her knees before Jame—the need for Jame to not turn her back on her after seeing the monster she once had been. But Jame never even considered the idea to give up on Tigh. She was ready to capture Tigh and drag her back to Ynit so she could be re-cleansed.

Argis never wanted to witness Tigh the Terrible again, but she wanted to grow old in the company of Tigh the queen's consort.

"We'll do everything we can to remove this magic," Argis said. "Out of curiosity. What would happen if she flashes back to being Tigh the Terrible?"

Jame rubbed her chin. "She'd be confused if she thought she were still in the Wars, but not overtly violent. You remember when Meah turned her into Tigh the Terrible. She didn't become some mindless monster with a need to kill everyone, she became very focused on the fact that Meah had insulted her by laughing at her."

"So you're saying, don't do anything to make her angry," Argis said.

"Right. But I don't think she'll turn into Tigh the Terrible." Jame looked down at Tigh. "With magic, it's hard to tell what it'll do to her."

Argis gave out a frustrated sigh. She hated uncertainty as much as she hated unseen enemies who were too cowardly to just stand up and fight.

Chapter 7

TIGH STARED AT the frozen snow-covered lake and then at Operal clinging to the edge of the cliffs that rose from the lake's northern bank. She brushed the snowflakes away from her face as she studied the extensive system of docks stretching into the lake.

She knew caves dotted the cliff, providing ways of getting supplies into the city and even an escape route if needed for the citizens of Operal. The lake and the cliffs, topped by high thick walls, made the city nearly invincible from invasion from the water.

But they weren't invading from the water . . .

"We need to cut off their supply route," Tigh said.

Meah shook her head. "We don't have the forces to watch the lake and set up the siege."

"We need to make it so they can't get the supplies, even if they're brought right to their back door." Tigh shaded her eyes against the sharp glints from the ice that seemed to cover the cliffs. "How many volunteers do you think we'd need to plug the caves and destroy the docks?"

Meah rubbed her chin. "For a quick quiet operation, a few hand-picked volunteers ought to do."

Then let's . . ." Tigh raised her hand to her head as her thoughts jumbled together. "Let's . . ."

"What's wrong?"

She looked at Meah but realized her second-in-command hadn't asked the question. In fact, she was studying the lake, unaware Tigh was having problems putting her thoughts together.

"Something's interfering." A strained voiced echoed in her head.

Tigh pressed her palms against the sides of her head as an indefinable pressure pushed more confusion to her brain. She had to somehow escape . . . the pain . . . too much . . . too much . . .

She sat up so fast she grabbed her spinning head with both hands and held it until the stomach-churning action stopped. She lowered her hands and blinked. The cave was dark except for the deep orange glow from the fires.

Cave. What was she doing in a cave? She squinted at the uniformed women gathered around the fires and sprawled on furs spread over the sandy ground. This wasn't her army . . .

A body close to her sat up. The body felt comfortable and familiar. Strange . . . "Where's my army?" Her voice was surprisingly soft.

She remembered this place but not from her time at Operal. How could she think of Operal as being in the past when she was there now? But she couldn't be there.

She raised her hands to her head again and pressed her palms against her forehead. Too much confusion.

"Your army has been disbanded for close to a decade," a soft voice tickled her ear.

That wasn't another disembodied voice . . . Tigh turned to Jame, and her world flipped right-side up. It felt so natural, she didn't even marvel at how easily it happened. "They wouldn't get along with anyone anyway."

Jame tried not to show her relief, but Tigh knew she probably scared the life out of her.

"This cave is crowded enough as it is," Jame said.

"So's my brain," Tigh said. "Something serious is going on in there."

"Operal again?"

Tigh nodded. "Stranger than that. I dreamed about something that never happened."

"What?" Jame pulled herself around so she faced Tigh.

"It was after the battle and after the snowstorm." Tigh concentrated on the remnant impressions from her dream. "I was standing on the edge of the lake—it was covered with ice and snow—talking to Meah. I came up with a scheme to cut off Operal's supply and escape route by destroying their docks and plugging their cave system."

"But you took advantage of it being winter and surrounded the city with your troops. You came up with those clever floats that protected troops and supplies when the ice weakened . . ."

Tigh stared at her astonished.

Jame shrugged with a sheepish look. "We heard many stories while the war was going on."

"I didn't think they were in such detail," Tigh said.

"Probably not out in the world, but I was at Ynit studying at the time," Jame said. "Not only did we hear just the stories but firsthand accounts of what was happening."

"You never—"

"I never wanted to." Jame took Tigh's hand. "There's nothing about what happened back then that has to do with us."

"Something else strange happened." Tigh frowned as she tried to make sense of her dream right before she woke up. "Someone asked 'what's wrong?' I remember it because I was talking to Meah but Meah didn't say it. Wait. Something happened before that. I was trying to give her orders, and my thoughts got confused but she didn't seem to even notice I was stammering. She just stared at the lake. Then I heard someone ask 'what's wrong?'" Tigh paused as she tried to put it together. "Another voice answered, 'something's interfering.'"

They gazed at each other for several heartbeats.

"Then what?" Jame asked.

"It felt like too many things were pressing against my brain at once, and all I wanted to do was escape the pain . . . then I woke up," Tigh said.

"Someone's trying to control your mind? Of all the horrible . . ." Jame frowned. "But you spent a part of your life under some kind of mind control."

"Yeah, but I knew who and why then," Tigh said.

"ADVANTAGES OF BEING in the south," Maure said as the Emorans and Ynitian soldiers helped the villagers remove snow from the roads and fragile roofs. "Snowstorms are swift, coming and going."

"But they leave as big of a mess." Argis shook her head as a pair of her warriors flung snowballs at a few unsuspecting soldiers.

Maure cocked her head at Argis. "Are your warriors always so mischievous?"

The soldiers reeled around in anger until they saw the grinning Emorans. Emorans somehow had the ability to make even a challenge to a snowball fight look like a flirtation.

Argis paused at the unexpected question. "Yeah, I guess we are. It's just our nature. Never thought about it before."

"Sometimes I think our style is a little too serious at Ynit," Maure said.

Argis shrugged. "You didn't grow up together. These warriors have been playing, fighting, working, and loving together since they were born. They've been training together since they could walk, and have lived together since they received their first braid for combat."

"Most of our soldiers come from villages," Maure said. "They came to Ynit with a serious determination to make something of their lives. I have to admit the number of girls wanting to join our ranks has increased considerably since Jame and Tigh have taken to wandering the Southern Territories."

"They're quite a pair." Argis' grin waned as she thought about Tigh's current troubles. "I never thought about how much Jame and Tigh will be missed when they settle in Emoria."

"I think we'll all be surprised by how much we miss their presence," Maure said. "From the moment they met, they were something special together."

Argis remembered her one-sided view of the situation at the time. "What do you mean?"

"Those of us in Ynit at the time got caught up in, first, Jame's determination for Tigh to get a fair first hearing and then their growing friendship and romance," Maure said. "Did you know when Jame went to Glaus, nearly everyone in the compound kind of looked after Tigh because she was so lost without her? We brought her food so she would eat, and she spent the nights working in the infirmary instead of sleep. When she fell asleep on her job in the archives, they let her sleep."

"I had in my mind the whole time she was a cruel warrior, just using Jame to get her freedom." Argis laughed at the irony.

Maure grinned. "And because of that you became a part of the story we followed that summer."

"Laur's waterfalls, I was so young then." Argis sighed. "I'm glad I didn't have the authority to drag Jame away like I desperately wanted to do."

"Hey!" Two Emorans, trying to avoid an avalanche of snowballs from the street, tumbled off a roof into a deep snowdrift.

"What do you think about the cross-training idea?" Maure quirked an eyebrow at Argis.

The skirmish in the street quickly erupted into a full-scale battle. Emorans and soldiers hurled insults at each other as they abandoned their work and converged on the main square in dozens of snowball skirmishes.

Argis made a show of thoughtfully considering Maure's question. She noted some of the gathering townspeople—keeping in the doorways and against the walls—were exchanging bets. "It sounds like a good idea. Someone has to teach your troops how to throw a snowball."

Maure crossed her arms. "Oh, really? They seem to be holding their own. Although your warriors' tactics are quite interesting. They don't seem to mind getting hit while they chase a particular enemy to put snow down her tunic."

"The down side of growing up together is letting someone know they're interested in being more than friends," Argis said. "So they had to come up with different ways of sending signals of interest, without getting teased for going soft."

"Snow down a tunic?" Maure asked, amused.

Argis nodded. "One of the more common signals since we get a lot of snow in Emoria."

"Jame's signals to Tigh weren't that subtle," Maure said. "Considering she was the one who asked Tigh out first—in public, in the middle of a crowded corridor in the fortress. Witnesses still talk about how bashful Tigh was when she accepted the invitation. Of course, she might have thought twice about it if she knew she'd end the evening with a bruised and bleeding lip."

Argis shook her head. "I was so wrong about that whole thing. I'm just happy both Jame and Tigh have forgiven me for it."

"As you said, you were all young at the time."

"Jame's not a warrior, so she doesn't have to worry about looking soft in front of other warriors." Argis winced as one of the solders tackled a warrior, sat on her, and smeared snow into her face. The soldiers were catching on. "If she had done that to a warrior in Emoria, the warrior would still be getting teased about it."

"No one seems to be teasing Tigh," Maure said.

Argis chuckled. "Uh, no one has dared to. It took some getting used to when she was in Emoria. Sixteen warriors challenged her because they couldn't believe she could be so . . . mushy, and still be a good warrior."

"Sixteen?"

"She took them all on at once and didn't even pull her sword." Argis grinned at the memory.

"That's the Tigh I remember." Maure looked up at a second-floor balcony overlooking the square. Tigh and Jame were visiting the mayor that morning, and the three of them were on the balcony watching the snowball fight.

"She'll be all right," Argis said with determination. "Goodemer is the greatest wizard in the Southern Territories, and she understands how magic works on Tigh."

Maure turned to Argis. "If you need an army to fight off this rogue wizard, don't hesitate to send word to Ynit."

"I'll keep your offer in mind." Argis nodded.

"WHAT IS IT with all the snow this year?" Tigh shouted over the howling wind.

The band had dismounted and were leading their horses through the pass north of Rihnon. The Rihnon pass on the southern flank of the Phytian Mountains usually stayed clear of heavy snow year around. It rarely if ever saw snow this early in the season.

"Unbelievable," Jame muttered as she pushed against the wall of wind and blizzard of snowflakes.

"A little too unbelievable." Tigh shaded her eyes as they stopped for the umpteenth time and could barely make out the warriors and soldiers ahead of them. The snow on the trail was drifting to shoulder height and the wind blew as much back on the trail as they tried to shovel away.

Jame shook out her leather cape and re-draped it around her shoulders. "If it's this bad this far down in elevation, what's Emoria like?"

"I hear something." Olet stopped in mid-scoop. "Up ahead."

Everyone stopped and listened for several heartbeats.

Argis frowned. "What's Tas doing here?"

The warriors and soldiers scooped and tossed with greater vigor until they saw dark figures through the blanket of falling thick snowflakes.

"We found them," Tas yelled over her shoulder as she trod through the snow, holding a snow shield.

"Aren't you supposed to be in Artocia?" Argis put her hands on her hips and glared at Tas.

"We were on our way back when the storms started up. We left Seeran's belongings in Rihnon and got to Emoria before this happened." Tas looked at the walls of snow on either side of them.

"How is the rest of the way?" Tigh asked.

"We're keeping it as clear as possible," Tas said. "But this new snow hasn't made it easy."

"Then why are we standing around here?" Argis rolled her eyes and gave her horse a tug.

"Hey, you look good in Emoran leathers," Tas said to Tigh.

Tigh looked down at her patchwork of winter leathers. "Thanks."

"I think they look good, too," Jame said, giving Tigh an affectionate squeeze.

Tigh grinned.

"Looks like you dragged half of Ynit along with you." Tas shaded her eyes at the long string of horses and soldiers waiting to get moving.

"It's a long story." Jame rolled her eyes.

Tas grinned. "I always did enjoy your stories."

CLAUDI KEPT NUDGING Fant as the band of travelers finally trudged through the southern gate and straggled into the expansive plaza of Emor. The Emorans seemed to have made efforts to keep the stone ground clear, but new layers of snow made the fountain and low walls and tables and benches in front of what looked like a tavern look like they were covered with white adobe. Claudi didn't mind because the effect of the falling snow cast the city sculpted from white stone in a magical glimmer.

Claudi, along with all the other Ynitian soldiers, gazed in wonder at the huge bright murals of ancient Emoran heroes. She squinted through the heavy snowfall at the towering bluffs rising high above them. Walkways seemed to be carved behind waist-high walls that snaked all over the walls pocked the windows and doorways.

"They live inside these cliffs," she said.

Fant was scribbling in her small journal. "I want to get down the soldiers' reactions. Just think, my history of Ynit will be the only one with a firsthand account of Ynitian soldiers entering the legendary Emoria for the first time."

The Emorans, dressed in leather and fur, emerged from the doors up and down the cliffs until the walls were filled with women and girls. An excited murmur filled the air as the Emorans chattered to each other.

"Is that the queen?" Claudi dragged Fant to the edge of the chaos of soldiers, Emorans, and horses for a clear view of what could only be the palace.

Fant squinted at the tall opened double doors in a sheer cliff wall pocked with enormous clear quartz windows. A where a golden-haired woman walked across the threshold and stood with arms crossed as she studied the scene in front of her.

"I can't tell if she's upset or amused by us being here," Fant said.

"Attention."

Claudi and Fant looked in the direction of the voice. Maure was perched on the fountain wall in the middle of the plaza.

"The horses have to be attended to first." Maure's voice rang out in the clear mountain air. "Remove all your gear and saddles. When the stable hands have taken your horses, get yourself and your gear to the barracks over there, where the nice ladies are waiting to show you where to bunk."

Claudi and Fant turned to the barracks and joined the others in a nervous laugh at the "nice ladies." A group of Emoran warriors, exhibiting their best tough attitudes, lounged around the opened doors leading into their domain.

"This is going to be a very interesting experience," Fant said.

Claudi opened her mouth but was struck dumb by a tall woman with blond hair and a bow and quiver of arrows strung on her back sauntering up to her. The archer eyed the colored patches sewn to Claudi's tunic.

"They tell me those patches are like our braids." Mularke ran her finger across the braids hanging from her belt. "Does that mean you're pretty good with that bow?"

"This is Claudi the dragonslayer," Fant said. "She killed the wizard who led the army of the Silver Dragon."

"Dragonslayer, eh?" Mularke casually raked her eyes over Claudi. "I'm Mularke, Master Archer. I'm afraid the most notorious thing I've ever done was pin one of Queen Jyac's banners to the bellybutton on that painting of Hekolatis." Mularke pointed to the dramatic mural that reached far up the cliff face. "I was aiming at the eyebrow but I was too drunk to keep my bow steady."

Claudi didn't know quite how to react to this astonishing confession but decided Mularke was an amiable enough character. "Then you must have been a little less drunk when you won those braids."

Mularke gave her a rakish grin. "A little less. Perhaps we can do some target shooting while you're here."

"On the condition that I stay well behind you."

Mularke threw her head back and roared out a laugh. "And they told me the soldiers of Ynit were boring and serious." She slapped Claudi on the back. "Let's get this gear off your horses, and I'll show you where you can bunk."

JAME COULDN'T KEEP away a grin as she trudges through the mounting snow to Jyac, who was half-obscured behind the thick flurries.

"I didn't know you'd be bringing half of Ynit with you." Jyac laughed as she embraced Jame. She held Jame at arm's length and brushed the snowflakes from her cheek.

Jame shrugged. "They wanted to come along for some reason."

Argis stepped next to Jame, brushing the snow off the patchwork of fur and leather covering her arms. "They wanted to make sure Jame made it home safely."

"And they didn't think your group was enough?" Jyac arched an eyebrow.

"It's one of those long stories that Jame is good at telling," Argis said.

"That's what these long winter nights are for." Jyac looked up at the sky. "This winter looks like the nights will be longer than usual."

"Before anything, we need to get Goodemer to take a look at Tigh's wound." Jame turned around and squinted through the thick flurry of snow. Tigh was exchanging a few words with Maure.

"Goodemer?" Jyac's brow creased.

"It's a part of that long story," Jame said. "Some kind of spell was on the sword that caused that wound on Tigh's head."

"I though magic didn't affect Tigh," Jyac said.

"That's what we thought." Jame sighed. "Hopefully Goodemer will have some answers."

"I'll go find Goodemer and bring her to your quarters," Argis said.

Jame laughed. "You just want to find Goodemer. We'll meet you in my quarters in half a sandmark."

Argis nodded and trotted across the square toward Goodemer's quarters.

"She's like a different person," Jame said.

"Goodemer has been a good influence on her." Jyac smiled at Jame.

"I'm just glad she found someone to spend her life with." Jame watched in amusement as Argis trotted up one of the cliffside paths.

"I'm glad you also found a devoted companion." Jyac put a hand on Jame's arm. "My only regret is we spent too many years resisting Tigh when we should have been embracing her as a sister."

"On the other hand, it gave us an opportunity to prove we belong together." Jame grinned at the unmistakable crunch of boots on the snow. She turned around just as Tigh stepped up to her. "Everything arranged for the soldiers?"

Tigh nodded. "It'll be a tight squeeze tonight while they prepare one of the practice chambers as temporary barracks."

"Hmmm. I'll make sure to have some extra patrols out tonight," Jyac said. "When the ale and the boasting start flowing, Laur only knows what will happen."

Jame looked up at the dark clouds that were expelling a seemingly impossible amount of snow. "The way this weather is going, the Ynitians may be here for quite a while."

Jyac laughed as she threw an arm around Jame's shoulder to lead her into the palace. She winked at Tigh. "Emoria is never dull with you two around."

"MAURE IS PROBABLY regretting helping us get our wagons up the mountain, instead of stopping in Rihnon," Jame said as she stood and gazed out the glazed window of her chamber at the chaotic activity in the plaza below.

"She may grumble about it, but deep down she's probably thankful for a bit of adventure," Tigh said as she carefully unpacked the saddlebags into the niches in the side wall.

"A year ago, they would have been stopped on the border and not allowed in—allies or not," Jame said. "This feels like the right thing for Emoria but . . ." She waved her hand and sighed.

Tigh stopped her work and gave Jame her attention. "If you start doubting these decisions then Emoria will never have the opportunity to grow. There's always a chance of failure, but there's an equal chance of success. Nothing comes without risk or a price."

"You'd better watch yourself before you turn into a philosopher," Jame said.

Tigh did a quick scrutiny of her body. "Hmmm. Maybe too late."

Jame laughed, almost missing the soft knock on the door.

Tigh went to the door and opened it. Jame rushed to Tigh's side, pulled a bemused Goodemer through the doorway, and gave her a hug.

"Congratulations on your upcoming joining." Jame grinned at the tall, wiry wizard.

"Thank you," Goodemer said. "And welcome home. Both of you."

Jame led Goodemer into to chamber. "Where's Argis?"

"She got waylaid." Goodemer rolled her eyes. "She'll be here if she can free herself from getting the visitors settled." She turned to Tigh and frowned.

"What?" Tigh asked.

"I think I'd better take a look at this wound," Goodemer murmured.

Jame grabbed Tigh's arm and took her to a chair at the table. "You can see something?" she asked as she sat adjacent to Tigh.

"Seeing, sensing, it blurs when dealing with spells." Goodemer stood behind Tigh and carefully removed the bandage.

"But isn't Tigh immune to magic?" Jame asked.

"There are different kinds of magic." Goodemer lifted her wolf's head amulet over the wound. "I don't recognize this trace."

"Another rogue wizard?" Jame sighed.

"At least a clever wizard who was able to hide the trace beneath a don't-look-at-me spell," Goodemer said.

"So this wizard isn't as powerful as the healer thought," Jame said as she took Tigh's hand.

"This looks like pretty ordinary spell casting to me." Goodemer inspected the wound area and then snapped her fingers.

"Agh." Tigh clutched her head with both hands, turned around, and gave Goodemer an evil look.

"Sorry." Goodemer shrugged with a sheepish look. "Removing the spell was going to hurt no matter what."

"So it's gone?" Jame asked.

"All gone." Goodemer rubbed her amulet and held it over Tigh's head.

"Were you able to determine anything from it?" Tigh gingerly fingered where the wizard's trace had been.

"Only that the spell was sloppily cast." Goodemer sat down at the table. "But I knew that before."

"Before." Tigh frowned. "It was you."

"Yes," Goodemer said. "As you know, it's hard to hide wizardry from other wizards. When I became aware of some interesting activity in Ynit, I set up a vigil spell to monitor it. I thought it odd that someone was attempting a sword spell. That kind of spell is difficult to pull off and is not performed very often because the use of wizardry is against the rules of combat. It wasn't until you sent for an escort that I realized the spell might have something to do with you two."

"I'll try not to take that the wrong way," Jame said.

"You do tend to attract some of the strangest kind of trouble," Goodemer said. "I couldn't tell if the spell had been cast but I did detect a secondary spell set up to influence the sword one."

"And you were able to break into this spell." Tigh grinned.

Goodemer shrugged. "Secondary spells are not very strong to begin with, and I don't think whoever cast it expected someone to interfere with it. That was the last dream you had, right?"

Tigh looked at Goodemer in wonder. "Yes."

"They knew if they tried again, I would have caught them," Goodemer said.

"Hmmm." Jame put a finger to her lips in thought. "Too bad, though. I'd like to know who's behind this."

"Anyone who goes to all that trouble to cast obscure spells is most likely not going to give up," Tigh said.

"But we're in Emoria now." Jame glanced around the chamber she grew up in. "We ought to be safe here."

"Let's hope so," Goodemer said quietly and then blinked at Tigh and Jame, who were watching her with expectation. "I didn't like what I was feeling from those others in your dream."

"Feeling," Tigh said.

"It's hard to put into words." Goodemer's expression became distant. "I want to use words like evil, unwholesome, almost an inhuman feel." She shook her head. "Like I said, not good."

Chapter 8

JYAC DECIDED TO open the great hall in the palace for an impromptu banquet for the unexpected guests from Ynit. She smiled in amusement at how many of her warriors were fascinated by the newcomers. What she found more interesting was the reactions of the warriors who went to Ynit to the attention the soldiers of the Southern Territories were receiving from the warriors who stayed home. She suspected a few attachments had already formed.

She looked to either side of her. How much had changed in a single year. Ronalyn and Goodemer were discussing the climatic differences between Maymi and Emoria. Jame was relating an apparently amusing story to a laughing Tas and Seeran. Tigh and Argis had interrupted their discussion on how to keep the visiting soldiers entertained to go break up a fight in the far corner of the hall.

Jyac felt strangely at peace at that moment. Like her world for the first time was comfortably settled. She looked at Jame, who had finished her story and was gazing out over the hall with an amused affectionate expression. All it took was Jame falling in love with an outsider, and Emoria's world had changed for the better. Amazing.

"Why so thoughtful?" Ronalyn asked, leaning into Jyac.

Jyac blinked out of her reverie and wrapped an arm around Ronalyn's shoulder. Goodemer had risen from her seat to get a better look at the commotion Argis and Tigh seemed to be caught in.

"I was just thinking how right all this feels." Jyac glanced in Jame's direction. "And to think we resisted this for all those years. Resisted Jame's choice of a life companion for so long. Hindsight . . ." She waved her hand.

The sound of heavy chairs crashing to the floor and shouts erupted from the far corner of the hall. Everyone else in the hall were on their feet, arching their necks and trying to see the scuffle.

Jyac stood with the other occupants at her table. Several warriors and soldiers engaged in a shoving and posturing match, their insults drowned out in the rising noise of the hall.

Tigh and Argis unsheathed their swords and pushed themselves between the brawlers.

"I think we'd better get some challenges set up before someone gets hurt." Jyac smiled as Tigh sheathed her sword, raised herself to her full height, and crossed her arms.

Jame laughed out loud as the warriors and soldiers stepped away from each other. They stared at Tigh in awe and even some fear. Tigh held her stance for several heartbeats before relaxing and grinning at them. Argis made some kind of comment to Tigh, and the group erupted in a nervous laugh.

Jyac turned to Jame and smiled. "She's going to be good to have around." Jame chuckled. "I've always enjoyed having her around."

"As much as I hate to admit, she's been a good influence on you," Jyac said. "I'm just sorry it's taken so long for us to see it."

"As Tigh and I have discovered while out on the road," Jame said. "A new world dawns each morning, you just have to be there to discover it and take advantage of it."

THE WATER IN the pool below the waterfall was soothing and warm but not as soothing and warm as the arms wrapped around her from behind. She always marveled how arms could be so strong, yet so soft and gentle at the same time. She felt safe in those arms.

Instead of being enveloped in the warm strong arms as she woke up, Jame was tangled in a warm nest of skins and furs in an otherwise empty bed.

She raised her head and looked around the dimly lit chamber. Tigh sat, wrapped in a fur, cross-legged in front of a fire, studying a small crystal of a waterfall—turning it different ways, creating explosions of color as it filtered the light from the low fire in the fireplace.

Jame knew Tigh's sudden interest in crystal waterfalls had nothing to do with the actual object. Tigh was mystified, curious, and a bit fearful of the powers of Laur.

No matter how much Jame tried to put Tigh's mind at ease, Tigh just couldn't wrap her mind around this child-gift Laur was capable of giving.

Jame selected a fur and covered her bare skin. The night had been filled with gentle kisses and lovemaking. Jame grinned at what the Emoran warriors would think of their preference for sweet, gentle love. Not keeping with the tough warrior image at all.

Jame padded across the fur covered stone floor and dropped cross-legged in front of Tigh.

Tigh gave her a sheepish look and shrugged at the crystal before putting it down.

"Laur wants us to have a beautiful child together," Jame said softly.

"A child of yours can't help but be beautiful." Tigh took Jame's hand and pressed it to her lips.

Jame grinned. "I'm hoping our child looks like you."

Tigh smiled and shook her head. "You have the looks and the bearing of an Emoran Queen. I did my research. Every queen in your history has been fair-haired."

"Really?" Jame cocked her head, intrigued.

Tigh nodded.

"So if our child has hair like yours, it'll be the beginning of a new and exciting time in Emoria." Jame laughed Tigh's expression. "My people will love our child and respect her as a princess and a queen no matter what she looks like."

Tigh slowly nodded and leaned forward and captured Jame's lips with her own.

"So you have nothing to worry about," Jame said. "Just putting up with me for nine months while I carry our child."

Tigh blinked up at her. "But Tas said Laur chooses who carries the child."

"There are royal privileges that only we know about. I get to choose who carries the next princess of Emoria," Jame said. "For many reasons, I'm the best choice."

A renewed look of worry flashed across Tigh's face. Jame scooted forward and wrapped her arms around Tigh's neck.

"Laur's gift doesn't hold the risks other mothers experience when carrying a child," she said. "Only some of the discomforts as our bodies change."

"Honestly?" Tigh asked in Jame's ear.

"Honestly." Jame closed her eyes as a warm tingle went through her. After all these years, Tigh could still set her on fire. "Hmmm. Want to practice some more?"

Tigh answered by lowering Jame to the fur-covered floor.

"THIS IS WORSE than the blizzard from when we were children." Gindor stood outside her door with Poag. The fountain in the plaza had disappeared during the night in the waist high snow. Efforts to clear pathways across the expanse of open space were useless in the unending snowfall.

"I'm glad our princess made it home before the worse of it hit," Poag said.

Gindor grimaced. "That girl has more luck than a mountain sprite."

Their attention turned to snow-deadened noises coming from the barracks. The soldiers from Ynit stepped into the only clear path close to the far stone wall and trudged with their gear toward the palace where two halls had been prepared for them.

Gindor scowled. "She did have to bring half the army of Southern Territories with her, didn't she?"

"They came as an escort," Poag said. "They didn't know it would be snowing like this."

"They didn't think our warriors could properly take care of their own princess?" Gindor asked.

"They escorted her out of respect for all that she and Tigh have done for the Southern Territories in the last few years," Poag said.

Gindor sighed. "Now they're stuck here for Laur knows how long."

"Jyac thinks the interaction between our warriors and these soldiers will be good for us."

"It's one thing letting a couple of outsiders into our country, but half an army?" Gindor threw up her hands. "All I see is continually breaking up brawls and endless challenges."

"And how is that different from life around here all the time?" Poag asked.

Gindor scowled at Poag.

Poag grinned. "You just don't like outsiders."

"What the . . . ?"

They stared in disbelief as the layers of snow on the plaza turned into wisps of white and then disappeared. Standing across the square was a grinning Goodemer and a smug-faced Argis.

"Sometimes outsiders can be useful," Poag said.

"Hmmph." Gindor couldn't protest since she was the one who brought Goodemer into Emoria.

"Look. The snow is melting as it touches the ground," a woman cried out in delight.

Poag simply grinned.

Dozens of warriors, whooping and yelling, ran onto the plaza and crashed down onto the hard stone, looking stunned. Laughter came from the front of the palace. The indignant warriors yelled protests at Goodemer and Argis.

Goodemer raised her hand and snapped her fingers. The ice covering the plaza melted away.

"Having a wizard around has been interesting," Poag said.

Gindor nodded. "She certainly has brought out the playfulness in Argis."

The warriors climbed to their feet and after wary glances at Goodemer, continued their frolicking in the snowless plaza.

"Argis was far too serious before. Far too serious with her relationship with Jame." Poag shook her head as some of the Ynitian soldiers joined the warriors in their celebration of Goodemer's spell.

Gindor sighed. "I hate to admit they were truly wrong for each other."

"I'm just glad we didn't force them into a joining."

Gindor raised a silent thanks to Laur.

CLAUDI STARED IN disbelief as Mularke drained the leather tankard of ale and threw it into the snowy night air, raised her bow, and let the arrow fly. It miraculously speared the handle, missing the body of the tankard.

"Amazing," Claudi said.

"Years and years of dedicated practice," Mularke said solemnly. "Don't want to ruin a perfectly good tankard."

Tas laughed. "Ask her how many tankards she had to repair for old Teniar during those years and years of practice."

Mularke straightened. "I learned enough from it to make my own tankards."

"An occupation for your old age, when you're too blind to see the tip of your arrow much less a target." Tas ducked as Mularke took a drunken swipe at her.

"Hey look it stopped snowing." Claudi squinted into the black night sky where moments before it had been white with thick flurries.

"Wait . . . What?" The three jumped around as flakes from a black blizzard whirled around them, stinging any flesh they touched.

Footfalls pounded and shouts arose as the handfuls of Emorans enjoying the evening in the snowless plaza rushed to the closest shelter.

Tas, Mularke, and Claudi ducked through the open palace doors with several other equally shocked women. Fortunately, the entry way was a large hall, created to hold an army if need be.

"Volcano?" Tas asked.

Mularke shook her head. "We would have felt the earth shake and a roar as it spewed this ash."

"But what else could it be?" Tas blinked at the black snow that quickly covered the plaza. She stared at the snow-covered thatch over the outdoor pavilions and the thatch overhangs that protected doors and the paths up the side of the bluffs. "Daughter of a shaggy goat. We need to find Goodemer. That stuff is melting through the snow."

Wisps of smoke already rose up from tiny flames as the ash touched anything that could burn.

"Find Goodemer," she shouted and was answered by a dozen footsteps running into the depths of the palace.

"Do you think it's some kind of magic?" Claudi asked as more Emorans, using the overhangs as cover, ran in from the sooty snow.

"What else could it be?" Tas shrugged. "Oh Laur, the temple offerings are catching fire."

"They're pumping water into the reservoirs," Argis panted as she skidded in through the doorway. "Where's Goodemer?"

"They're looking for her," Mularke said.

"The plaza is like a lava pit. There's no way anyone can get the water near the fires." Argis turned around at the sound of pounding footfalls coming from the hallways within the palace.

Tigh and Jame ran up to them and simply stared out into the deep black covering the everything, punctuation by flaring orange glows.

TIGH STEPPED FORWARD until she was at the edge of where the falling flakes could touch her.

"Tigh," Jame said as she and the others followed as close as possible. "What are you doing?"

Tigh looked back at Jame, turned to the falling soot, and raised her hand to it. The others swallowed a gasp.

The black flakes melted to nothing as they touched Tigh's hand and leather-clad arm. She turned to the others. "It's magic. It doesn't have any effect on me."

Jame let out her held breath. "Don't scare me like that."

Tigh gave her a sheepish look. "Sorry."

Argis frowned. "But who would be doing this to us?"

Tigh and Jame exchanged significant glances. "I hope to Laur I didn't bring this to Emoria."

"It could be me," a voice—part amiable and part amused—said behind her. Goodemer strode up to the edge of the overhang. "I'm not particularly popular with rogue wizards. But it doesn't matter. This is something that can be easily stopped. A fact that will surprise whoever is doing it because my spellcasting is being probed. Meaning they are ready to adjust their spell to counter mine."

All but Jame and Tigh looked confused.

"Tigh has her uses." Jame grinned.

"Thanks a lot." Tigh shook her arm out, let curiosity overtake her, and stepped into the black blizzard, producing a snow-like crunch beneath her boots. "Interesting." She picked up a handful of the black stuff and molded it into a ball. She threw it at a wooden pole holding one of the many lanterns that lit up the square.

Flames flared and died down into an orange glow on the post.

Tigh raised an eyebrow at the thought of being able to throw a flame ball without being burned. Useful skill.

Argis crossed her arms. "Why don't we do something about this before Tigh gets carried away and burns all the light posts?"

Tigh turned around with a sheepish look. "Sorry."

Goodemer rubbed her chin in thought, a devilish look lighting her eyes. "I could just stop the black snow or . . ." She gazed at Tigh, who was building a sooty snow person. "Reverse it."

Jame turned to Goodemer, mirroring her devilish look. "You can do that?"

"So what will stop them from reversing it back?" Tas asked.

Goodemer shrugged. "A non-reversal spell."

"Can you figure out where this wizard is?" Jame asked.

"That depends," Goodemer said. "Hmmm. I could tack a little tracking spell onto the reversal spell . . ."

Argis broke out into a delighted grin. "Is she good or what?"

"And we're lucky to have her as our own personal wizard," Jame said.

Goodemer straightened. "I hate to tear you away from your creation . . ."

Tigh looked up from putting some rather creative features on her snow person. "Uh, no problem." She stepped back under the palace overhang.

"You're pretty good at that." Tas studied the sculpted image of a mountain sprite.

"Huh?" Tigh looked at her sooty sculpture and shrugged.

"She's rather handy to have around," Jame said.

Goodemer grasped Tigh's arm and held her amulet with the other hand. She murmured a few words and spent several heartbeats in silent concentration. A tiny frown appeared, and she mumbled a few more words. After several heartbeats she gave a satisfied nod and looked out into the plaza.

"It's still black," Mularke said.

"Patience," Goodemer said. "They made the spell complicated so they'd have time to detect anyone tampering with it."

"Does that mean they had time to discover you tampering with it?" Jame asked.

"I don't think so," Goodemer said as she studied the still-black snowflakes. "But you never know how these things will work."

"What if the other wizard detects your spell too soon?" Tas asked, walking to the edge of the overhang. She just as quickly stepped back as the black snow turned to a sheet of sleet. "Sorry I asked."

All eyes turned to Goodemer who had a huge grin, even as everything in the plaza seemed to be flaring in intense flame. She held out her amulet, said a few words, and the sleet turned a watery white long enough to snuff out the fires then fluff into snowflakes.

Argis let out a held breath and turned to Goodemer. "What was that all about?"

"Wizard games." Goodemer raised her amulet for a heartbeat then released her hold on Tigh. "There. That ought to keep things under control."

"What did you do?" Jame asked.

"I put out a mouse spell," Goodemer said. "It will hopefully detect any magic aimed at us without being detected itself. Like a mouse in the wall."

Tigh grinned. "Ah, clever."

"Are you able to find out who the other wizard is?" Jame asked.

"If they don't find my tracking spell in the chaotic mess of useless spells I tacked onto the one that reversed their spell," Goodemer said. "I'm hoping the wizard will be too occupied to stop the black blizzard to notice."

Argis whooped in delight. "You should have been a warrior. Good strategy."

"So the reversal spell worked?" Tas asked.

"It hasn't been stopped, so I'm presuming it's working."

"Fire!" Shouts came from the west tower—fortunately made of stone, so the guards did not have to abandon their posts. "In the valley forest."

"I think we found that wizard," Tigh said.

Argis gave Goodemer a sound kiss and ran into the plaza, shouting orders to gather the warriors for a little nighttime hunt. A grinning Tas and Mularke trotted after their old friend.

Tigh blinked a question to Jame.

"No," Jame said.

The blue eyes turned to a sad pleading.

"Tigh." Jame bit her lip. "You can bet that wizard is going to use more magic. Goodemer needs you here."

Tigh sighed but nodded that Jame was right. "Sometimes it's not fun being useful."

Jame almost laughed at Tigh's pout. "Maybe Goodemer will make a few of those black snowballs for you."

Tigh gave her a wonderful hopeful grin.

Chapter 9

ARGIS WAS GETTING used to strange sights fast that night as they stood on top of the ridge that marked the western boundary of Emoria. They were in several feet of snow in an unrelenting blizzard, and rain came down in sheets in the valley below, causing the burning trees to smolder and hiss.

"Their wizard is going to cause a flood." Tas knocked packed snow off of her wood webbed snowshoe.

Before Argis had a chance to respond, she felt a warmth and looked down to see the crossed-sword amulet that Goodemer had given her glow orange. She wrapped her hand around the amulet and waited.

"Enjoying yourself?" Goodemer's voice popped into her mind. She was getting used to the odd sensation but it still jarred her senses when it happened.

"Having the time of my life." Argis concentrated on mentally sending her words through the amulet.

"You don't have to rush into the rain to capture our wizard friend," Goodemer said. "I put a scatter barrier spell around the forest. It can't be detected until the wizard tries to go outside the tree line."

"You have quite a bag of tricks there." Argis grinned.

Tas rolled her eyes. "I can only imagine what you're talking about."

Argis punched her in the arm as Tas laughed unrepentant.

"Minchof was a good teacher." Goodemer laughed. "Now this spell will last only as long as it takes for the wizard to realize that it's a scattered barrier. I'm also bombarding the wizard with a teasing spell to draw her energy from making spells."

"Teasing spell?"

"A spell that creates miscellaneous illusions that look real," Goodemer said. "Little things like a mountain cat ready to attack, an army of warriors, gaping holes in the path."

Argis could almost see Goodemer's casual shrug. "So how come the wizard isn't using those kind of spells on us?"

"The shortcuts for these kinds of spells are taught during an apprenticeship with a wizard," Goodemer said. "Most rogue wizards usually wash out of school before they get to an apprenticeship. If you don't know the shortcut, it takes many sandmarks to prepare even a simple teasing or scattered spell."

"So you think it's another rogue wizard?" Argis asked.

"Either that or one of those foreign wizards, but they seemed to be more skilled that this one," Goodemer said.

"So how do we catch her?" Argis squinted into the blanket of steamy fog that covered the forest.

"The scatter spell is forcing her to go northeast."

"Where the only way to go is on our land and into our tunnel. You're brilliant. But won't she get suspicious that she's going toward Emoria instead of away from it?" Argis scratched her head.

"Do you think she's going to be able to keep track of direction trying to avoid the scattered spells, the teasing spells, and not being able to see two paces in front because of the smoke and rain?" Goodemer couldn't keep the good humor out of her voice.

Argis grinned. "You have a point there."

"The wizard is casting people finding spells," Goodemer said, "so you'll have to stay up there until she enters the tunnel. Then you'll have to move fast."

"How close can we get?" Argis looked at Tas, who touched her arm and nodded at something with her chin. "Are you expecting company? Because there is"—Argis squinted through the snow-rain-smoke—"a sizable army falling into place on top of the Kaderin plateau. They don't look like they're here for the winter festival."

"I've been keeping an eye on them," Goodemer said.

Argis sighed. "And you were going to mention them at some point, right?"

"They seem to be having a problem finding a way down off that plateau," Goodemer said. "All the rain has washed out the trails into the forest valley. That's the other wizard's doing, not mine."

Argis chuckled. "Probably not what she had planned to do."

"You can go safely to the path above the tunnel and wait," Goodemer said. "The wizard is only casting for people around her not above her. Tigh is leading a group to greet the wizard on the other side of the tunnel."

Argis smirked. "I bet she begged for that assignment."

Goodemer's warm laugh echoed in Argis's mind.

TIGH BOUNCED ON the soles of her feet, like a child who had been promised a toy if she was good. Sometimes the idea of leading a group of soldiers, even if it was just to ambush a silly wizard flashed Tigh into the feelings she most enjoyed and missed about being a Guard. She was a leader and needed to be allowed to indulge that every once in a while.

Jame grinned at Tigh as they waited for Goodemer to finish her conversation with Argis.

They stood at the entrance of the hall that was to be the temporary home of the soldiers of Ynit.

"They look like they're ready for a little fun," Tigh said.

"Warriors always look like they're ready for a little fun." Jame gave Tigh a knowing look.

Goodemer released her wolf's head amulet and turned her attention to them. "All is going as planned."

Tigh couldn't keep the grin away as she waved Maure over to them.

Maure, wearing a curious expression, approached them. "Do we know what's going on yet?"

"A wizard who's about to get caught between a rock and a hard place," Tigh said as Jame rolled her eyes. "Do you think your soldiers want to volunteer to be the hard place?"

"We were hoping you'd ask," Maure said.

"We're moving out as soon as you can get assembled in the plaza," Tigh said.

Maure grinned as she strode to the soldiers who had clustered in the middle of the chamber when she went to talk to Tigh.

Tigh and Jame followed Goodemer back up to the main foyer of the palace where Jyac and Sark had joined the curious crowd gathered there.

"Wolfie's making progress digging a path to the tunnel," Jyac said. "They're churning up snow like a torchlit fast-moving tiny blizzard snaking across the valley."

"Argis is getting into position above the other tunnel entrance," Goodemer said.

"Makes me wish I was twenty years younger," Sark said with a sigh.

"What's the word from your scouts?" Tigh asked.

Sark grinned. "The army on the Kaderin plateau seem to be stuck up there for a while."

"I'll make sure they don't go anywhere until we're ready to deal with them," Goodemer said.

"Excellent," Jyac said. "You did a great job of coming together in such a short bit of time to stop what could have been a serious situation. Having a resident wizard had its uses."

Goodemer looked at her feet, embarrassed.

A steady rhythm of footfalls sounded from deep within the palace. They turned around in time to see the soldiers of the Southern Territory emerge from the staircase at the far end of the main corridor. They marched in rows of three across through the foyer and out into the crisp night air. They turned and fell into formation, facing the palace doors.

Maure strode up to Tigh and grinned. "We're ready when you are."

Tigh turned to Jame. "I'll be careful."

Jame shook her head and pulled Tigh into a hug. "Enjoy yourself."

Tigh grinned and kissed Jame. "Keep a warm space for me in the bed," she murmured in Jame's ear.

"Don't worry, warrior," Jame said. "I'll make sure there's a hot bath first to warm up those frozen feet."

"ENJOYING YOURSELVES?" TIGH sauntered up to Wolfie and her companions, who were sculpting strange beasts from hastily rolled mounds of snow near the tunnel's entrance.

"Uh, we're just practicing for the winter festival contest." Wolfie flashed her an innocent look.

Tigh looked over their handwork. "Good idea. Practicing that is."

Wolfie turned to the snow sculptures. "I thought they were pretty good."

Tigh laughed. "I'm kidding."

Wolfie's relieved look was almost comical.

"Anything going on in there yet?" Tigh nodded at the tunnel entrance.

"It's been quiet as mice whispers," Wolfie said.

"That'll give us time to give the wizard a little surprise," Tigh said with a wicked grin.

"How will we stop her from just doing some magic on us?" Wolfie asked.

"That's the surprise." Tigh waggled her brows. "Let's clear the area around the mouth of the tunnel. Large enough for all of us to stand in but keeping a bit of a distance from the tunnel."

A half sandmark later, the soldiers of the Southern Territories were adding their own creative twists to the snow creatures. Much of a soldier's life was waiting, and each soldier had to figure out a way of dealing with the boredom. The desert-based soldiers rarely had the opportunity to play in the snow.

Tigh and Maure stood to one side of the mouth to the tunnel listening for any activity.

"Someone's coming," Tigh whispered. "Fast. Argis must be on the other side." She signaled the soldiers to take their places on either side of the entrance.

Uneven stumbling footfalls preceded a cloaked figured emerging from the tunnel. The soldiers quickly moved to block the tunnel and form a wide circle around the startled woman. The woman lifted her hand to throw a reactive spell. Tigh moved lightning quick and touched the exposed skin on the woman's arm with a small amulet.

"Aghh." The woman grabbed her arm and fell to her knees. Her face was contorted in anguish. "What did you do to me?" she whimpered like a wounded animal.

"Was that the surprise?" Wolfie asked.

"Yep." Tigh grinned as she stood over the wizard. "Your powers have been neutralized."

"That's not possible," the wizard gasped.

"Obviously it is." Tigh shrugged. "It only works with rogue wizards who haven't completed their training."

"I've never heard of such a thing," the wizard said.

"That's because you never finished your training." Tigh crossed her arms. "Now you get to tell us why you and that army are here."

"Yes. Why are you here?" Argis asked.

The soldiers blocking the entrance stepped aside to let Argis and her warriors into the valley.

"They hired me to remove the enhancement spell from your warriors," the wizard said, shivering from being on her knees in the snow.

"Then why did you announce your presence with the black snow?" Argis frowned as she sauntered up to the wizard.

"Because she really can't remove the enhancements," Tigh said as the wizard hesitated. "They must have promised a large sum of money."

"Yes," the woman breathed.

"So you thought you could destroy the warriors and Emoria another way and those who hired you wouldn't be the wiser," Tigh said.

"Yes." The woman, shaking uncontrollably, bowed her head.

"Now, the question is, who are they and why do they want to invade Emoria." Argis rubbed her chin.

"I don't know." The woman bowed her head lower.

"Guess we'll have to ask them ourselves." Tigh grinned at Argis.

"I think that's an excellent idea." Argis got the same look in her eye.

A nice little battle would bring a pleasant end to the night's activities.

"YOU'RE BARELY A woman." The wizard's eyes widened in disbelief as Goodemer and Jame entered the cell deep in the dungeons of Emor.

Goodemer raised an eyebrow. "I'm nearly of age and I've completed my apprenticeship. And I've earned the Master Wizard's staff," she lifted the ornate staff in her hand, "for defeating a rogue wizard . . . like yourself."

"Misner," the woman muttered.

"What's your name?" Goodemer asked.

The woman looked as if she wasn't going to answer for a heartbeat. "Denle."

Goodemer sucked in a breath. "We thought you were dead."

"No," Denle said, sounding bitter. "Minchof didn't quite finish me off during our last encounter."

"Someone had to have helped you." Goodemer stepped forward. "Someone has been helping several rogue wizards. Were you the one who enchanted the sword that wounded Tigh?"

Denle held her chin up defiantly. "There are those who have the power to squash you and to squash the Southern Territories."

"And they're doing such a fine job of it, too." Jame crossed her arms. "I suspect all their power is simply enough silver to buy as many lackeys to do their dirty work as needed to get the job done. What was the purpose of invading Emoria?"

Denle clenched her teeth and glared at Jame. "To destroy the strongest army in the Territory. The army of the Southern Territories is nothing without the strength of the Emoran warriors."

"And you thought you could outsmart these powerful people by what? Setting the city on fire with black snow?" Goodemer shook her head. "You must have known the enhancement spell is a permanent one. Even I can't reverse it."

"I didn't think that you'd still be here," Denle muttered.

Goodemer smiled and spread out her hands. "This is my home now. Now were you the one who enchanted that sword?"

"What does it matter?" Denle sneered at Goodemer.

"It matters when we bring you to justice," Jame said.

"It doesn't matter if you tell us of not." Goodemer polished a bit of her staff. "I'll have no problem extracting the truth from you. I just thought you'd want to be spared that experience."

Denle gave the staff a wary look. "I wasn't the one."

"So there are other wizards involved in this?" Goodemer asked.

Denle put her head in her hands. "The ones who hired me aren't going to make an effort to rescue me. They're not going to help that army out there when it falls either. The wizard that cast the spell on the sword . . . I can only imagine what happened to her when the spell was detected and reversed." She raised her head. "If I tell you everything I know, what will happen to me?"

"What will happen to you if we just let you go?" Goodemer asked.

Denle's eyes widened with fear.

"The one who hired you is not the forgiving type, I see," Goodemer said.

"I think we should wait until Tigh is here," Jame said.

"Good idea." Goodemer nodded and then looked at Denle. "You tell us everything you know, and we'll keep you from harm."

Denle let out a grateful cry, buried her head in her hands, and sobbed tears of relief.

"WHAT DO YOU think?" Argis crouched low behind a jumble of boulders on the western edge of the Kaderin plateau.

Tigh thoughtfully twirled a brown leaf, thinking through all the ways to have fun with the force of five hundred bored and shivering soldiers who were obviously mercenaries. They had built little fires to keep warm and looked as if they weren't expecting any visitors. She wondered if they really believed they would just march into Emoria and take over.

"Let's give them something to take back to their leader," Tigh said.

Argis cocked her head. "What do you have in mind?"

"Something simple but effective." Tigh looked at the thirty-odd warriors tucked behind boulders around them. "We're going to stand up and face them."

Argis stared at Tigh. "We just stand up?"

Tigh smiled. "Yep. Stand up and look like you could defeat them without any effort. Goodemer won't let anything happen to us. Remember Balderon."

"If I'd known beforehand half of what she did there, I would have been petrified," Argis said.

"But you weren't. Even after you were suddenly enhanced. You just adapted and kept going without hesitation." Tigh almost laughed at the look of realization on Argis's face.

"We did, didn't we?" Argis shook her head in disbelief.

"The enhancements made you invincible," Tigh said.

Argis stared at Tigh in startled shock. "Really?"

"A Guard had never been lost in battle because we truly could not be defeated." Tigh grinned. "Now I think it's time to show this puny army how foolhardy it is to even think about invading Emoria."

Argis peeked at the oblivious army. "Their leaders don't look very happy."

Tigh watched the small group gathered around a fire in the center of the plateau. "They look like they're planning some counter strategy to whatever plan they had made with the wizard."

Argis turned to her band of expectant warriors. She motioned Tas over with her head. "Tigh just informed me we're invincible."

Tas grinned. "So what's the plan?"

Argis grinned back. "We're going to stand up and dare them to fight us."

Tas blinked at Argis. "We're that invincible?"

"Yep. Now pass the word that we stand up and act like big bad invincible Emoran warriors who'd rather be home in our nice warm beds," Argis said.

"Sounds like fun." Tas crept to the other warriors to spread the word.

Tigh and Argis gave the startled warriors around them reassuring looks and then waited until they were all watching them.

Argis took a deep breath, rose to her feet, and stepped around the boulder. Tigh and the other warriors did the same until they were lined up not fifty paces from the closest enemy.

"Hey. You want to fight or should we just take you prisoners and go home?" Argis shouted.

Tigh shook her head. Argis certainly had a knack for capturing the attention of the enemy army. The scramble for arms and falling into formation reminded her of the chaos of Misner's army on the plain of Balderon.

The knot of leaders warily pushed through the hastily assembling lines of troops. Their expressions were disbelieving as they realized no more than thirty warriors, standing with a casual mocking attitude, faced their sizable army.

A woman with a battle-hardened face stepped in front of the enemy army, her stance echoing the confidence of the Emorans. "It's obvious you haven't been home lately. Our first wave of attack has brought destruction and terror to your city."

"I have to admit the black snow was kind of interesting." Argis shrugged. "Tigh was having fun throwing black snowballs."

"Tigh?" The woman's confident expression faltered as she recognized Tigh. Then she straightened. "The black snow burns everything it touches."

"Because it's magic." Argis crossed her arms and sauntered up to the woman. "Have you ever known of a wizard who has defeated Tigh?"

The woman stared at Argis. "Being immune to black snow isn't the same as defeating our wizard."

"True." Argis rubbed her chin. "But capturing her and disabling her abilities is." She held up the wizard's amulet. "Now, do you want to fight or surrender? Your choice. But my warriors wouldn't mind a little exercise tonight."

"Emorans are known for their smooth talk," the woman said.

"A reputation greatly enhanced by our princess," Argis said. "Emorans have no reason to be anything but truthful. There are enough of us right here to defeat ten times your number and still be home in time for the morning meal."

The woman gazed at the line of Emorans. "How do we know you're not bluffing? No one believes those rumors you've been enhanced."

"Why would you risk your lives to find out if it's true or not?" Argis asked. "You're here because you're being paid to fight, not because you have any conviction to a cause or to a people. We're giving you a choice to fight because your wizard was more in fear of whoever hired her than of us. She feared her fate if she returned without delivering Emoria."

Tigh raised an eyebrow at this. That must have been what the last communication with Goodemer was about. Interesting.

The woman relaxed a bit. "We've heard you are an honorable people. If our wizard doesn't succeed, our leader's wrath will be toward her not us. We're here to follow her orders."

Argis nodded. "We don't take acts of violence against us lightly. We'll track down who's behind this and when we do, we'll defeat whoever stands against us. If you're smart, you'll walk away from here and walk away from this army because your wizard will tell us everything she knows about who hired you. It's only a matter of time before we meet again in battle."

The woman gazed at Argis. "Is it true you have the enhancement of the Guards?"

"Yes," Argis said. "We were given the enhancements during the battle of Balderon."

The woman looked at Tigh. "Do these warriors have Guard enhancements?"

"Yes," Tigh said. "I don't have the skill to defeat them."

Argis blinked at her, startled.

The woman sucked in a breath. "If you don't have the skill to defeat them, then this plateau will become our graveyard." She reached over her shoulder, and the hiss of her sword slipping from its sheath cut through the tense cold air. "Might I ask the name of the warrior I give my sword and my army to?"

Argis straightened. "Argis, Master Warrior of Emoria."

"Argis, Master Warrior of Emoria, I surrender my army to your mercy." The woman laid her sword on the ground.

The army behind her drew swords and dropped them as if they couldn't surrender fast enough.

Argis picked up the surrendered sword. "I return this sword to you if I have your promise that you and your army will leave this land. I also request you take a message back to your leader. We see this attempted invasion as an act of war, and we'll not rest until we've tracked down and defeated whoever is behind it."

The woman nodded. "I accept your terms."

Argis held the sword, and the woman took it.

The woman saluted Argis with the sword. "You know, I've been a mercenary for so long, I've forgotten the satisfaction that comes from doing something honorable."

Chapter 10

EVEN FOLLOWING THE directions, Fant got lost twice roaming the corridors and galleries of the palace before she found the archives tucked away on an upper floor. The archives were the safest driest place in Emor. For all their warrior traditions, the Emorans valued their written histories and documents.

The middle part of the chamber had several study tables with shaded oil lamps on them. The walls were pocked with carved out holes and shelves filled with scrolls and bound volumes. An occasional doorway led to other rooms holding the written treasures of Emoria. She went to the row of windows of semi-clear glass through which she could see the plaza and found a table covered with unrolled scrolls and opened volumes and sheets filled with neat handwriting. She'd been told this table was Seeran's permanent domain in the archives.

Seeran was supposed to spend the mornings working in the archives, but Fant didn't know where to start looking for her. She peeked through one of the doorways and was surprised at range upon range of scrolls in the large chamber. She wandered into the chamber and marveled at all the history surrounding her. History the scholars at the University of Artocia could only dream of seeing.

She pulled a scroll from a shelf made of stone. It depicted recent events involving the return of Jame and Tigh to Emoria and the defeat of Misner. She never realized Jame had been estranged from her home country because of her relationship with Tigh.

"Interesting place isn't it?"

Fant started and looked up.

Seeran stood at the end of the row of shelves.

"I never imagined an archive like this," Fant said.

"You're a long way from Artocia." Seeran led Fant back to her cluttered table in the main chamber.

"I'm writing a history of Ynit and decided to follow the escort to Emoria," Fant said. "I thought it would make an interesting chapter."

Seeran laughed. "One lesson I've learned. Anything involving Tigh and Jame makes not only an interesting chapter, but many interesting books. I am forever grateful to them because they saved my life, and now I've devoted my career to chronicling their lives and to chronicling the events here in Emoria."

"You're also to be joined to an Emoran," Fant said.

"Yes. A warrior no less." Seeran smiled. "It's been interesting living here. Did you know Emorans don't have a monthly cycle. They don't have to. They don't need a man to reproduce. Laur gifts them with a child."

"So that's really true?" Fant sank into a chair, her enchantment of Emoria growing by the heartbeat.

"Oh yes," Seeran said as she settled into her chair. "That's why Jame and Tigh came back. Jame has to produce an heir."

"So the child will be both of theirs?" Fant asked.

"Yes. Laur takes a bit from each partner when creating a child." Seeran almost laughed at Fant's incredulous expression. "Tigh fits in here better than I do because she also doesn't have a monthly cycle. The Guard enhancements took that away."

"So no former Guards can have children?"

"Only those joined to Emorans," Seeran said.

"Would it be all right if I spent some time here? Reading." Fant glanced around the chamber.

"Of course," Seeran said. "I'll be able to have someone to talk to then. Every day I seem to uncover something new and interesting about Emorans and Emoria."

"It looks like we may be here all winter if this weather keeps up," Fant said. "But I'm not complaining. This is an archivist's dream."

Seeran looked out the window with a fond expression. "Exactly what I thought when I first entered this country."

TIGH DUCKED AND then cringed as the sponge splat against the polished stone wall behind her. "That didn't come out right."

"You bet it didn't come out right." An irritated Jame splashed through the warm water toward Tigh. "Now would you care to rephrase that?"

"I meant I'd rather get this latest threat to Emoria out of the way before we go through with the ceremony, not that I'd rather be out chasing the army than chasing down the finer points of the child-gift ceremony." Tigh put her arms up to protect her face.

Jame stopped and gazed at Tigh. "Sorry about the sponge. You do realize you'll have to put up with greater mood swings."

"I'll just keep all the sharp objects hidden," Tigh said as she sank back into the water of the private warm water pool in the corner of Jame's chamber.

"I didn't think the mood swings would start before the ceremony." Jame gave Tigh a sheepish look. She retrieved the hapless sponge and picked up a piece of soft soap.

"I think you've been under a lot of pressure you've been trying to keep under control," Tigh said softly as she took the soap and sponge from Jame. She soaped the sponge and lovingly ran it down Jame's arms. "You know you can let out your frustrations on me."

"I know and for that I'm forever thankful," Jame said. "You know you drive the warriors crazy. They can't understand how you can be so gentle and even-tempered and still be the best warrior they've ever seen."

"They didn't know me before I became a Guard." Tigh scooted around Jame so she could wash her back. "My mother was sure I'd never make a good merchant because I wasn't ruthless enough."

Jame's shoulders shook with laughter. "What an irony. And she thought the Wars would toughen you up. But you aren't any more ruthless now than you were then."

"What if our child inherits my passive traits?" Tigh asked.

Jame turned around and gave Tigh a loving smile. "Then our child will be blessed with the best disposition to be queen."

"Even if her peers tease her for being overly sentimental and all mushy over some pretty girl?" Tigh breathed in Jame's ear.

"She's going to break every heart she comes in contact with," Jame murmured back, "if she has any of your traits."

Tigh solemnly shook her head. "Only if she's like you." She kissed Jame's cheek.

"I'm glad you're my partner, and you're willing to give up the outside world just because I have to be here," Jame said.

"There's only one world for me. The world that has you in it." Tigh kissed Jame's lips. "Besides someone has to teach these warriors how to fight."

Jame laughed. "I'm sure Argis would appreciate hearing that."

"They need to understand what it means to be enhanced." Tigh nuzzled Jame's wet hair. "Before we track down whoever is trying to attack Emoria."

"I HAVE WARDS all along the border," Goodemer said as she ran her finger over the irregular line on the map in the palace war chamber. "Although I don't think whoever it is will try any more magic."

"Whoever it is." Something kept flicking through Tigh's mind she couldn't quite bring into focus. "I feel like I know who it is. Something from when they were in my head."

Goodemer strolled around the map table, studying the contours of the mountainous lands. "Perhaps someone who has been in your head before."

Tigh snapped her attention to Goodemer.

"You were flashing back to when you were a Guard. You were interacting with people you knew back then. Was there anything unusual about those interactions?" Goodemer asked.

Tigh tried to recall what seemed so real to her when she dreamed them. "The only people in my dreams were Meah and Ardhat."

"I know Meah but who's Ardhat?" Goodemer asked.

"She was the Federation Council's chancellor," Tigh said. "She was the one who relayed the Council's orders to us."

"And you did what she told you to do," Goodemer said. "I got the feeling from your attitude in your dream that she wasn't necessarily liked."

"We tolerated her because she was the Council's voice. But we didn't like her," Tigh said. "She was too arrogant and smug and enjoyed the life of luxury too much."

"Sounds like she also enjoyed controlling you." Goodemer rubbed her amulet. "Do you know what came of her after the Wars?"

Tigh scratched her head. "Never gave it much thought. By the time I was captured and brought back to Ynit she wasn't around at all."

Goodemer smiled and cocked her head at Tigh. "The first time I saw you and Jame was right after your first hearing during your rehabilitation."

Tigh blinked at her. "You were in Ynit? You couldn't have been very old."

"I was one of the group of apprentices who accompanied Minchof. We had just arrived, and our carriage was stopped by the crowds who attended your hearing," Goodemer said. "I was in Ynit all that summer. I even showed Argis where Jame lived. She's still amazed that skinny fourteen-year-old was me."

Tigh shook her head. "I guess it *is* a small world."

"I learned a lot about Guard enhancements," Goodemer said. "That's how I was able to cast the spell that enhanced the Emoran warriors."

"I always wondered how you were able to do that," Tigh said.

Goodemer walked around the map and put her finger on Maymi. "I was also in Maymi when you were there."

"You mentioned that when we met a year ago," Tigh said.

"But I never mentioned I was the one who showed you the magic chamber beneath Cadryn's shop," Goodemer said.

Tigh squinted at her. "That was you?"

"I had volunteered to help Cadryn and felt the magic when I walked into the shop," Goodemer said. "When I saw you and the other Guards enter as if you were looking for something I couldn't resist following you."

"We never had a chance to properly thank you for that," Tigh said. "If it wasn't for you, we would have never been able to rescue those children in time."

"You did thank me," Goodemer said. "I was more than happy just to help."

Tigh rubbed her chin and gave Goodemer a speculative look. "Did you volunteer to investigate the rogue wizard up in these mountains last year?"

Goodemer looked a little embarrassed. "I admit I asked to be the one to come here. But I didn't know you and Jame were here. I was just curious about Emoria from when I saw the Emorans in Ynit. I never imagined I'd be getting joined to one."

"I would have never imagined Argis going for a wizard," Tigh said.

"Don't tell her this, but she caught my eye the first time I saw her in Ynit," Goodemer said. "I almost ran into a rain barrel when I saw her strolling down the lane. Never had I seen a warrior who looked as if she was born to it and couldn't possibly be anything else."

Tigh nodded. "Argis is a natural warrior. Emoria is lucky to have her, and we were lucky she led the warriors at Balderon. She may not think she did anything outstanding, but many a battle leader would not have taken all the magic and the enhancements in stride and immediately adapt her strategy to it."

"We'll just have to work on getting her to see what a great warrior she is," Goodemer said with a smile.

JAME HAD NEVER felt nervous walking into the Temple of Laur, but she was nervous as she stepped into the airy main chamber. Waterfalls of different sizes cascaded into clear pools, adding to the usual peaceful, calming atmosphere of the temple. For the first time, Jame didn't feel calmed by the water.

"I'm acting like Tigh," she muttered as she strode across the chamber to a small doorway behind the main waterfall. She entered a chamber of crystallized rock with water gently flowing down and around the many-sided sparkling walls to a channel that emptied into a central pool.

"Sit, Jame," came a voice from a waterfall.

Jame sat on one of the many large cushions scattered on the floor. She glanced around the chamber, trying to settle her unsettled nerves.

Panilope, the head acolyte to Laur, appeared from behind the waterfall, holding a silver chalice. Her dark purple robes flowed across the crystal floor as she approached Jame.

"Welcome home," Panilope greeted with a joyous smile. "I was pleased to hear that you are home for good." She gracefully dropped cross-legged onto the floor without even causing a ripple in the liquid in the chalice.

"We felt it was time," Jame said.

"Ah, time." Panilope nodded. "It does catch up with us." She touched Jame's cheek with her finger. "Has Tigh agreed to you carrying the child?"

"Yes. After I convinced her that I wouldn't be at risk." Jame smiled fondly at Tigh's concern.

"It's not a bad thing that Tigh is very protective," Panilope said. "You and your child will be queens of Emoria."

"She'll make a great parent," Jame said. "She's a little nervous about the ceremony though."

"It's only natural, not being raised here." Panilope gently swirled the water in the chalice. "To prepare your body for Laur's gift, you must drink this."

"But we don't know when we'll be going through the ceremony," Jame said, as she caught the delicate scent of winter flowers from the liquid. "Tigh thinks that whoever is menacing Emoria should be stopped before we commit."

"It would be less stress for both of you," Panilope agreed. "You only have to drink this mixture once before you receive Laur's gift. Once it's in your system it stays forever."

Jame took the chalice and looked into the liquid. It was clear like water but the fragrance hinted at exotic ingredients. That the liquid was something that stayed in her forever was kind of frightening.

"It's a big step to drink of this chalice," Panilope said. "You must be completely sure in your heart you're ready to take on the responsibility of receiving Laur's gift."

Jame took a deep breath and looked up at Panilope. "I never gave it much thought until I met Tigh. I never envisioned sharing a child with Argis. But Tigh and I discussed it on the way to Ingor for our joining. Tigh has always been open to the idea, even if she's been a bit daunted by it."

Panilope smiled. "You were lucky to find someone who is willing to follow your path and who is strong enough to protect you."

"I thank Laur every day Tigh is in my life." Jame returned Panilope's smile and lifted the chalice to her lips. The fragrance drifted up from the liquid and bathed her senses with calm and a feeling of well-being. She drank until the chalice was empty.

Panilope took the chalice and touched Jame's forehead with her fingers. "I give you Laur's blessing and when the time comes, she will bless you with a child."

Jame's breath caught in her throat as the reality of what she and Tigh were about to do enveloped her. "Thank you, Panilope. I look forward to that time."

ARGIS, TIGH, AND Tas, all in search of their respective better halves, finally decided they were in the feast hall for the midday meal. They entered the hall, still half-empty but noisier than if it were full. Warriors and soldiers were shouting challenges between tables and one table seemed to be engaged in a tankard pounding contest.

Tigh arched an eyebrow at Argis. "Whoever gets the worse headache wins?"

Argis rolled her eyes. "These soldiers have made them crazy."

"Perhaps it's time to start training as one army," Tigh said.

Argis studied the noisy groups. "As long as they're here, they might as well be useful."

Tas grinned. "I like the way you think."

"You realize we'd better get this little war out of the way or else our partners are going to think we're getting cold feet about the upcoming ceremonies." Argis nodded at the table at the end of the hall. Jame, Goodemer, and Seeran were engaged in an animated discussion, punctuated by fits of laughter.

Tas gave the trio a wary look. "Wonder which one of us they're talking about."

Tigh's and Argis' eyes widened as a new round of laughter reached their ears.

"Maybe Jame's telling a story of our adventures," Tigh said.

Three sets of eyes saw them at the same time and the attempt to stifle the laughter was halfhearted at best.

Argis scowled. "Nothing is stopping us from sitting around and telling funny stories about them."

Tigh and Tas gave Argis uncomprehending looks.

"Yeah. I couldn't do it either," she mumbled.

Tigh sighed and led the way to their jovial partners.

Argis and Tas dragged chairs from the ends of the table and squeezed them in to sit next Goodemer and Seeran. They sat down with warrior casualness, careful not to betray too much affection beyond a grin at their partners. Argis couldn't help but glance at Tigh as she sat next to Jame and planted a gentle kiss on her lips. She then grasped Jame's hand and kept hold of it.

The noise in the hall subsided, and Argis noted her warriors watching Tigh with a profound puzzlement. The young warriors-in-training were positively wide-eyed. Argis knew without a doubt Tigh's actions were going to impact the younger generation.

Tigh squeezed Jame's hand. "So how did it go?"

"I had to drink something to prepare my body to receive Laur's gift," Jame said.

Tigh blinked at her. "Prepare your body?"

"To put in my body what is necessary to make a child," Jame said as she squeezed Tigh's hand. "What it takes to allow the child to grow within me and be born."

Tigh took in a ragged breath. "Did it taste bad?"

Jame's grin widened. "It was like sweetly fragrant water that calmed the soul."

"But awakened the body." Tigh kissed Jame tenderly on the cheek.

"If you two don't stop that, I'll have to challenge you to prove you're still a warrior," Argis muttered.

Jame turned to Argis. "And when Tigh beats you, all the warriors will start spewing mushy words to their sweethearts and openly show affection to them."

Argis tried to scowl but couldn't keep away a smile. "I can't protest because you're probably right. The young ones are already watching your big tough warrior with interest."

Tigh grinned as she wrapped her arms around Jame. "I wonder how bad an influence I can be on them."

Argis sighed and shook her head.

"Just wait. If Goodemer carries their child, Argis will be changing her tune," Tas said. "That's the only time warriors can be openly affectionate without being teased or constantly challenged."

"And what if Argis is chosen to carry the child?" Tigh asked.

Jame, Goodemer, and Seeran collapsed in a fit of laughter.

"Now we know what they were talking about," Tas said. "But Argis probably won't carry the child because she's so much older than Goodemer."

"Hey, I'm the same age as Argis," Jame said.

"But you're younger than Tigh," Tas said then turned to Tigh. "Laur usually gives the gift to the youngest."

"If Laur gives us her special blessing our children will grow up together," Argis said.

"I can see it now," Jame said. "Our daughters competing for everything."

"And becoming the best of friends," Goodemer added.

"I don't care how many braids you have, I bet you can't beat Kine here at hand to hand," a voice cut through the noise.

A muscular warrior stood up and flung a braid at a soldier. "The armory. Tomorrow at nine sandmarks. Be there to learn what it means to earn a braid in Emoria."

Argis sighed. "It's going to be a long winter."

"ARDHAT." TIGH PAUSED in brushing Gessen.

"What?" Kas's head popped up from a nearby stall.

Tigh turned and looked at Kas. "Uh, nothing. Just, uh, talking to myself."

Kas nodded and disappeared behind the stall wall.

Tigh ran the brush across Gessen's fair neck as she rolled through her mind everything she knew about Ardhat. She realized she knew very little about the woman who had controlled her during the Wars. Truth was, the Guards were never even curious about her. They only tolerated her because they had to.

Satisfied that Gessen was thoroughly groomed, Tigh wandered out of the stables perched at the top of the eastern cliff of Emor. She crossed her arms and gazed at the city below, then looked around her and at the western side of the canyon. More snow than she had ever seen was piled everywhere, obscuring the practice ground and the ceremonial circle, even burying smaller trees and larger boulders. A group of stable hands were constantly clearing new snowfall from the stables.

She sighed. The information she needed was in the archives in Ynit. She smiled sadly at the irony. She thought moving to Emoria would put their lives in the outside world behind them. The outside world simply followed them there. Jame didn't need this. She needed to settle down to a peaceful life, learning how to lead Emoria and raising an heir.

How was she going to get the information she needed from Ynit? The few reports they received said nearly the whole Southern Territories was blanketed with snow. They had been hit with the worse string of snowstorms that anyone could remember.

She turned her attention to the city below her at the sound of shouting from one level of the cliff side to another. Shouting seemed to be a common form of communication in Emor.

"She's in the archives with Seeran." Tas leaned over the ledge of one of the many shrines to Laur that could be found on the paths that snaked around the sides of the cliffs.

Tigh scanned the rather crowded square and saw a wave of acknowledgment from Claudi. Who would Claudi be looking for who would be visiting Seeran? The moment the answer touched her mind, Tigh was crunching on a fresh layer of snow down the path that led to the archives.

Chapter 11

"THE NEXT THING I knew, Tas was shuffling her feet and acting like a bashful girl with a crush." Seeran laughed. "She offered to fill me in on Emoran traditions but spent most the evening walking me around Emor and listening to me talk."

"But wasn't it a big decision?" Fant asked. "I mean to leave Artocia forever and to live here."

"I once thought life in Artocia was perfect, and I felt Bal's blessing every day I was there," Seeran said. "I have to admit my life changed after I met Tigh and Jame. Imagine having your life saved by those legendary heroes and then getting a chance to come to Emoria and get caught up in the most incredible adventure. And Tas just kind of crept into my heart until I realized I couldn't imagine a life without her or without Emoria."

Fant sighed and fidgeted with her pen before looking across the table at Seeran. "I'm, uh, feeling the same about Ynit."

Seeran grinned. "This doesn't have anything to do with that young archer I've seen you with, does it?"

Fant looked down at her hands. "Uh, I mean, we're friends and uh—"

"You'd like to be more than friends," Seeran said.

"I thought we were heading that way. Until we came here." Fant's shoulders slumped in defeat.

"One of these warriors showing some interest?" Seeran had witnessed more than a little flirting between warriors and soldiers the last few days.

"That's just it," Fant said, frustrated. "I can't tell what's going on. These Emorans are so afraid to show any kind of affection and, according to Tigh, they show interest by playing practical jokes and picking fights and making challenges, I just can't figure it out."

"Is it someone in particular?" Seeran asked.

"That master archer, Mularke." Fant waved her hand. "She's always wanting to talk to Claudi."

"Is Tas usually with her?" Seeran asked.

Fant frowned. "Sometimes."

"Has she challenged Claudi?"

"She said she'd like to do some target practice with her," Fant said.

"I don't think you have anything to worry about," Seeran said. "Mularke just wants to be friends. She probably feels Claudi is a kindred spirit because she's also an archer. Besides Mularke has been so unlucky in love she's about given up on it."

"But how can you really tell for sure?" Fant asked.

"I've lived here for about a year now, and I've come to understand Emoran courting behavior very well." Seeran shook her head in amusement. "Mularke is Tas's closest friend. Tas would have told me if Mularke was mooning over a soldier. In fact, Tas would be teasing her without mercy about it."

The sound of boots hurrying down the corridor captured their attention. Tigh rushed through the opened doorway, paused, and walked to Seeran's table. "Sorry to interrupt."

"We're just talking," Seeran said. "Have a seat."

TIGH SAT DOWN, her attention drawn to the walls filled with scrolls and volumes of books. A pang of regret always fleeted through her when she was in an archive. If not for the Wars, she and Seeran and Fant would have been colleagues at the University of Artocia. She wondered if she would have met with Jame somehow. It wasn't such an outlandish idea. Seeran, after all, ended up in Emoria.

"Impressive isn't it?" Seeran asked.

"I didn't have a chance to visit it the last time I was here," Tigh said.

"Now you'll have plenty of time to spend in here," Seeran said.

"I haven't had much time to spend in an archive since I was rehabilitated." Tigh picked up a scroll on the table. "I was studying to go to the University." She looked up at Seeran and Fant. "If it weren't for the Wars, we could have been classmates."

"Do you regret not being allowed to do what you wanted to do in life?" Seeran asked.

Tigh blinked at her. "If it means never meeting Jame, I don't regret anything."

Seeran and Fant grinned.

"Now you can indulge that long dormant scholarly bent," Seeran said. "These archives have many treasures from all over the Southern Territories."

"Really?" Tigh asked.

"It seems there have been more than a few Emorans with a scholarly bent," Seeran said. "Ronalyn spends several sandmarks a day in here."

Tigh grinned. "It'd be one more thing for Argis to complain about what warriors shouldn't do."

"That didn't stop you from paying a visit," Seeran said.

"Actually I'm here to see Fant," Tigh said.

"Me?" Fant reacted in surprise.

"You're writing a history of Ynit?"

"Yes." Fant straightened.

"Do you know what happened to Ardhat? She was the Council's voice for the Elite Guard." Tigh leaned forward on the table.

"Ardhat." Fant frowned in thought. "When the Wars were over the Federation Council made her a part of the transition team in turning Ynit into a peacetime military compound. She had gotten used to having an important role during the Wars and was not happy when she was not put in charge of the transition team. She thought she understood the Elite Guards better than anyone—even though she was only an assistant to the healers who developed the enhancements in the first place. She, uh, had ideas about what to do with all of you that, uh, weren't in agreement with the Federation Council and the healers in Ynit."

"Ideas." Tigh drew out the word.

Fant took a breath and looked at Tigh. "She was against the cleansing."

Tigh and Seeran stared at Fant in disbelief.

"What did she think they could do with us?" Tigh asked, unable to fathom being Tigh the Terrible in peacetime. The two years she spent in hiding after the Wars was torturous without being able to channel the need to fight.

"She thought you could be kept in reserve somehow as an elite special unit," Fant said.

"Elite special unit," Tigh said. "We could never be controlled well enough to just stay quietly somewhere until we were needed."

"She, uh, had some ideas about that, too." Fant fidgeted with her pen.

"Let me guess," Tigh said. "She wanted the healers to come up with a way of controlling us."

"Uh, yeah. Something like that." Fant glanced up at Tigh.

"So what happened?" Tigh asked.

"The Federation Council wouldn't agree to putting her in charge, and they were dead set against any idea other than cleansing the Guards," Fant said. "She resigned in protest of their shortsightedness with the parting words that they'd be begging her to return after they realized what a mistake they were making."

"Which they never did." Tigh rubbed her chin in thought. "So do we know what Ardhat has been doing since then?"

"According to the chronicles she returned to her home in Rihnon."

"Rihnon." Tigh sat back as she envisioned the closest city to Emoria. "Do we know how she supports herself?"

"When she was young, she apprenticed to a healer but then she became one of the aides to Winsle, the Rihnon representative on the Federation Council. Her background in healing made her a good candidate for the team who created the enhancement program," Fant said. "When she returned to Rihnon, she became a healer."

"A healer," Tigh said. "In Rihnon."

"Why are you asking about her?" Seeran asked.

"She was in the strange dreams I had when the magic was in my wound," Tigh said. "I think she may be behind our latest troubles."

"Sounds like she certainly has a grudge against the Federation," Seeran said.

"But why would she be going after you and now, Emoria?" Fant asked.

"She wants what she couldn't have at the end of the Wars." Tigh stood. "She wants to rule the Southern Territories. She first tried to discredit me through Iksoc because of the pledge the former Guards made to me after the encounters with the armies of the Silver Dragon."

"He's from Rihnon," Fant said.

"That's one coincidence too many, then." Tigh walked to the window and stared out at the plaza, overcrowded with the addition of the visitors from Ynit. "She came after Emoria because the most powerful warriors in the Southern Territories live here. But she underestimated Goodemer's enhancement spell. I don't know what she'll try to do next, but she's got to know we're going to track her down and defeat her. Using the combined forces of Emoria, Ynit, and the former Guards, with the Lukrians thrown in because they won't want to miss out on the fun."

"You have the element of surprise on your side," Seeran said. "She doesn't know you know she's behind all this."

Tigh turned around and leaned back against the window, feeling the bitter cold through the thick glass. "She'll be surprised all right."

"IT'S BEEN SEVERAL generations since a princess has returned from a life of adventure," Jyac said as she led the way down a narrow corridor deep within the palace.

"Sometimes more adventure than we bargained for," Jame said with a rueful grin.

Jyac slipped a small key into the lock of a door made of opaque glass with an ornate engraving of a crossed sword and bow on it. "Every princess, when she turns eighteen years enters this chamber." She pushed the door open and gestured for Jame to enter first. "Some wandering princesses entered this chamber when they were older than eighteen summers."

Jame walked into the chamber and was surprised to find that its walls and ceiling were made out of sheets of quartz. Jyac lit lamps inset in the walls, giving the room an orange crystallized glow.

"How many princesses didn't enter at eighteen summers because they had been estranged from Emoria?" Jame asked, trying to keep a lingering sadness from her voice.

Jyac gave her a sad smile. "One, other than you. Trigo."

Jame stared at her aunt in shock. Trigo is considered the greatest of Emoran Queen. "Why was she estranged? And why isn't that in the chronicles?"

Jyac's smile changed to amusement. "She fell in love with the wrong woman and certain things are meant only for the private chronicles—for royal eyes only."

"But her partner was greatly admired and respected," Jame said.

Jyac nodded. "Yes. I find the similarities comforting."

Jame blinked at her in confusion for a heartbeat. "Similarities?"

"You and Tigh are very much like Trigo and Nyte." Jyac walked to a shelf carved in the wall. Several boxes crafted from quartz were piled on the shelf.

"How can you say that? She was a hero. Tales of her life are still told throughout the Southern Territories . . ." Jame took several long breaths, realizing that she wasn't pointing out differences at all. "It's not the same."

"Time will tell," Jyac said. "If it makes you feel any better, Trigo was thirty when she entered this chamber."

"I still feel too old at twenty-six," Jame said. "I sometimes feel like I got too caught up in my life as an arbiter to even try to reconcile with you."

"It's funny." Jyac rubbed her chin. "I feel that everything happened when it should have happened."

"Really?"

"When I entered this chamber, I thought I knew everything about being mature and grown-up." Jyac laughed. "I didn't have a clue about life or about what it took to be a queen."

"I find that hard to believe," Jame said.

"I had as much sense as Mularke did at that age," Jyac said.

Jame winced. "Ouch."

"The truth is, you had a maturity and confidence at nineteen that was so unexpected we didn't want to believe it," Jyac said. "Attending the arbiter's school and working with the Guards helped you grow up quickly."

"I couldn't understand why Argis was acting so childish," Jame said. "But she was just acting like a warrior of nineteen years."

"And you were acting like someone getting ready to go out into the world as a judge in legal cases," Jyac said. "We just didn't understand how important that was to you. But I'm glad you had the strength to stand up to us. When you returned last year, I was so proud of how you turned out."

Jame stared at the polished stone floor, trying to find some kind of response.

"It is now time for you to take your place as my heir." Jyac lifted the lid off of a box and pulled out a delicate strand of silver with a crossed sword and bow pendant dangling from it. "You came to Ronalyn and me soon after we were joined. Because you were of royal blood, Laur didn't bless us with a child of our own. You've always been our daughter in every way."

"I have always been grateful to you and Ronalyn for raising me," Jame said.

"This pendant has been worn by every princess since the beginning of our history." Jyac lifted the strand of silver over Jame's head.

An intense emotion bubbled up from somewhere deep within Jame as she wrapped her hand around the pendant. "I feel blessed and honored to receive this."

"May you and Tigh be blessed with a daughter to pass this pendant to when she reaches her eighteenth summer."

Jame wiped away unexpected tears and smiled. "If she's anything like Tigh and me, we'll probably have to send scouts throughout the Southern Territory to find her."

Jyac shared the grin. "Let's hope you do."

THE SIGHT OF soldiers and warriors practicing drills made Tigh smile. Their precision was still a bit rough but the determination on each face showed the natural rivalry between the groups. Argis looked less than pleased at the performance of her warriors. *Emoran pride.* Tigh shook her head as she approached the scowling Argis.

"They need a lot of work," Argis said.

Tigh studied a particularly intricate drill. "They'll be perfect before the day is out."

Argis cocked her head at Tigh. "They'll be lucky if they can do it in precision by the end of tomorrow."

"You know your warriors, I know the soldiers from Ynit." Tigh scratched her head. "I think the soldiers will have it by the end of today."

Argis turned to Tigh and put her hands on her hips. "I was talking about the soldiers."

"So you think your warriors will have it by the end of the day?" Tigh asked.

Argis straightened. "Of course. They're almost perfect now."

Tigh spent several heartbeats observing the dazzling sword work from both groups. "So are the soldiers."

Argis studied the group trying to stomp in unison and then whip their swords into a salute. "How much are you willing to wager on that?"

"What are you willing to part with?" Tigh adjusted the sleeve on her leathers. Winter Emoran leathers were a stranger patchwork than the summer ones.

Argis shook her head. "On second thought I don't think I should make any wagers with you until I get to know you better."

A shout in perfect unison bounced off the walls. Tigh grinned, and Argis sighed.

"Where do you think our current adversary is keeping her army?" Tigh asked.

Argis frowned. "How did that army get to that plateau in this weather?"

"So, you think their base of operations is close by?"

"If it is, we haven't been as diligent in patrolling these mountains as we thought we were," Argis said. "Between the Lukrians and us, we've kept track of every traveler and settler from Balderon to the wilds of the eastern slopes."

Tigh watched the flashing of swords for a heartbeat. "I think the person behind all this lives in Rihnon."

"How did you reach that conclusion?" Argis asked.

"I believe it's the person who used to act as the liaison to the Elite Guards during the Wars," Tigh said. "She was in my dreams while the magic was still in my wound."

"Rihnon." Argis paused to watch a particularly well-performed drill. "That's the one place around here where you could hide an army."

"What?"

"During the Wars, they opened up access to caverns with good size rooms to be used to protect the citizens if Rihnon was invaded. They used to have drills every few moons. Orderly evacuations of the city into these caves." Argis shrugged. "We would sit on top of the bluffs overlooking the city and watch. We were young and easily entertained."

Tigh chuckled. "Jame's told me stories of how you used to entertain yourselves."

"She was still with us at the beginning of the Wars," Argis said. "Jyac was so angry when we snuck down to Rihnon that first time after one of the scouts told us about the drills. She was always very protective of Jame even though Jame could take care of herself."

"If Jyac was so protective, why did she let Jame leave Emoria to go to school?" Tigh asked.

"Jame can be very persuasive when she wants to be." Argis grinned. "But I don't have to tell you that."

"I never had a chance against her," Tigh said.

Argis laughed. "I'm sure you did a lot of struggling."

Tigh shrugged and grinned.

"So are we planning a little trip to Rihnon?" Argis asked.

Tigh waggled her head. "A little scouting party to begin with."

"How about accompanying the delivery of knives and swords to our shop in Rihnon?" Argis said. "We have to stock it for the winter festival there."

"Winter festival."

"In three weeks," Argis said.

"Wonder what Ardhat plans to do with her army during that time." Tigh stared at the intricate sword drill that was very close to being perfect. "We have to make sure she's the one behind this and find her army as quickly as possible."

Argis turned to Tigh. "Ardhat. That's her name?"

"Yes. She's now a healer—"

"In Rihnon." Argis snapped her fingers. "Pranor, the proprietor of our safe house down there, just had a bit of a run-in with her."

"What?"

"It seems this Ardhat was a part of a small group of local merchants having an evening meal at the safe house, maybe a week or so ago," Argis said. "She got a little drunk and started bragging about how she had worked with the Elite Guards during the Wars and how Emorans were helpless children compared to them. Needless-to-say, this wasn't well received. Our warriors there, of course, wouldn't lift a hand against someone who wasn't a warrior and this just encouraged her to keep up her taunts. When Pranor finally had her removed by force, Ardhat hurled one last insult that had every warrior in the place out the door after her. Only their honor prevented them from killing her then and there."

"What did she say?" Tigh asked.

"Everyone who witnessed it took a pact not to say—except if Pranor pressed charges against Ardhat for disorderly conduct and several other minor offenses."

Tigh gave Argis a curious look. "Why isn't Pranor pressing charges?"

Argis sighed. "Too much trouble. We have to petition Ynit for an arbiter and they usually send an assistant arbiter doing field work to achieve their medallion. Most of them don't understand our code of honor."

"Why don't you just ask the arbiter representing Emoria?" Tigh asked.

"We don't have . . ." Argis caught the mischievous glint in Tigh's eye. "Jame?"

"When she stepped down as arbiter-at-large, they gave her Emoria and Lukria," Tigh said. "The official papers to Jyac and Kylara are probably in Rihnon, waiting for the weather to clear to be delivered."

"You think bringing this suit would be enough to take Ardhat's mind off of whatever she's doing with that army?" Argis asked.

Tigh raised an eyebrow. "You heard about how Jame eliminated the crime and corruption from Maymi?"

"Oh, yeah," Argis said. "We are forever thankful you didn't actually send those prisoners here."

"Jame didn't want you to know what she was doing down there," Tigh said. "She was still worried Jyac would order her home—estrangement or not. She had already made one difficult decision to go against Jyac's wishes, she didn't want to be faced with another one. Not so soon."

"Jyac surely would have gone crazy," Argis said. "But in hindsight, she's proud of what Jame's done over the last few years—once the stories finally reached us."

"Then I think we ought to give Jyac a chance to see Jame in action first hand." Tigh smiled at the perfectly executed drill.

"Glad I didn't wager anything," Argis mumbled.

Chapter 12

"HOW ARE THE drills going? Have they started using the weapons on each other yet?" Jame asked.

"It's like they've been drilling together all their lives," Tigh said as she joined Jame at a small table outside the tavern.

Bright torches lit the late afternoon darkness that came in deep winter. Fireplaces surrounding the outside seating area were enough to keep the bitter chill off the patrons. The potent Emoran ale added an extra layer of warmth. Emorans liked being outdoors as much as possible, so they found ways of spending even the coldest days on the plaza that was, more often than not, lit up like a winter festival in the evening.

Tigh touched the pendant around Jame's neck.

"It's been worn by every princess of Emoria since the beginning of our history," Jame said.

"Jyac is proud of you and what you've accomplished," Tigh said, softly.

Jame nodded. "I know. Hard for me to believe but I know it's true."

Teniar put tankards of ale in front of them. "Just tapped a new keg of the special brew in honor of our newly initiated princess visiting my establishment."

"News travels fast," Jame said wryly to Tigh.

"But you've always been their princess," Tigh said.

"The wearing of the pendant shows a princess is ready to settle down and learn the royal duties," Jame said.

"We can now treat her like a princess, and she can't refuse what is our duty to her," Teniar added.

"Like the tents and the escort," Tigh said.

Jame sighed. "Yeah."

Teniar laughed. "You'll get used to it, princess." She shook her head at a rowdy shout from inside the establishment. "Enjoy the ale and let Rilce know if you want more." She ducked through the doorway.

"So does that mean a royal procession, even when you're called upon to be an arbiter in, let's say, Rihnon?" Tigh breathed in the strong aroma of the ale before taking a sip.

Jame narrowed her eyes at Tigh. "And why would I happen to be called upon to be an arbiter in Rihnon?"

"Because the proprietor of the safe house there may want to bring charges against a local healer for disorderly conduct, plus other offenses." Tigh stared at the fire in the fireplace near the table.

"But she doesn't know that I'm the arbiter for Emoria," Jame said.

"The scout leaves first thing in the morning," Tigh said and took another sip of ale.

"And why are you so anxious for Pranor to press this suit?" Jame asked.

Tigh captured Jame's eyes. "The local healer is Ardhat."

Jame widened her eyes and then laughed in delight. "Whatever you're thinking, I love it."

"Pranor was content with just removing Ardhat from the establishment when she got drunk and started taunting the resident warriors," Tigh said. "But Ardhat said something that made the warriors angry enough to follow her into the street. Only their honor prevented them from killing her on the spot."

Jame straightened and frowned. "What did she say?"

"They took a pact to only tell if Pranor brings suit against her."

Jame took a long sip of ale. "It must have been something beyond insulting, beyond shocking . . ." She sucked in her breath. "I wonder if Iksoc was working for Ardhat."

Tigh grinned. "He's from Rihnon."

"I may be wrong, but I can think of only one thing an outsider could say that would both anger and upset an Emoran," Jame said. "I don't even dare utter it out loud. Just the thought disturbs the safety and peacefulness of this place. Was anyone from here there that night?"

"We can ask." Tigh wrapped an arm around Jame, who ignored the looks from the warriors at the other tables. They were just going to have to get used to Tigh's unabashed affection for her. "From what I remember of Ardhat, this insult you have in mind would be in keeping with her attitude toward us."

"Because you had been physically altered to imitate Emorans." Jame rubbed her chin in thought.

"I've never thought of it that way before, but it's true," Tigh said. "You were the model for the superior warrior. We were chosen because we were physically suited to be warriors based on what they knew about the Emoran warrior."

Jame took another sip of ale with that look in her eyes Tigh knew so well. Ardhat won't know what hit her going up against Jame.

GINDOR HAD A way of looking as if she was about to explode when she was more than displeased with something. Jame saw this look the moment she and Jyac looked up from behind the ancient crystal table Jyac used for official business. A princess traditionally shadowed the queen to learn the ways of the country and to learn how to rule, so Jame had to spend several sandmarks a day with her aunt.

"Yes, Gindor?" Jyac asked as a bristling Gindor stood in the doorway.

Gindor stomped into the chamber, shaking an angry finger at Jame. "What is this about you serving as arbiter for Emoria and Lukria?"

"Isn't that what you wanted me to become in the first place?" Jame asked.

"With restrictions we'd have negotiated with Ynit," Gindor said. "Being an unrestricted arbiter for Emoria is just as bad as being an arbiter-at-large. Every safe house is considered a part of Emoria."

"Do you expect Jame to be imprisoned here for the rest of her life?" Jyac asked.

"It's one thing going to Ynit and visiting her friends every once in a while and quite another thing gallivanting off to all parts of the Southern Territories at the drop of a helmet." Gindor paced in frustration around the rather spacious chamber.

"She'll always have the royal escort with her," Jyac said. "Even when she returns to Ynit to renew her credentials and for Tigh's yearly meeting with the healers."

"And the royal guard will have to pick up and go whenever and wherever Jame has to go," Gindor said.

"Which is their job," Jyac said.

"Spending too much time away from Emoria," Gindor said.

"I think the problem is not with me being an arbiter but with having our people continually exposed to the outside world," Jame said.

Gindor stopped pacing and glared at Jame. "Emoria has had too much attention brought to it lately."

"Meaning I've brought too much attention to it over the years," Jame said. "But you can't blame the battle of Balderon on me or Tigh. You were the one who sent Argis out to find us."

Gindor's jaw tightened. "What will you do when you're with child? When you have a baby to take care of?"

Jame shrugged. "What every other traveling arbiter does. We take a leave of absence until we're ready to resume our duties."

"Gindor," Jyac said. "Jame has enough sense to know when her work as an arbiter becomes too much for her and for Emoria."

"It's not just Jame I'm worried about," Gindor muttered.

"What do you mean?" Jyac exchanged glances with Jame.

Gindor waved a wrinkled hand. "You can't tell me all this mixing with outsiders has been good for us. Argis and Tas are even being joined with outsiders. And all the attention these soldiers from Ynit are getting—"

"Is a good thing." Jame stood and stepped around the table. "Either that or you officially present your gripe to the Emoran people so we can have it out once and for all. So just make it easier for all of us and accept the fact that you're in the minority on the subject and you must make the effort to get to know and appreciate our visitors."

Gindor blinked at Jame. "You're used to getting your own way, aren't you?"

"Yes," Jame said. "I'm used to passing judgment on a case and having people carry out my judgment."

"Your job has given you a rare confidence," Gindor said.

"I've heard every excuse and every lie and seen every absurd thing people want to dispute about," Jame said with a sigh. "So much is wasted on not getting along. Let Emoria set a better more dignified example to the world. Let Emoria show the rest of the world how to get along with each other and foster the spirit of cooperation."

Gindor stared at Jame. "It's difficult for an old woman like myself to see good in what we've always considered a bad thing for Emoria. I have not allowed myself to be convinced the benefits we've witnessed from being exposed to the outside world have outweighed the harm."

"We can never know for sure what will work and what will not," Jame said. "But simply living is taking a series of risks. We cannot stop living because something bad might happen. We also prevent all the good things from happening."

Gindor turned to Jyac, who was staring at Jame with an expression that mirrored Gindor's own astonishment. "If Jame is an example of what an outside influence can do to an Emoran then perhaps I'm being too hasty in my opinions."

"In Jame's case," Jyac said, "I don't know how much is outside influence and how much is just Jame."

"I have no idea of what you're talking about," Jame muttered.

Jyac simply smiled at her.

Gindor stepped up to the window overlooking the plaza. The warriors and soldiers were engaged in a rambunctious pickup game of Glak. "I'll accept that you want to continue to be an arbiter. But why go out in this weather for a case that can wait until spring?"

"Because we think the person the case is against is building an army with the intent of conquering the Southern Territories," Jame said.

Gindor turned to her. "Isn't that what that wizard, Misner, was trying to do?"

Jame shrugged. "It's a popular ambition."

Gindor let out a bark of laughter. "I bet you're a wonder in the arbiter's hall. So how do you know this person is trying to take over our fine Federation?"

"Tigh discovered it during her research," Jame said.

Gindor cocked her head. "Research?"

"Tigh's the scholarly one in the family." Jame grinned at Gindor's sour expression.

"No one's more bookish than you, short of those historians from Artocia," Gindor said.

"I'm bookish for an Emoran," Jame said. "Tigh's the real thing. She reads everything she can get her hands on. That makes her very handy when needing to quickly learn everything about a town or a case."

"I thought the enhancement and then the cleansing took all that away from her," Gindor said.

Jame shook her head. "She was just too much of a warrior after the Wars to become a scholar."

Gindor sighed. "Does that mean we're going to have to get used to seeing a warrior in the archives?"

"She's pleased that it contains so may scrolls from the outside," Jame said.

"Laur help us." Gindor threw up her hands.

"Maybe she can teach a special research class for the warriors," Jame suggested with a straight face.

Jyac stifled a laugh.

"You joke"—Gindor pointed a finger at Jame—"but the way things are changing I wouldn't be surprised."

TIGH BLINKED IN the torch lit corridor as solemn golden eyes blinked back at her. She squinted into the gloom next to a wall beneath a torch. The crouching beast stared back with an arrogance and disdain that was its birthright. It then casually stood up and leisurely stretched, turned, and sauntered in the direction Tigh was headed.

Tigh shook her head and followed the muscular, red-furred feline. The cats of Emoria were rumored to be the most pampered cats in the Southern Territories. They were certainly large and healthy looking.

She looked around the long corridor, which opened to an occasional chamber. In most of these chambers, women were gathered around fireplaces engaged in conversation or peaceful contemplation. Some were hunched around tables playing Wits—a mystifying game to Tigh involving carved sticks and painted stones. The night sky had opened up with another blizzard, sending the women indoors.

She was pleased at how at home she felt walking the corridors of the palace after just a few days. She was a bit surprised at her contentment but not surprised at how relaxed she was. For the first time since she had become a Guard, she didn't need to maintain a shield against how other people perceived her. Everyone knew who she was, and she didn't have to worry about strangers wandering into Emor. The initial meeting with strangers was always the hardest part of being out in the world.

"Hey, Tigh." A pair of scouts walked by.

Tigh nodded and smiled at them, no longer taken aback by the Emorans' genuine friendliness toward her. She walked up the steep incline cut in wide curves and lined with torches to the upper floor of the palace. The cat scampered ahead of her and disappeared somewhere. Cats had an enviable freedom even as they depended on humans to keep them warm and fed.

Tigh negotiated the maze of corridors and rooms until she came to a rather wide corridor. Down near the end, in the light of an opened door, the cat lounged as it licked a paw. Tigh got ten paces away from the door, and the cat rolled to its feet and sauntered into the chamber. Tigh got to the door in time to see the beast jump up on the bed and curl up in the middle of it.

She also noticed several crates of different sizes stood next to the door.

"Have we adopted a cat?" she asked.

Jame turned from her efforts to consolidate her old belongings in the shelves and holes carved into the wall to make room for the stuff they had brought from Ynit. "I think it's adopted us. It wandered in while our things were being delivered."

Tigh studied the sleeping red tabby for a heartbeat. "Maybe it belongs to someone else."

"Probably not," Jame said. "Most of the palace cats don't attach themselves to any one person. Every once in a while one will take a liking to someone and make themselves at home in that person's chambers. Come to think of it, they often attach themselves to someone who's preparing for motherhood. Something in the way our bodies change attracts them."

Tigh raised an eyebrow. "It's a boy cat?"

"That has nothing to do with it," Jame said. "The cats that take up residence in the palace are caught and neutered. He's just decided he likes it here. I've prepared a little place in the corner for his food and water."

Tigh wandered over to Jame and took the pile of leathers from her. "This sounds suspiciously like nesting."

Jame laughed as she pointed to where the leathers should go. "Maybe it is. If it is, I'm not complaining. In fact I'm feeling very good right now."

"That probably has something to do with that potion Panilope had you drink," Tigh said. "Are we going to have enough room here for all of our stuff?"

"Timaral said if we need more space, she'll come in and drill out some more holes on that wall." Jame pointed to the wall with the fireplace sprawled from its center.

"The walls are thick enough between chambers?" Tigh asked.

"A couple of arm spans thick." Jame piled several relics from her childhood into Tigh's arms.

"I guess some of this is going to get some use again." Tigh looked down at the stuffed animals, miniature wooden weapons, and bags of stones and sticks for table games.

"We should be thinking about fixing up the chamber across the way." Jame nodded toward the open door. "When our daughter turns four summers, we'll move her in there. It's always nice to have it prepared as the playroom so she gets used to it being her room before she moves into it."

Tigh bit her lip as she put the toys onto the shelf Jame pointed to. She was just getting used to the idea of having a baby, but the idea of a child playing, talking, walking around . . .

"Tigh?"

Tigh blinked out of her distracting thoughts and gave Jame a sheepish look. "Uh, I just got overwhelmed a bit."

Jame grinned and wrapped her arms around Tigh. "Don't worry. It's been happening to me, too."

Tigh lifted Jame up and spun her away from the wall and gently put her down. "At least it's a good kind of overwhelmed."

"Yeah." Jame sighed as she nestled Tigh's shoulder.

"Meeeoooow."

They looked at the bed. The cat sat scowling at them.

Jame separated herself from Tigh, walked to the bed, and gave the cat a scratch behind the ear. The cat arched into her hand, the scowl softening into a blissful expression and a purr rumbled from that place of complete contentment only found in cats.

A fascinated Tigh approached the cat and gently brushed her fingers behind the other ear. The cat looked as if he was floating on the mist of Laur's waterfalls. Tigh exchanged a wry look with Jame.

Jame grinned. "Looks like he's adopted both of us."

"YA KNOW, TIGH, you have a cat following you around." Argis crossed her arms as Tigh entered the strategy room next to the chamber where several challenges were being met—noisily with an enthusiastic audience. "You also spent the morning rummaging through the storage chamber for, let's see, a cradle, baby chairs, a games table, several stuffed animals, a box of toys, several stick horses, and a rocking unicorn. The cat got tired following you."

Tigh gave Argis a puzzled look.

Argis raised an eyebrow. "We usually wait until our partners are actually with child."

"I, uh, just did it while I was thinking about it." Tigh shrugged.

Argis relaxed and stared down at the table covered with a model of the southern range of the Phytian Mountains. Emorans were masters at creating three dimensional replicas of the world around them. "I guess it's different with you two. You've been together for so long. For most of us, we have to adjust to being joined and expecting a child at the same time."

"That's tough," Tigh said. "Of course, Jame and I had a lot of other things to deal with after we were joined. Her first case, my learning how fight again."

Argis picked up a small carved figure of a soldier. "On the other hand, you're both a lot more secure in your relationship than the newly joined."

Tigh walked to the side of the table opposite from Argis. "Are you sure you're not having second thoughts?"

Argis straightened. "No. Not me. I'm just making a general observation."

"I can tell you speak the truth, but does anyone else believe you?" Tigh chuckled at Argis's look of resignation.

"Getting cold feet is so common no one believes you when you say you don't feel it—even just a little bit." Argis placed the soldier on the upper meadow above Rihnon. "Not everyone takes a nap right before their joining ceremony."

Tigh grinned. "Give it a try. Maybe you'll start a new Emoran tradition."

Argis laughed. "You've never seen a young Emoran warrior before her joining. We've contemplated banning some of them from Emoria until the day of the ceremony."

Tigh choked down a chuckle. "I can imagine."

Argis shook her head as she turned her attention to the model. "We've sent out word to all the safe houses and the larger populations of Guards. Looking at this, I'm not sure if we're going to need so many troops."

Tigh sucked in a breath. "I'm, uh . . . I'm going to try to make a point. One that will hopefully discourage anyone else from these attempts to take over the Southern Territories. I don't want to be dragged away from Jame and my family every other season because some crazy fool has delusions of power. That's the downside of being involved in stopping all the attempts to conquer and invade since the Wars. Jame wouldn't want me to go alone, and I wouldn't want her to go along—"

"And I wouldn't want to be around here while you two were having that discussion," Argis said.

"It's a discussion I hope we never have," Tigh said. "So if I can demonstrate that I can pull together an army of Emorans, former Guards, Ynitian soldiers, and Lukrians at the hint of a threat—without leaving Emoria—then maybe we'll be left in peace."

"Good plan," Argis said. "If I didn't know better, I'd think you were thinking about retiring from being a warrior."

Tigh shook her head. "Not retiring, just being aware I'm gradually losing my edge."

"Which means in ten summers everyone else may be as good as you are," Argis said.

"At least here in Emoria, my sparring partners will keep me on my toes." Tigh grinned.

"You know, I think I'm going to need a better challenge than these eager young pups to get warmed up before our upcoming confrontation with Ardhat's army," Argis said. "And the only exercise you've been getting, lately, is hauling baby furniture and toys from the storeroom and building snow creatures."

"You want to spar?" Tigh didn't know why this surprised her. The only times they'd ever scuffled were when they weren't friends.

"Yeah. Unless you think I'll whup you in front of everyone." Argis nodded in the direction of the noisy challenges.

Tigh rubbed her chin. "I'm just making sure you won't be too embarrassed when you can't keep up with me."

"You, yourself, said we can't beat you," Argis said.

"That's true. But that doesn't mean you can out spar me," Tigh said. "After all, you've been lazing around here all year."

"Yeah, but I'm not about to turn thirty years," Argis countered, crossing her arms.

Tigh tried to ignore the reminder of her next birthday. "Tomorrow morning?"

"Tomorrow morning." Argis nodded then caught a movement at the door. "Have you named your shadow yet?"

Tigh turned around. The cat sat watching her. "I leave the important decisions to Jame."

Chapter 13

"I GUESS IT was bound to happen sooner or later." Jame stood in the middle of their chamber, taking in Tigh and the cat. Both gave her identical looks.

"We're only going to spar." Tigh and the cat looked at each other.

Jame couldn't help but laugh. "You and that cat are so cute together."

"It's the cat's fault," Tigh said. "He keeps following me around."

"He has good taste in companions." Jame walked up to Tigh and put her arms around her waist. "Argis is capable of hurting you, isn't she?"

Tigh looked down into Jame's eyes. "Yes. I've only sparred with cleansed guards, never someone with true enhancements."

"Why are you going to spar with her then?" Jame pushed Tigh's shaggy bangs out of her eyes.

"So, she learns she can fight without hurting someone." Tigh smiled at Jame's touch. "She knows she can hurt me but when she spars with me, she won't that to happen. She'll figure out very quickly the skill it takes to wound someone is the same as the skill to prevent hurting them."

Jame sighed and stepped away from Tigh. "I guess you're the only one who can help her through this reluctance to engage in friendly fighting."

She took Tigh's hand and led her to the fireplace. She had created a nest of soft leather cushions in the amber glow of the fire. On a small stone table with legs only a finger length in height was a gleaming silver tray with a crystal decanter and a pair of tiny delicate crystal cups. A nearby wooden tray held Tigh's Ingoran dishes filled with heavenly smelling food. The cat had already found a cozy spot on one of the pillows.

"What's this?" Tigh gave Jame a mystified look.

"We're celebrating my first case as an arbiter for Emoria," Jame said.

"Pranor decided to press the suit?" Tigh grinned in delight.

"Without hesitation," Jame said as she pulled Tigh down onto the cushions. "Emorans celebrate special occasions with a special wine."

Tigh arched an eyebrow. "And my favorite foods and a romantic spot by the fire?"

Jame smiled as she leaned forward and gently kissed Tigh's lips. "Just giving the celebration my own personal touch."

Tigh stretched out her legs with a relaxed contented expression on her face. "I've always been fond of your personal touch."

Jame couldn't resist stealing another kiss from Tigh. "Let's begin the evening meal with a toast." She lifted the lid off the decanter, releasing a floral fragrance, and poured the pale liquid into the small cups. She picked up both cups and offered one to Tigh.

"I didn't know Emorans indulged in such delicate wines," she said.

Jame, feeling a bit lightheaded as the special floral fragrance filled the room, smiled at Tigh, who looked as contented as the cat. Not for the first time did Jame think the Emoran leathers fit Tigh like they were a part of her skin. She always marveled how Tigh's hard muscular body was compacted into a slender graceful frame.

"The warriors will indulge in private moments of celebration with their partners or closest friends," Jame said.

"Are there any special words for such a toast?" Tigh's soft voice tickled Jame's ears.

"The wine says it all," Jame whispered as they brought their heads close together and sipped from their own cups but could breathe in the fragrance from each other's breath.

Tigh leaned close to Jame's ear. "How does the wine go with Ingoran food?"

Jame closed her eyes as she drank in Tigh's presence. "That's territory that's never been explored."

Tigh smiled as she pressed her lips against Jame's cheek. "We've had some experience with the exploration of new territory."

Jame reached behind her, picked up a dish, and held it between them. Tigh pulled off the lid and revealed thinly sliced cucumbers in a light sauce. Tigh returned the lid to the tray and then took the dish from Jame. She picked up a slice and lifted it so Jame had to tip her face up to receive the delicate food.

"Well?" Tigh purred as Jame savored the cucumber.

Jame sighed. "I think the wine was made for Ingoran food."

"I'd better give a second opinion." Tigh pressed her lips against Jame's. "Hmmm. I think you're right."

"But it doesn't hurt to keep testing that opinion." Jame picked up a cucumber slice.

Tigh grinned and then deftly took the slice from Jame's fingers with her teeth. "Emoran's certainly know how to celebrate."

"YOU HAVEN'T LECTURED me about why I shouldn't spar with Tigh," Argis said as she and Goodemer strolled down a palace corridor after the evening meal.

"I think it's a good idea," Goodemer said. The slight frown she wore all evening briefly went away as she turned and smiled at Argis.

Rather than be reassured, Argis felt more unsettled. Something was bothering Goodemer. But fear that it was something she had said or done, prevented her from asking out right. "You really think so?"

"As long as you don't hurt her." Only the twinkle in Goodemer's eye betrayed her light teasing. "Jame would not be pleased."

"Tigh wouldn't be very happy about it either." Argis scowled. "It's kind of a strange feeling, knowing I can beat her. The first time we were face to face, I punched her, and she didn't even have it in her to fight back."

"Now you can face each other and have a friendly sparring match," Goodemer said.

Argis sighed. "I hope so. Speaking of . . . Jame and Tigh weren't in the dining hall."

"I met up with Jame earlier on her way to the kitchens. She said she was arranging a cozy meal in their chamber to celebrate her first case as an arbiter for Emoria." Goodemer smiled.

"Those two don't need much of an excuse to celebrate—alone," Argis said.

"They've learned to fully appreciate their lives together," Goodemer said. The slight frown return to Goodemer's face. Then she grasped her amulet.

"What's wrong?" Argis asked.

"A wizard has been trying to probe the city all evening," Goodemer said.

"What? Why didn't you say anything?" Argis asked, relieved that Goodemer wasn't mad at her, and a bit put out she didn't say anything about the potential trouble to Emor.

"I wasn't sure what it was until this moment," Goodemer said as she concentrated on her amulet. "I think this wizard is more skilled than the other ones."

Argis mentally kicked herself for thinking Goodemer would keep something as important as another wizard probing Emoria from her. "What do you think this wizard is up to?"

"I can't tell yet." Goodemer released her amulet. "All I feel is a gathering spell."

"Gathering spell?"

"A spell that collects information such as the physical layout of Emor, how many inhabitants, things like that," Goodemer said. "I sense this spell is a little more sophisticated—possibly trying to determine how many enhanced warriors are here."

"I can't believe they're still thinking that they can invade Emoria," Argis said.

"It's possible this is a diversion," Goodemer said. "Something to keep me distracted while they're doing something else."

"Something else?"

"Such as exploring the caverns north of Rihnon in search of a passage into Emoria."

Argis scratched her head. "It still sounds like they want to invade."

Goodemer fingered her amulet. "I feel something deeper than just trying to destroy the strongest military presence in the Southern Territories. A zealousness, even though the chance of succeeding is nonexistent."

"Why can't anything be straightforward?" Argis hated people who won't stand up and fight. "The ideas in the outside world are too complicated."

Goodemer gave her a sidelong look. "You can't tell me you don't enjoy the opportunity to engage in battle—something Emorans haven't done for many generations. With the exception of skirmishes with the Lukrians."

Argis wanted to protest Goodemer's words. But it was true. She reveled in all the new adventures the outside world had introduced into her life.

THE WATER WAS so warm and soothing Jame felt she could float in it forever. Even the water flowing from the falls hit the pool with muted gentle splashes. She looked up at a flat stone ledge and smiled. Tigh was curled up on her side in a deep contented sleep.

"I will float in the water for a time while you stay on solid ground," Jame whispered. "You are the rock while I'm the water."

Jame opened her eyes. The fire had diminished to an orange glow and the peace in the chamber was so profound and deep it stole her breath away. The fragrance from the wine still hung in the air. Tigh was wrapped around her in a deep sleep. Jame sighed at the wonderful warmth of being in Tigh's arms.

She smiled and pressed her lips to Tigh's cheek. "You did everything just right. You were perfect."

JYAC QUICKLY REALIZED a friendly bit of sparring between Tigh and Argis would draw practically everyone in the city, so the night before, she had a section of the plaza cordoned off to be the sparring area. As soon as the area was marked, the citizens of Emor and their Ynitian guests staked out prime spots from which to watch. The result was a rowdy outdoor all night celebration.

As dawn barely lightened the sky through the thick winter clouds, the celebrants were either still dosing or just waking up.

Fant huddled between Claudi and Mularke who were sleeping off a spirited impromptu archery contest and way too much Emoran ale. She was freezing, sitting on cold stone with a master archer snoozing on each of her arms. Yet another situation she never envisioned herself in when she set out to chronicle the history of Ynit.

The two leather blankets draped over them didn't warm her southern blood, and she shifted to adjust the blanket over her hands.

Mularke lifted her head and then huddled under the blankets. "We usually don't have blankets when we end up passed out on the square. You outsiders are very resourceful."

"You mean you do this a lot?" Fant asked.

"We never need much of an excuse for a party or celebration," Mularke said. "We only have ourselves to keep entertained, and you can go crazy in the wintertime if you don't light up the long dark nights as often as possible."

Fant stared at Mularke in amazement. Who would have thought the master archer was at her most articulate just heartbeats after awakening from a drunken stupor. "Very interesting."

"You know what we find interesting?" Mularke crossed her legs to get more comfortable. "How you outsiders show affection to each other."

"You mean Tigh?" Fant grinned.

"Tigh." Mularke nodded. "You and Claudi."

"What?" Fant blinked at her.

"If any of our warriors were caught looking at another woman the way she looks at you when you're not paying attention, they'd be teased without mercy," Mularke said.

Fant stared at Claudi asleep on her arm. "Really?"

"Oh, yeah. I mean I can tell you two are still just friends. But that's only because you're still getting to know each other," Mularke said. "The warriors don't fault the way you look at her. You being a scholar and not a warrior."

Fant was speechless and felt a little foolish for suspecting Mularke had more of an interest in Claudi than just friendship.

A deep gong filled the air.

"What the—?" Fant looked at Mularke, and Claudi raised a sleepy head.

"The temple bell," Mularke said. "The acolytes must have received a blessing from Laur last night."

"A blessing?" Fant asked.

"Sometimes it's a favor, sometimes it's for an upcoming joining," Mularke said. "Sometimes it's a baby. Most of the favors granted at night are babies."

"A baby?" Claudi sat up and pushed the hair out of her eyes.

"Laur blesses Emorans with a baby," Fant said.

"Just like that?" Claudi huddled under the blanket.

"Whoever Laur chooses to carry the child has to prepare her body first by drinking a special mixture," Mularke said. "When her body is ready she usually doesn't tell her partner because they tend to get nervous about the idea. She entices her partner into a night of lovemaking, and Laur then blesses them with a seed of a child."

"When does the mother-to-be break it to her partner she's with child?" Claudi asked.

"That's up to her." Mularke shrugged with a twinkle in her eyes.

"So who is it?" Claudi sat forward.

"The festival of Fall Time begins in a fortnight." Mularke pulled her skin of water from her belt and took a swig. She then offered it to a grateful Claudi. "Many couples are joined during the festival because Laur never denies the gift of a child for those who ask on or before Wintermas Eve. It's also a tradition for women to prepare their bodies and conceive right before Fall Time, so her child can receive the blessing of the Wintermas Eve."

"Do we know who's preparing her body for a child?" Fant asked.

Mularke gave them an amused looked. "I know of one. And I also happen to know she had a private evening meal with her partner in their chamber last night."

Fant frowned, and Claudi looked equally unenlightened.

"They've been adopted by an arrogant four-footed beast."

Fant and Claudi exchanged wide-eyed looks.

"So, you think . . . ?" Fant remembered Seeran telling her Jame had returned to Emoria to produce an heir.

Mularke grinned. "I'd say it was a sure bet."

A clanging of metal against metal came from the direction of the palace.

"Now what?" Claudi asked.

"Food," Mularke said. "They're passing out bread and tea. That means Tigh and Argis are going to spar before the morning meal."

"So why is the festival called Fall Time?" Fant asked.

"The official name of the festival is The Time of the Waterfall," Mularke said. "But only Panilope ever calls it that. We've always just called it Fall Time."

Several women put large baskets of warm aromatic bread and jugs of spiced tea in the spaces between huddled groups of women. Mularke reached out her long arms and grabbed three loaves and the jug. Claudi and Fant unhooked their leather cups from their belts. Mularke poured the tea into their cups and unhooked her own cup and filled it, then passed the jug to her closest neighbor.

The hot tea tasted wonderful to Fant. She sighed as it warmed her from the inside. The bread was the sweet kind Emorans favored for their morning meal.

"Do you think anyone will believe any of this?" Claudi leaned into Fant and asked.

"I don't even believe it," Fant said.

Their eyes met, and they laughed, then turned quickly lowered their eyes to their simple meal.

Mularke shook her head in amusement.

"There's Argis," someone said.

Everyone looked in the direction of the palace.

"She doesn't look very happy," Claudi said.

"She's just put out at us for turning a simple bit of sparring between friends into an excuse for all night partying," Mularke said.

"Simple bit of sparring." Claudi grinned. "You Emorans have a rare gift for understatement."

"There's Tigh," Mularke said, almost laughing at Tigh's bemused look.

A grinning Jame sauntered through the opened palace doors behind Tigh. Fant noted Jame looked very pleased with herself about something.

"CAN YOU BELIEVE this?" Argis waved her hand at the crowded plaza and the paths up the cliffs filled with women and girls.

"How did everyone find out about it?" Tigh asked.

"Were you ever able to keep a secret in Ynit?" Argis arched an eyebrow.

"Uh, no," Tigh said.

"It's equally impossible here," Argis said.

"They seem to think that something worth watching is going to happen," Tigh said.

"I guess that's up to us." Argis pushed down a rise of nervousness. She never got nervous when she was about to fight and that made her feel even more unsettled. She concentrated on looking relaxed and casual.

"Don't have too much fun," Jame said. "I expect to have my morning meal sometime before the midday meal."

"Hmmm." Tigh rubbed her chin. "So, you want us to spar long enough to work up an appetite."

"Something like that." Jame wrapped her hands around Tigh's arm. "I want to spend a nice quiet day with you before we go to Rihnon. I don't want to be putting ice on too many bumps and bruises."

Argis pushed down the reminder she was capable of injuring Tigh and appreciated Jame's effort to lighten her apprehension. "I'll try not to inflict too many wounds."

She expected some kind of retort from Tigh and was surprised at how amiably passive she was. Something had put Tigh in a good mood, and it wasn't the prospect of doing a bit of sparring. Argis shifted her observation to Jame, who looked up at Tigh with unabashed love. They must have had some celebration the night before.

"That's good to know," Goodemer said. She approached them by skirting the edges of the plaza.

"You actually got up this early to watch?" Argis asked.

"It was difficult to sleep with all the gonging and clanging going on out here," Goodemer said.

"Gonging?" The word died on Argis' lips at the dumbfounded look on Tigh's face.

Jame slipped her arms around Tigh. "Laur blessed us last night. I was waiting to tell you after the sparring. I didn't want you to keep hitting yourself in the head with your own sword."

Tigh turned to Jame. "You're . . . you're . . ."

"Yes." Jame smiled.

"If you faint on us, you'll never be able to live it down." Argis could imagine what Tigh was feeling and wondered how she would react when Goodemer broke the same news to her.

Tigh took a breath and gazed at Jame. "Faint? I feel like I could take on every enhanced warrior here without breaking a sweat."

"Just have fun," Jame said. "And Argis, have pity on her, she's in shock at the moment."

"I'd suggest postponing the sparring, but everyone will be mad at both of us," Argis said. Then she grinned. "Congratulations to you both. Emoria has truly been blessed today."

Jame released Tigh and took Argis' hand. "Thank you, Argis."

Goodemer gave Jame a hearty hug. "I'm so happy for both of you." She couldn't keep the tears from her eyes and sheepishly wiped them away. "In some ways I'm still the hero-worshipping girl back in Ynit when Tigh was being rehabilitated. I'm happy I've been able to witness many important events in your lives."

"We're hoping to be witness to the most important events in your life." Jame grinned at Goodemer and Argis.

Argis sighed and nudged Tigh. "We'd better go out and spar before they get even more mushy on us."

Tigh answered with a silly grin.

Chapter 14

ARGIS FLIPPED HER blade a few times as she and Tigh circled each other. The gathered women were on their feet, quiet with anticipation. Neither she nor Tigh were accustomed to making the first move, but they both knew they couldn't circle each other all day. They would have Jame's empty stomach to answer to.

She caught a slight lift of Tigh's chin and didn't have time to register Tigh decided to make the first move. She got her blade in place to stop Tigh's graceful swing. Not for the first time did Argis wonder about Tigh's sense of honor. By making the first move, Argis didn't lose face with her warriors.

Argis spun around and whipped her blade at Tigh and was surprised at the sting in her hands as it met the infamous black blade. She may be invincible, but Tigh had an unrivaled power behind her strokes.

Tigh grinned as she flipped over Argis and tapped her on the shoulder. Argis swung around but Tigh was airborne again. Argis swung back around to find Tigh standing two paces away with her blade resting on her shoulder.

Tigh grinned. "I didn't want to make it too easy for you."

"You're so considerate." Argis flipped over Tigh who whipped her blade over her head to stop Argis's blade. She then twisted her body and blade against blade until she faced Argis and forced the weapons so they were hilt to hilt.

Argis realized being invincible wasn't enough for someone who not only knew all the moves, but invented countless numbers of them along the way. Tigh's speed was as big a factor as her skill with a sword. Argis had never thought she wasn't as fast as Tigh when it came down to a direct comparison.

The surrounding spellbound women had yet to utter a sound.

Tigh's eyes twinkled as they pushed away from each other and casually stalked the other in a circle. By voiceless mutual consent, they kept the next flurry of strikes and parries rather subdued as they learned each other's rhythm and style. Argis tried not to think Tigh was holding back on her speed, while she was pushing hers. Just sparring with Tigh would increase her reaction time.

"Ready to give them a reason for spending the night out here?" Tigh asked in a quiet voice.

"What do you have in mind?" Argis flipped her sword between her hands.

"You start and then follow my lead."

"Start and follow your lead?" Argis wrinkled her brow as she swung her sword and was in the middle of a carefully controlled but spectacular looking exchange of hits, flips, and everything in between before she realized what had happened. Tigh somehow was able to hold back on her speed and keep Argis from going full strength and letting her enhancements kick in—in a sense equalizing their skills. They kept it up long enough to shame some of the younger un-enhanced warriors-in-training.

The crowd erupted in cheers and shouts as they voiced their appreciation for this wild display of skill. Argis knew Jame and Goodemer were holding their breaths and praying she and Tigh really knew what they were doing.

Argis and Tigh increased their rhythm until the blades were a blur and neither of them decreased the flips and jumps or the inventive moves.

All of a sudden they stopped in mid move and stared at each other in disbelief. The last echoes from the puzzled crowd died away.

TIGH APPROACHED ARGIS and inspected a rip in a patch of leather on Argis' arm. Blood seeped from a thin scratch.

"I thought we couldn't be hurt," Argis said.

"You can't. Goodemer understands the enhancements as well as the healers who created them." Tigh frowned, trying to grasp what her mind insisted was impossible.

"Then how do you explain this?" Argis twisted her arm to study the scratch.

Tigh stepped away and dropped to her knees, so lightheaded she fought not to pass out.

She heard rapid footfalls, and Jame knelt in front of her. She tried to focus on the eyes gazing at her in concern. She finally took a deep breath and blinked, but still felt dazed and confused.

Jame wrapped her arms around her and held her close.

Argis knelt next to them. "What happened?"

"Tigh was struck with a very startling revelation," Jame said.

"What?" Argis asked. "She didn't even say anything."

Jame kissed Tigh's cheek and then looked at Argis. "She's still enhanced."

"THIS IS RIDICULOUS." Jame threw up her hands at the Council. Just a year before, she stood in that chamber shaking her head at another ridiculous reaction from the ancient women seated in a semicircle in front of her. Even Argis was there to defend Tigh as she had the year before.

Gindor stood up and pointed at Jame. "We're not in the outside world, and you're not arbitrating a case. Show the proper respect to your Elders."

"A trial can be arranged if that's what it takes to stop this constant arresting of Tigh every time her notorious past rears its ugly head," Jame said.

Gindor straightened. "We're just taking precautions."

"She's the same person she was yesterday, and the previous seven years I've known her—six of which we've lived together," Jame said. "If she hadn't sparred with Argis, we would've been having the nice relaxing day I planned for us instead of having to deal with this nonsense."

"It could be a warning from Laur," Gindor said. "I've sent word to Panilope to consult her."

Jame rolled her eyes and sighed. "Then she shouldn't have given us her blessing last night."

Jame had never seen Gindor look so dumbfounded as she sank onto her chair.

"Blessing," Gindor said.

"Blessing," Jame said.

Gindor exchanged looks with the women around her. "The blessing?"

"Why are you so surprised? That's why I'm here after all." Jame was sure she'd never understand Gindor.

"Yes, of course. I just didn't think the blessing would come so soon."

Jame crossed her arms. "Because . . ."

"Tigh's an outsider, and it's not unusual for Laur to spend time getting to know outsiders before giving a blessing," Gindor said.

"We spent quite a bit of time here last year," Jame said.

"But still, I just thought Laur would wait longer." Gindor fidgeted with the papers on the half circle table.

"She was pretty insistent with her dreams," Jame said.

"Dreams?"

"You know, Gindor." Jame walked up to the table, put her hands on it, and leaned forward. "You're the only one in Emoria who hasn't accepted Tigh into our society. I'm curious about why."

"I'm just remembering the laws of the Southern Territories," Gindor said. "All enhanced Guards must be taken into custody."

Jame shook her head. "Everything about Tigh's enhancements, everything about her cleansing, and everything about her rehabilitation was different from all the other Guards. Tigh is the exception in every way. But everyone is in agreement about one thing. Whatever it was that made her Tigh the Terrible is gone. Everything else left within her has been to the benefit of, not only the Southern Territories, but to Emoria." She leaned closer, capturing Gindor's eyes and unleashing the full force of her compelling personality. "So whatever thorn you have in your leathers about Tigh, you'd better get over it because I'm not going to take any more of these incidents in such a calm and reasonable way."

Gindor could only stare at Jame.

A grinning Argis sauntered up next to Jame. "By the way. Tigh has never been considered the dangerous one in their partnership."

Realizing she was actually making Gindor squirm, Jame relaxed, lifted her hands from the table, and straightened. "I'm sorry. That was most disrespectful of me."

Gindor sucked in air and rose a bit unsteadily to her feet. "I always try to keep the welfare of Emoria in mind."

"As do I," Jame said.

"I seem to keep forgetting you're not one of these young pups who has never faced the realities of life," Gindor said.

"So what can we do so you'll remember?" Jame crossed her arms.

Gindor studied Jame for several heartbeats before relaxing a bit. "Every time I catch myself forgetting, I'll remember what it feels like to experience what made you the successful arbiter you are."

Jame stared at her, surprised. "Uh, will that be enough?"

Argis chuckled, and Gindor allowed a small smile.

"Let's just say, you've got quite an effective weapon there," Argis said.

"THAT WIZARD HAD some very interesting things to say about Ardhat," Tigh said as she folded her extra set of black leathers and put it in her pack. They had decided to wear their nonEmoran clothes when they were outside of Emoria for other than official Emoran business. The cat rubbed up against his favorite warrior and purred.

"Don't try to justify Gindor's behavior." Jame still simmered from her encounter with the Elder that morning.

Tigh blinked up at Jame. "I just said that wizard had some interesting things to say. The reason I was within earshot of her is between you and Gindor."

Realizing she was possibly acting a bit irrational, Jame relaxed and pulled her extra set of brown leathers from the wall shelf. "It's funny how I'm not intimidated by her."

"According to Argis, it's the other way around." Tigh took the leathers from Jame, folded them, and put them into the pack.

"I actually intimidated her." Jame wandered to the window and looked out at the soldiers going through their drills in the plaza. "When did I ever develop the ability to do that?"

Tigh walked up to Jame and wrapped her arms around her from behind. "You've always had the ability. You've just never had to use it on someone who wasn't trying to obstruct justice."

Jame frowned at the thought. "I guess I've gotten used to being able to intimidate as a part of my job. I just never thought about it being a part of me, the everyday person."

"You've certainly gained a lot of respect around here with your fearlessness," Tigh said. "I think Gindor will leave you alone now."

"What makes you say that?" Jame cocked her head so she could look up at Tigh.

"Because you're carrying the heir to the Emoran throne." Tigh gently kissed Jame's lips. "Thank you for not telling me that last night was the ceremony."

"We have a tradition here," Jame said. "We have a story for outsiders about how our conception happens. They seem to accept it better than the simpler truth. We are sworn not to tell outsiders the truth, even if those outsiders become our life companions, until the time of conception—if the Emoran is chosen to carry the child. If the outsider carries the child, then Laur's acolyte initiates them to our ways."

Tigh pulled Jame closer. "I'm just glad we don't have to spend the night in the temple."

Jame turned around in Tigh's arms. "I liked our way much better."

Tigh just grinned.

"IF YOU DON'T stop laughing, Tigh's going to stuff you into the next snow drift," Tas said. "You're going to fall off your horse."

"I can't help it," Argis managed to say. "You didn't see the expression on her face."

"Give her a break," Tas said. "She just found out she's going to be a parent."

"I've never seen her pout like that before." Argis's shoulders shook as another bout of laughter overtook her.

Tas rolled her eyes. "You didn't have to tease her about it."

They broke into a trot as they cleared the last jumble of rocks that marked the southern boundary of Emoria. The layer of snow was thin in the meadow from the hot springs flowing close to the surface. The rest of the group of travelers were still a distance behind them—the coach Jame had to travel in now when she left Emoria couldn't move through the pass as quickly as being on horseback or on foot.

"I can't believe how attached she is to that cat," Argis said.

"She certainly thought the palace rules were absurd," Tas said.

"As far as I know, no one has ever wanted to travel with a palace cat before." Argis pulled her horse into a walk, circled around, and stopped. Tas walked her horse a bit around Argis.

"If you think about it, it *is* an absurd rule," Tas said.

"No doubt one Jame will try to get changed." Argis shaded her eyes against the glare of the midday sun on the snow. A group of Emorans and Ynitian soldiers on horseback rode onto the meadow followed by a snow coach. "Finally."

"Jame did tell us Tigh sometimes has strange reactions to new emotional experiences," Tas said.

"I wonder if the combination of Jame with child and bonding with a cat was just too much for her." Argis fought to keep the laughter away.

Tigh poked her head out from the coach and gave Argis a curious look.

Tas grinned. "I think she thinks you've lost your mind."

Argis just shook her head as they moved out of the way of the riders and coach.

"You'd better watch all that laughing," Tigh said. "You may set a bad example for the other warriors."

Argis straightened. "Says the warrior who travels in a coach."

"I travel any way Jame does." Tigh grinned. "Every heartbeat away from her company is too long to spend."

Argis sputtered in disbelief Tigh would actually utter such words of affection in public without the excuse of too much ale.

A laughing Jame poked her head out next to Tigh's. "I predict you two will be discussing this same subject when our children are old enough to get their braids."

The reminder of Jame's condition subdued Argis. A part of her heart would always have a whisper of what could have been between them. "Fortunately for Tigh, she's allowed to act unwarrior-like while you carry your child."

"I happen to know Goodemer has paid a visit to the temple. I'm sure Laur will bless you on your joining night," Jame said. "Then the two biggest baddest warriors in Emoria will be forgiven for their mushy behavior."

Argis straightened. "I'll never be as mushy as Tigh."

"Argis!" Tas, who had trotted ahead of the group, galloped back. "Something's wrong."

"Wrong?" Argis repeated.

"Ambush, I think," Tas said. "My enhanced hearing picked up too many noises that don't belong in the forest ahead."

Argis rode ahead of the group and put her hand up for them to stop. "We're going to take a break. Give the sledge horses a chance to rest and have a bite to eat."

The riders dismounted and formed a protective circle around the coach. Argis and Tas went to the coach as Tigh and Jame climbed out of it.

"I should go and check it out," Tigh said.

"You?" Argis said.

Jame grinned. "Tigh needs to run off some excess energy."

"Besides, we have a plan to fool whoever's watching." Tigh scanned the line of trees of the forest that blanketed the lower slopes of the Phytian Mountains.

"You think they're watching?" Argis squinted at the trees.

"I know they're watching," Tigh said. "Now I've got to see if they know we've spotted them and what they plan to do."

"How do you plan to do that without being spotted yourself?" Argis asked.

Jame chuckled. "After six years, we've probably played every trick possible. So go about eating your midday meal and just react to whatever we do as you would without knowing anything else was going on."

Argis and Tas could only stare at Tigh and Jame as they climbed back into the coach.

Less than a quarter sandmark later, Tigh's and Jame's voices, raised in an animated discussion, came from inside the coach. They finally climbed out and made a show of looking around the area where they had stood before.

The warriors and soldiers looked up from their conversation and meal and watched in curiosity.

"Is there a problem?" Argis asked from where she and Tas lounged against the front of the coach.

"I seem to have lost my favorite dagger." Jame pointed to the empty sheath on her belt.

"Maybe it fell when you had to get out when we went over the pass," Argis said with a twinkle in her eye.

"I'll go check." Tigh kissed Jame on the cheek. "I'll be back before you know it." She trotted in the direction they just came from and disappeared around a group of boulders.

Jame grinned affectionately after Tigh. "Our bit of news has her wanting to run all the way to Rihnon."

"It must be strange after it just being the two of you all these years." Argis scuffed a patch of snow. "This life changing event."

"You know, I think in a lot of ways, we did it right." Jame leaned against the coach. "We spent our most energetic years having adventures and creating an unbreakable bond between us. Now we can settle down with a family without feeling like we missed out on something."

Argis stared in the direction Tigh had gone. "I worry a bit Goodemer will feel like she settled down too soon."

Jame and Tas exchanged alarmed expressions. "What makes you think that?"

"She's so young, and she's such a skilled wizard," Argis said. "Sometimes I feel like I'm taking her away from what she spent her life studying to become."

Jame blinked at Argis. "Goodemer is not me."

Argis looked up at Jame startled. "Do you think—?"

"I think you're feeling some old guilt," Jame said. "That's all right. So do I. Tigh understands, and I think Goodemer will also understand. I also think she feels she has found her place in life in Emoria and with you."

"Not everyone can talk about stuff like you two can," Argis said.

"It's up to you." Jame shrugged. "But ask yourself this. Do you want to spend your life worrying about something that may not even exist or talk it out and maybe discover more about each other that you like?"

Argis cocked her head. "I'll think about it." And strangely enough she felt better about it. Maybe talking was useful sometimes.

Chapter 15

WITH THE GRACE and stealth of a mountain cat, Tigh got close enough to the leader of the band of soldiers to be able to tell what she had for her morning meal. Ardhat must be running out of mercenaries because the band hiding along the path looked as if they came straight from their mothers' firesides. She doubted they could hit what they were aiming at with the bows slung across their bodies or had the guts to go blade to blade with anyone much less an enhanced Emoran warrior.

Tigh sighed. She could imagine what lie Ardhat had told them about the enhancements. No one with half a thought in their brain would try to ambush the equivalent of Elite Guards. Their inexperience made this situation serious for Jame and the soldiers from Ynit. Something she didn't want to risk.

Tigh rubbed her chin in thought. She did have some excess energy to burn. She could either render the band unconscious one at a time or . . . This whole trip and confrontation were about sending a message to the world she had the ability to pull together an army quickly and efficiently.

"How long does it take to eat a meal?" The leader stamped down a clump of snow.

"Emorans do things on their own time," her companion muttered.

"Ardhat thinks they're unnatural," the leader said.

"She's been talking like that for years," her companion said. "I just hope she's right that their enhancements are just a story they've started to be left alone."

"Of course it is," the leader said. "No wizard is good enough to enhance one warrior much less a whole country of warriors."

Tigh grinned as she ghosted through the trees and around boulders to the path. She paused behind a boulder and then stepped out onto the path. With arms crossed and an expectant expression, she waited for some reaction from the ambushers.

Several tense heartbeats passed. At least they had learned to keep still and quiet. "Come on. We don't have all day. Come out and let me beat you so we can get on with our journey."

The leader stepped out onto the path. "You think you can beat thirty of us?"

"I'm a former Guard. We aren't able to lie." Tigh shook out her arms. "We can do this a number of ways. I can track down your poor excuse for a band of ambushers one at a time, or you can all come out and let me fight you here or," she took several steps forward, her eyes twinkling as the leader struggled not to step back, "you can just assemble everyone on the path, turn around, and march away."

The leader quickly reviewed the route back down off the mountain.

"Soldiers. Assemble." The leader looked around and thirty nervous soldiers fell into two lines behind her.

"Just remember as you're going down the mountain ahead of us," Tigh said. "The Emoran warriors and Ynitian soldiers with us would love the chance to do a little fighting. I don't think you'd find it a very enjoyable experience."

"We understand what you are saying," the leader said.

Tigh watched the band march out of sight, wondering what other little surprise Ardhat had waiting for them.

ARGIS TRIED NOT to glare at the curious citizens of Rihnon as the entourage of Emorans and Ynitian soldiers wound its way around their festival preparations. She didn't know how many in Rihnon were followers of Ardhat.

The stopped in front of the door with the sword and bow etched on it.

"The swords and knives go next door." Argis nodded at an opened doorway next to the safe house.

Several soldiers picked up the bundles of weapons and took them to the shop.

"All the gear goes in the basement of the safe house. There's plenty of room down there for us."

Tigh handed their packs out to a pair of Emorans. She had to get used to being a part of Emoran royalty now and follow Emoran protocol when circumstances required it. She climbed out of the coach, turned around, and put out her hand. "My princess."

Jame smirked, took the hand, and allowed herself to be helped out. "You're going to enjoy playing consort aren't you?"

Tigh grinned. "It could be kind of fun."

"Hmmm. Knowing us, we'll make it fun." Jame smiled as she grabbed Tigh's arm.

"My princess." Pranor stepped out of the safe house. "Welcome to Rihnon. I'm Pranor."

"I'm glad I can be your arbiter," Jame said as she clasped Pranor's arm. "This is Tigh."

"Well met, Tigh." Pranor had to look up her.

Tigh nodded. "Well met, Pranor."

"I have rooms prepared for you. The royal suite." Pranor grinned. "This is the first time it will ever be used."

Jame almost protested. The reflex was so automatic. She sighed and worked on what she knew would be a continual mental adjustment of the consequences of finally accepting her duties as a princess. It helped she was carrying the Emoran heir. If she determined the formality needed loosening up, she'd pursue it later, after the birth of her own princess.

"Thank you, Pranor," Jame said. "We feel honored to be the first to use it."

"I also have rooms for your master warriors and for the commanders from Ynit." Pranor led the way through the door.

"Thank you, again," Jame said. "I'm sure they'll appreciate not having to sleep with the troops."

They walked down the long narrow corridor found in all Emoran safe houses—a way to control unwanted visitors, if need be. The main room was good size, Jame noted with some relief. Accommodating her entourage could be a problem if there wasn't enough room in the public parts of the establishment.

"There's also a private tap room on the third floor where the royal suite is," Pranor said. "For yourself and the commanders, if you want."

Tigh and Jame exchanged bemused glances as they followed Pranor up the back stairs.

"Wonder how Argis will react to all this special luxury," Jame said.

"It'll make her think twice about volunteering to lead the royal entourage," Tigh said.

They stopped at the top of the third floor landing and just stared at the public room. Pranor and her staff had obviously worked hard at making the area more than presentable for their royal visitor. The wood on the tables and chairs were polished to a golden shine and the stone and tiles around the large fireplace were so clean, they brightened the whole room.

"You didn't have to go to so much trouble," Jame said. "We're used to roughing it."

Pranor turned to them and almost laughed at their puzzled and almost embarrassed expressions. "We're delighted to be able to fuss over our princess a bit. In fact everyone has been excited by the idea since we heard you were coming."

Jame's puzzlement deepened as they followed a grinning Pranor to one of the doors. A carving of a crossed sword and bow hung from the knocker.

"This is the royal suite." Pranor opened the door and stepped back to let Jame and Tigh enter.

Jame sucked in her breath at the simple but elegant sitting room. "Thank you, Pranor. It's perfect."

Pranor grinned as she walked across the chamber to a side door. "This is the bedroom."

Tigh and Jame exchanged glances, and they approached the door a bit warily. Pranor stepped back as they peeked into the chamber.

"Thank you, Pranor." Jame put a hand on Pranor's arm. "It's wonderful."

"We heard you were with child," Pranor said. "Congratulations. We don't often get a chance to dress a chamber in the royal colors. So this is our gift to you in celebration of your good fortune."

"You did a beautiful job." Jame stepped into the chamber, pulling Tigh with her.

The large chamber was a study in shades of purple and white and in the corner was a marble pool filled with steaming water pumped up from the hot springs Rihnon was famous for.

"That pool will come in handy after a day of arguing your case." Tigh turned to Pranor. "Jame tends to get a little tense in the shoulders when she's dealing with idiots and fools."

Pranor sighed. "I'm afraid Ardhat is more than that. She has some kind of fanatical ideas about Emorans. How we're not natural somehow because we can conceive without a man." She gestured at Jame's stomach. "That what you have growing inside you is not a beautiful gift of nature from Laur. I don't understand how she can think that. What is worse, she's convinced others what she thinks is the truth."

"I know. That's partly why we're here," Jame said. "She's put together an army with the purpose of invading Emoria."

"I know there's been evidence of an army forming in the cliff area but for invading Emoria? She's crazier than I thought." Pranor laughed.

"She's already tried to invade once," Tigh said. "Gave the warriors some practice on their night tracking."

"Unbelievable." Pranor turned at a noise in the outer room. She looked through the doorway. "Your things are here. I'll let you get settled in."

"Thanks," Jame said. "And thank you for allowing me to argue this case for you."

"If it brings down Ardhat, it'll be worth it."

ARGIS STROLLED INTO the tavern room and almost laughed. Tigh was seated at a sizable table in the back, which in itself wasn't unusual. All the stuffed and wooden toys on the table was quite unusual for an Emoran tavern room.

Tigh was in an intense discussion with a woman seated across from her. The gestures were in the direction of a stuffed horse with a strong resemblance to Gessen. Tigh's expression had the same intensity as when she was fighting.

Argis put on her most serious expression and went to Tigh's table.

"If you include this rabbit," Tigh said, pointing to an embarrassingly cute stuffed rabbit.

Argis was already working on how to hide it when they traveled back to Emoria.

The toymaker made a show of considering the counter offer before giving a quick nod. "Deal. The horse and the rabbit for three pieces of silver."

Argis choked back her reaction. Jame was obviously the one who did the bargaining in the family. On the other hand, she had no idea how much toys cost. She scanned the assortment of toys with a sudden panic. She was going to have to get toys for her own daughter—soon, if Laur gave them her blessing.

Tigh gave the toymaker the coins and took possession of the stuff animals.

The toymaker stood and gathered her toys into leather bags. She turned around and was face-to-face with Argis. Who stood with her arms folded, seriously studying her. The toymaker froze and stared at Argis.

"You're the toymaker here in Rihnon?" Argis asked.

The toymaker blinked in surprised. "Yes."

"What's your name?"

"Jerey. My shop is just two doors down." She pointed in the direction.

Argis nodded. "Thank you." As Jerey started walking past her an idea came to Argis. "Do you have stuffed alligators?"

"Why, yes. Three sizes." Jerey gave Argis a puzzled look.

"Two doors down?"

"Yes." Jerey smiled and carried her bundles to the door.

"Stuffed alligators?" Tigh lifted an eyebrow as Argis sat across from her.

"Asks the woman who just bought a stuffed horse and a disgustingly cute rabbit." Argis signaled a server for ale.

"My partner is with child," Tigh said. "I'm allowed to buy toys."

"Three pieces of silver seems steep." Argis picked up the horse and studied it. She had to admit it was very well made with precise intricate detail.

"Nice toys are generally more expensive," Tigh said. "But the funny thing is, they become more valuable as time goes by."

"Even after your daughter has loved the stuffings out of them?" Argis asked.

"She will love the rabbit to death," Tigh said. "But she'll cherish the horse because it looks like Gessen and hopefully an offspring of Gessen."

Argis sipped her ale and then nodded. "Good idea. We have good strong breeding stock."

Tigh took a sip of her own ale. "So, what have you learned?"

"You wouldn't believe how many former Guards have managed to sneak into town," Argis said with a grin. "They're staying with the Guards who live here and are camped out in a cave just north of here that is used by the local Guards for sparring. Also staying there are out-country Emorans. From all over. You and Jame certainly got around and made quite an impression."

Tigh frowned. "Emorans?"

"From Maymi. From Artocia. From Balderon. From Ynit. From Glaus . . ."

Tigh held up her hands. "The Emorans outside of Emoria were always very good to Jame—even when she was out of favor in Emoria."

"I know. And I'm thankful she was treated with honor and respect." Argis held up her tankard of ale. "Here's to Jame. The most amazing woman in the world."

Tigh grinned and lifted her tankard. "To Jame."

JAME STOOD BEMUSED as Tipca, the blades shop owner, proudly showed how the knives and swords were displayed to show off their finely crafted hilts and blades.

"Very nice," she said. "I'm actually looking for a dagger."

"We have several nice ones over here." Tipca walked to a table displaying daggers with ornate hilts. "The stone in this one matches your eyes."

"Actually it's for Tigh." Jame looked the daggers over. "Just a little gift."

"Ah." Tipca put a finger to her cheek. "Maybe something matching her black-bladed sword. Like all the weapons for the soldiers of the Southern Territories, that sword was forged in our blade shop in Ynit."

"I wonder what Ardhat would think if she realized the weapons of her so-called army were forged and crafted by Emorans," Jame said.

Tipca grinned. "Life is full of little ironies."

"Would you be able to forge a black-bladed dagger?" Jame asked.

"Of course," Tipca said. "The secret was passed to all the blade shops so any of us can produce a blade on demand."

"I'll want the hilt to be of the same design as Tigh's sword," Jame said.

"So you want the dagger to be a miniature version of the sword."

"Yes." Jame smiled at the idea. "That would be wonderful."

"We have the patterns for all the Elite Guard swords so it should be easy enough to do," Tipca said.

"Great . . ."

They turned at the sound of shouts and a scuffle at the door. Tipca grabbed Jame and pulled to her to back of the shop. "Get back to the safe house. Quick."

Jame knew better than to argue and went through the connecting door between the establishments. She ran down the small corridor and hurried past the kitchen into the tavern room. "There's something happening outside."

Tigh and Argis and a half dozen Emorans got to their feet and rushed out of the room.

Jame watched them go with belated worry. It was her job to send her people into what could be a dangerous situation. She sighed and sat down on the bench Tigh had just occupied. The stuffed pale, yellow horse caught her attention, and she couldn't help a smile through her worry. She held the horse and waited. The others in the room also watched the doorway.

They didn't have to wait long to hear the pounding of boots in the narrow corridor leading to the front door.

"We need Frira," Argis shouted as the group ran into the chamber. Olet was being held up between Tigh and Tas. Blood seeped down the scout's arm.

"What happen?" Jame got to her feet and rushed to them.

"Ambushed," Olet said as Jame followed them to a back room. "Half dozen of them. Dressed like ruffians but fought like soldiers. It was well organized."

"Why would they ambush you?" Jame asked.

Tigh looked back at her. "To get to you," she said in a soft voice.

"What?"

"They were just rushing into the shop when we got to them," Tigh said.

She and Tas eased Olet down on a pallet. Frira ran into the room took one look at Olet and shooed everyone out.

Jame backed against a wall and stood, still holding the horse against her chest, grasping what had just happened. It wasn't the first time someone attempted to get her out of the way, so to speak. But someone close to her had never been hurt before. She wasn't carrying the Emoran heir before. She had always felt safe surrounded by Emorans or Guards or soldiers—just their presence deterred potential assailants from trying anything. But now.

"Jame?"

Jame blinked up and saw identical expressions of concern and the kind of panic that warriors experienced when they were faced with a situation outside their comfort zone. "Sorry. Just thinking." She held out the horse. "Nice choice. It'll make a great hug toy."

"It's become too dangerous for you here," Argis said.

"And it's too dangerous for me to return home," Jame said. "So let's do what we came here to do so we never have to worry about it again."

Argis opened her mouth but Tigh put a hand on her arm. "As much as we hate to accept it. She's right. We've worked in dangerous situations before. Fortunately, this time we have a lot of help."

Argis studied Jame. "You can't leave the safe house. Not for anything."

Jame fought back her own protest. She knew Argis would have to answer for it if anything happened to her. "It won't be the first time I've been confined to a safe house. So agreed—until the trial."

Chapter 16

"YOU LOOK LIKE you had something sour for the evening meal," Tas said as she and Argis waited for a slump-shouldered, unhappy-looking Tigh to catch up with them on a small side road that led out of town.

Tigh's misery deepened as did the slumped shoulders. "Jame was unhappy about this little trip."

"Unhappy," Argis repeated.

Tigh sighed. "Very unhappy."

"Pregnancies are hard on the partners who aren't pregnant," Tas said. "Whatever she said, she didn't mean it."

Tigh nodded as she fell into pace with Argis and Tas. "I know. It still makes me feel guilty."

"You mean she's never made you feel guilty before?" Tas asked.

"Every time she's unhappy about something, even something small, makes me feel guilty," Tigh said. "Jame has put up with enough in her job without me adding to it."

"You know being in Emoria isn't going to change the pressures from her job. A queen in training takes on more and more duties as the queen grows older." Argis pointed out the route where the road split at the foot of a bluff.

"I know," Tigh said. "My hope is I can be the one part of her life that won't cause too much stress and worry."

"Good luck," Tas said as they trudged around large boulders that hugged the craggy bluff. "I guess Argis and I will find out what it's like to be joined quick enough."

"But not to Emorans," Tigh said.

"Maybe not born to it, but Seeran is learning Emoran ways very quickly." Tas sighed. "In some ways it's good, in other ways . . . let's just say, she's learning a little too well the traditional way non-warrior partners handle their warriors."

Argis choked back a chuckle. "Goodemer doesn't need any coaching on how to handle warriors."

"That's the truth." Tas laughed.

Argis stared at Tas and furrowed her brow. "What do you mean by that?"

"Uh, maybe you should continue this discussion some other time." Tigh, who had moved a pace ahead, turned around and put her hands on her hips. Tas and Argis stopped walking. Argis glared at her, and Tas looked pathetically grateful.

"All right. But you'd better have a good answer when we discuss this later." Argis tromped past Tigh.

"Thanks," Tas whispered as they followed after Argis.

Tigh felt something odd. They all stopped walking. Argis turned around and gave Tigh and Tas a questioning look, seeing the same look returned to her. They pulled their swords from their sheaths.

Tigh tuned her mind to the very air as they looked around them. She knew if all of them didn't feel it, they would have thought they were just jumping at shadows. But they were surrounded by nothing but shadows. The only thing that felt out of the ordinary was just a feeling.

"Magic?" Argis asked in a low voice.

"I can't detect magic," Tigh said.

"If not magic, then what is it?" Tas asked.

"Something that is the result of magic." Tigh ran her hand over the rough stone of the bluff. "Something that is meant to be felt by those who know to look for it." Her hand disappeared into the rock face.

Tas and Argis eyes widened.

"What . . . ?" Argis stepped closer to inspect Tigh's hand as she pulled it from the rock.

"I think we found the entrance to where that army is hidden," Tigh said. "They can find it when they feel whatever we're feeling."

"Clever." Argis slowly put her hand through the rock.

"Let's keep moving," Tigh said.

They sheathed their swords and continued along the bluff until they came to a large lake filled with night-darkened water. A stone bridge, wide enough for three horses to ride abreast, spanned the lake. Anyone who wanted to use the bridge in the past week would have found it difficult getting around the large boulders blocking the way. When Emorans wanted to take over an area, they learned to do it without bringing attention to themselves. The Emorans in Rihnon had convinced the mayor the bridge had become unusable from the weight of all the snow and ice and should be barred from traffic until it could be repaired in the spring.

Argis pressed one of the boulders with a finger and it effortlessly pivoted until it created an opening wide enough for them to walk through, then Argis pushed the rock back into place.

The reason the Emorans wanted the bridge barred was several paces away. The bridge had been fashioned from a natural divider between two lakes, crossing the larger lake then following a low cliff wall that hid the second lake, which was underground. Tas slipped her hand between cracks in cliff wall, releasing a knot at the end of a rope that allowed her to lower a thin, light stone onto the bridge, revealing a passage in the wall. They jumped down into the passage. Argis found and lit one of the little lanterns stashed in the cavern walls throughout Emoria. Tas pulled on the rope, raised the stone back into place, and looped the knot back into the crack.

The passage went downward and away from the Rihnon side of the lake. Over the generations, the Rihnon Emorans flattened out the walls and ceiling and even etched sign posts at intersections and where passages opened onto chambers.

They stepped into a large chamber several stories high. Tigh wasn't surprised to see the second lake inside. Emorans liked to fashion their homes away from home around bodies of water. As with Little Emoria of Maymi, residences pocked the upper walls, and the ground level was devoted to an eating establishment, a tavern, and a good-sized chamber where weapons were fashioned for both Emorans and for sale to the outside world.

Fortunately, the area looked spacious enough to accommodate the influx of visiting Emorans and former Guards—being warriors, most were used to living in cramped conditions on occasion.

Tigh sighed as the women on the other side of the lake spotted them and spread the word. Warriors started appearing from everywhere and gathered in every visible space.

Just as quickly, a young warrior jumped into a small flat boat and floated it across the lake to them. "Welcome to our little Emoria," she greeted as she pulled alongside a narrow wooden pier.

"Thank you," Argis said as they climbed into the boat.

"How many troops do we have here?" Tigh asked as she took in the mix of Emoran leathers and the black garb of the Guards.

"Three hundred strong," the young warrior said. "More than enough to tackle that so-called army next door."

"Next door?" Argis asked.

The young warrior grinned. "You'll see." She tossed a rope to one of the warriors on the pier that jutted out from a sizable flat area teaming with women.

Tigh, Argis, and Tas climbed out of the boat into the crowd.

Iklas stepped forward and saluted Tigh with her belt knife. "The peacetime regiment of the Guards reporting for duty, Commander."

Tigh took in her old friend, pleased to see time had been good to her. "Aren't you getting a little old for these get-togethers?"

"The chance to fight a real enemy keeps me young," Iklas said. "And I'll never pass up a chance to fight alongside Tigh the Terrible, even if we're hobbling around with canes."

"Haven't you heard?" Argis grinned. "Tigh's going into semi-retirement."

Iklas laughed. "I have the feeling the semi part of that retirement will go on for a long time."

Tigh shook her head. "Iklas is my second in command of the peacetime regiment of Guards. This is Argis Master Warrior and her second in command, Tas."

"Well met, Argis. Tas," Iklas said.

"Well met, Iklas," Argis and Tas returned.

"I'm going to be busy keeping our daughter out of trouble while Jame learns how to be queen," Tigh said. "That's why I called this little party. Jame and I are out of sight in Emoria. We want outsiders to know we can still put together an army at a moment's notice and squash any threat to the Southern Territories."

"Anyone who is crazy enough to try to conquer the Southern Territories while you're still able to lift a sword deserves the humiliating defeat they'll receive at your hands," Iklas said.

Tigh just shook her head and studied her feet.

"What's this about the other army being neighbors?" Argis asked.

The women within earshot crumbled into laughter.

"Come on," Iklas said. "I'll show you."

The women parted to let the small group through. Former Guards stopped Tigh and pulled her into an embrace and whispered, "Thank you" when they could find voices to speak. Tigh was startled at first and then accepted their need to let their feelings out to her. She glanced back to see Argis and Tas looking bewildered at these uncharacteristic emotional displays from the former Guards.

They finally ducked into a small corridor and escaped the crowd.

Tigh gasped for air as memories crashed down on her. After all these years, she again saw the comrades she wept for when she sat on the steps of the all-but-deserted fortress at Ynit before her first meeting with Pendon Larke. She brushed away tears, thankful the small corridor was not brightly lit.

"What was that all about?" Argis asked.

Tigh looked at her feet, uncertain she had a voice to speak.

"They were just thanking Tigh for the miracle," Iklas said.

"Miracle?"

"Because Tigh allowed the healers at Ynit to study and test her through the years, they finally figured out how to correct the flaws in our cleansings," Iklas said. "Over the past year, the healers visited each of us and performed a second cleansing. We are whole again. We can live normal peaceful lives and be called upon to serve the Southern Territories and fight with the same joy we possessed during the Wars. The best of all worlds for us who loved everything about being a Guard."

Argis studied Tigh's bowed head. "Life is full of strange ironies, isn't it?"

"What do you mean?" Iklas asked.

Tigh took a deep breath and raised her head. "A few days ago we discovered something the healers never considered when my cleansing didn't seem to work the way it did with the rest of you."

"What was that?"

"I was never cleansed."

Iklas looked as if the shock of the words hit her with a physical force. "No. That's not possible. You're nothing like Tigh the Terrible."

"With you, everything but your necessity to fight had been cleansed," Tigh said. "With me, everything but the necessity to fight remained. I just didn't know it until I wounded Argis while sparring."

Iklas shook her head. "You know, I think we all knew that. Somewhere deep in here." She patted her gut. "In that place we learned to listen to when nothing else registered danger. When we finally reached that part in you that was the fighter, so long ago in that warehouse in Maymi, we knew on every level except the conscious one. It wasn't possible so we convinced ourselves it wasn't true."

"I'm still getting used to the idea," Tigh said.

Iklas continued to lead them down the corridor. "You're right. Life is full of ironies. The greatest fear everyone had was Tigh the Terrible couldn't really be cleansed. And that's exactly what happened." She pushed open a door and put a finger to her lips.

It didn't matter if they shouted to each other because the noise in the empty chamber was almost deafening. Argis, Tas, and Tigh exchanged baffled looks as they walked into the middle of the chamber and glanced around. Two black clad Guards were seated at a small table against the far wall, listening and scribbling.

Iklas beckoned them back out of the chamber and closed the door.

"It's some kind of trick with how the caves are shaped," Iklas said. "The cave next to that one is used for meals and meetings. We've been able to get a lot of information from just listening in."

"Who would have thought?" Argis grinned with an impish gleam in her eyes.

"The best is still down here," Iklas said as she led them to another door and opened it. This chamber was small and quiet except for a few voices engaged in a discussion.

Two Guards sat at tables within the chamber, listening to the conversation with pens poised. They looked up and acknowledged Tigh with a nod before returning their attention to the disembodied voices.

Tigh wasn't surprised to see Patch Llachlan and Meah acting as scribes, given the nature of the discussion on the other side of the wall.

Iklas motioned them back out into the corridor and carefully closed the door.

"Wasn't that—?" Tas began.

"Meah and Patch." Tigh nodded.

"I remember Patch. Brrr." Tas shuddered.

"So we have an ear to their operations chamber," Tigh said.

"They thought they were being safe by putting it deep into that system of caves," Iklas said.

"And you got a pair of brilliant military tacticians analyzing what they are going to try to do," Tigh said.

"I asked politely," Iklas said. "They were nice enough to agree."

Tigh laughed. "They would have begged for the job."

"So how do we know they can't hear us in any of our caves?" Argis asked.

Iklas's grin was so wide, she had to keep from laughing. "There's only one other chamber we share with them, according to the maps you Emorans drew when you originally explored these caves. We have regular meetings in that chamber, making it sound like our own war room. All we've been doing so far is to discuss very unlikely scenarios to attack them, to protect Jame . . . You get the idea."

"How do you know they heard you?" Argis asked.

"Because they discuss them in their own war room," Iklas said.

"And how do you know they aren't playing the same game on us?"

"First, I don't think they're clever enough." Iklas had an amused twinkle in her eyes. "Second, no map exists to outsiders of the caves inhabited by Emorans. They don't know where our caves are, other than that one chamber. And we haven't made any noise they can hear in the other two chambers."

"They have another surprise coming to them," Tigh said. "We found the entrance to their cave while coming here."

"Really? We can add that to the final surprise for them. The maps have shown us all the back ways out." Iklas scratched her head and gave Tigh a speculative look. "You know, we thought an earthquake or something had covered the front entrance, since those maps were drawn centuries ago. And the local Emorans rarely go that way because it's a main travel way, so no one can remember ever seeing the entrance."

"You would have noticed a rather large mouth to a cave disappearing overnight," Tigh said. "It has been concealed by simple magic."

"So, they're trapped and don't know it," Tas said.

The other three exchanged that look . . . the one they got when they had an idea just crazy enough to work.

"So," Tigh said, "what do they think we're going to do?"

Iklas led the way to another corridor that opened into the tavern. "They think we're going to focus on a show of force during the trial."

"Sounds like a believable option for us."

"That's why they're preparing to block the way out this valley before we said we were going to get into position," Iklas said.

"Jame doesn't like interruptions when she's arguing a case," Tigh said as they entered the tavern and found an empty table.

"And I don't think the people of Rihnon want two armies engaged in battle disturbing their festival preparations." Argis smiled as a server put tankards of ale on the table.

"Do you know what their wizard looks like?" Tigh asked.

"Yes." Iklas nodded. "But it's not as simple as that. We just found out tonight she's acting as Ardhat's arbiter. That's one of the things we needed to tell you."

"What?" the others reacted.

"From what we could gather, when she washed out of wizard training, she went to Ynit to become an arbiter. This was a good twenty years ago," Iklas said.

"Bal's Children." Tigh breathed and then straightened. "I want her and that army neutralized tonight. This nonsense of Ardhat's can't be allowed to continue for another day. Protecting Jame will be impossible."

"That's the one glitch in stopping that army," Argis said. "That wizard will interfere with anything Goodemer does to help us."

"Do we know where this wizard keeps herself?" Tigh asked.

"She's hiding in plain sight. As Ardhat's arbiter, she's staying at the Rihnon Inn," Iklas said. "That's how we found out so easily who she really is. She and Ardhat discussed some of their plans in the wizard's room."

"No lookouts lurking about?" Argis asked.

"They don't want to do anything to make anyone suspicious," Iklas said. "One more thing we learned. Ardhat has gotten rather upset with her soldiers turning tail every time they came up against you. The wizard has done something to them. Something that won't fade if anything happened to her. A special kind of spell that once cast, it stays until it's removed."

"She's probably convinced them she's enhanced them, and we can't beat them," Tas said.

"If they think they're enhanced, that means they're going to want to fight. Better to do that out in the valley than in the caves." Tigh took a sip of ale, feeling a bit better than she did a few heartbeats earlier.

"If the wizard is neutralized, Goodemer can block all ways out except the way into the valley and everyone can get a good workout," Argis said.

"But how do we neutralize the wizard?" Iklas asked.

Tigh opened up her belt pouch and pulled out a small wolf amulet. "A small present from Goodemer. It only works on rogue wizards, and only I can use it, because I'm immune to magic."

"We can be ready to greet that army when Goodemer forces them out of the caves," Iklas said.

Tigh nodded as she studied the dark ale in her tankard. "Something is still bothering me about this. It's too easy, too pat. Ardhat hasn't done anything to indicate she understands military strategy at all. She's just focusing on her goal—showing the world Emorans are unnatural and Emoria should be destroyed because of that."

The others at the table stared at Tigh in shock.

"You're kidding?" Argis asked.

Tigh sighed. "That's what the trial is about. That was the insult Ardhat made in the safe house, that had the warriors there ready to kill her."

Argis pushed down her anger. "I'm glad Jame has a chance to correct her thinking legally, in a public forum."

"That thinking also tells us we're not dealing with a sane mind," Tigh said. All the pieces quietly fell into place, and she had a plan. "Where are the Lukrians?"

"They're in their safe house," Iklas said.

"I didn't know they had safe houses," Tigh said.

Iklas shrugged and raised an eyebrow at Argis and Tas.

"Only a few. They usually use the Emoran safe houses when they need one," Argis said. "Outside our borders we've always maintained a truce to keep us safe from the rest of the world."

"That explains why the Lukrians were allowed to stay at the Emoran safe house in Balderon." Tigh nodded. "So where is their safe house located?"

"On the next street over from the Emoran safe house—across the back alley, two doors down," Iklas said.

Tigh's eyebrow shot up. "That's convenient. Perfect in fact."

"You have a plan?" Argis asked.

"Yeah," Tigh said. "We can have this little mess cleaned up by sunrise."

Chapter 17

JAME READ THE simple, brilliant plans Tigh had devised for that night. She read through them three times, carefully noting Tigh's participation. She had assigned herself to do the tasks only she could do.

All right. Just calm down. At least she'll be in town doing what she does best—sneaking around.

She then looked at the second sheet of parchment. A note from Tigh. Begging Jame to understand why they decided to take Ardhat's army out that night. That she couldn't stand having this threat against Jame out there, filled with too many unknowns and uncertainties.

Jame did understand and knew what Tigh was going through. She was a little worried about her own safety after the attack in the blades shop.

She had to admit the plan was brilliant and the element of complete surprise made it as foolproof as anything could be under the circumstances. The enhancements to Ardhat's army were a potential problem. And why did Tigh think there was such a strong threat lurking in the city? Enough to call in the Lukrians to guard the safe house instead of sending them out to fight the army.

Jame had learned to trust Tigh's instincts, although she sometimes felt Tigh's protective reflex as far as Jame herself was concerned influenced that instinct. Never mind it more often than not proved right, much to her eternal thanks to Laur.

She sank into the chair in front of the fire. The noises of preparation wafted up from on downstairs. She felt . . . alone. And lonely. Worse, she felt not needed. She envisioned the combined forces of Emorans, Ynitian soldiers, former Guards, and Lukrians getting efficiently into position to do what they had all gathered there to do. To protect her and to protect Emoria.

She didn't like it. She didn't like the way she felt, being the eye of the storm, surrounded by a protective cocoon. She didn't like not being able to join in. She especially didn't like not being able to help Tigh or Argis or anyone who needed an extra hand or a fresh idea.

She knew her choice to return to Emoria to take over her duties as princess would put her in situations such as this. But she didn't know the feeling would be so . . . empty.

Slow footfalls sounded on the steps, and Jame looked back to see a dejected-looking Olet wander over to the fire.

"What's wrong?" Jame asked.

Olet sighed and lifted her arm in a sling. "They won't let me back on duty."

Jame gestured to the chair next to her. Olet sat and then slumped into the chair.

"I was just sitting here thinking how I really hate not being allowed to do anything," Jame said.

Olet turned to her in surprise. "But . . ." She looked a bit sheepish. "I was going to say, but you're our princess."

Jame returned the smile. "I enjoyed the adventure and danger that's been my life as an arbiter—that's been my life with Tigh. Even though I was getting frustrated with the arbiter part and it was suddenly a little too dangerous for me out there, I wasn't ready to give up . . . this." She waved a hand at the noise downstairs. "Tigh and I are alike in that respect. We love doing things that are on the edge of danger, of excitement. We get our thrills from taking risks to make sure what we need to get done, gets done."

"You used to love leading us on adventures when we were young," Olet said.

"I can imagine what our daughter is going to be like." Jame ruefully patted her stomach.

"She's going to be a special child." Olet shook her head. "Imagine a child with both you and Tigh in her. Wonder what she'll look like."

"According to Tigh, every Emoran queen has had blonde hair, so she's convinced our daughter will be blonde." Jame grinned. "Whatever the hair color, I hope she has Tigh's blue eyes."

"Your hair and Tigh's eyes." Olet sighed. "She'll be a heartbreaker. Of course, she'll break hearts no matter what with the two of you as parents."

"If she looks anything like Tigh, she'll have to leave Emoria just to get some peace." Jame laughed.

"Like Hekolatis," Olet said. "I love the stories about how she couldn't turn around without being challenged or being face to face with a love-sick apprentice archivist or acolyte. She must have been something."

"But she had the good sense to find her soulmate," Jame said. "Even if she came from outside of Emoria."

"You know . . ." Olet cocked her head at Jame. "While you were out there being an arbiter, you were often compared to Hekolatis."

Jame gave her an incredulous look. "We are nothing alike. She was a great warrior and battle leader. If anything, Tigh is probably more like her."

"It's not what you do, it's who you are," Olet said. "You seem to have the same . . . I don't know . . . essence. Her blood flows strongly in you, and we told and retold the stories of your adventures with the same awe and reverence we tell her stories."

Jame could only stare at her childhood friend. "You all know me, not some myth. I could see you gossiping . . ."

"Not gossip," Olet said. "Because you were out there, experiencing a world we could only imagine, you were like a myth. You and Tigh. Like you were two different people. The Jame we grew up with and Jame the peace arbiter."

"I thought I was not to be spoken of," Jame said.

"If Gindor had her way, that would have been true," Olet said. "But the day Jyac announced your decision not to accept the terms of compromise, we all went to the ceremonial circle to pray for your safety. Gindor and the Elders showed up and had us pray to Laur that you come to your senses and return to Emoria—without Tigh."

Jame rolled her eyes and shook her head.

"Jyac and Ronalyn found us." Olet straightened and captured Jame's eyes. "What she said has become legend, and we all have it memorized. This is what she said. 'You are gathered here to entreat Laur to give Jame guidance to bring her home to Emoria. I ask that you pray for a safe journey for Jame as she pursues her life outside our borders.' Then Argis stepped forward and asked, 'How can you ask us to give her our blessing? She's chosen to wander all over the place with that woman as a companion. She's going to be joined to that woman in a foreign ceremony.' Jyac responded with, 'We had a choice. We had a choice whether to bring Jame home against her will or let her decide what she wants to do with her life. Bringing her home against her will risked breaking her down emotionally or causing her to completely rebel and leave us forever. Jame is destined to be the Queen of Emoria, we must learn to trust her decisions and she must learn from her mistakes.' Then she read the last letter you sent to her."

Jame sat back as the old hurt crashed over her. She wondered if the hurt would ever completely fade. Now she had to accept that much of what she felt was based on something she carried around in her own head. She blinked back tears as she studied the crossed swords above the fireplace. "I, uh . . . I never knew that."

"Would you have come back sooner if you had?" Olet asked softly.

"I thought . . ." Jame took a calming breath. "I didn't know she had said that."

"For what it's worth," Olet said, "we thought you had all the luck. Roaming around the countryside getting into all kinds of adventures, while at the same time maintaining the peace and becoming a hero. You gave us a lot a stories to tell on long winter nights."

Jame sighed, her earlier surge of emotion ebbing quickly away. She had never heard Jyac's words, but she knew in her heart Emoria hadn't really completely turned its back on her. She had stayed away because she hadn't been ready to go back. But even if Argis hadn't come looking for her, she would have known when it was time to return and would have started the process of rejoining Emoran society with Tigh at her side.

"Thank you for telling me. I think that one sore spot in my past can now start to heal."

Olet smiled with relief. "We never lost our trust in our princess."

They sat for a while, just watching the fire lick around thick logs. The noise downstairs died away into the silence of waiting. Jame glanced at the sand clock in the corner of the chamber.

"Waiting is the hardest thing to do," she said. "I think that's what I hate the most about this. If I'm not with Tigh, I worry about her. If I can't be with her, then I need something to do to keep from spending every heartbeat in worry."

"She'll be fine," Olet said. "She's invincible."

Jame looked into Olet's steady eyes. "I've spent all these years thinking of her as being vulnerable, that, as great a warrior as she is, someone younger and faster had a chance of coming along and defeating her. Now. Nothing can hurt her. It's funny, she thought she was slowing down and losing her edge when that crazy person got her with the magic enhanced sword. She really thought she would have been able to stop the blow with her hands and feet shackled when she was enhanced. Now we know a fully enhanced Guard would have been as defenseless against that kind of attack as anyone else."

"So let's just sit here and enjoy each other's company until the others come back with enough tales to fill the nights for the rest of the winter," Olet said.

Jame smiled and settled back into the chair. She still didn't like it, but she could probably get used to it.

"I'M SURPRISED CADRYN let you come," Tigh whispered to Vorkin as they crouched in the shadows next to the stables behind the Rihnon Inn.

"She owes you and Jame her life and her livelihood," Vorkin said. "She was glad I could come and help you."

"Every time I see a scroll shop with the Cadryn and Rend insignia on the sign, I feel fortunate to have been a part of making that happen."

Vorkin grinned. "Scroll shop owners still can't believe we don't want to take over the shop, but to protect it and help support it by offering scrolls to them at a discount, so they can offer a wider selection to their patrons."

"After Jande, the idea of sharing the wealth takes time to get used to." Tigh looked up and frowned at the darkened third floor window. "Still not there. Iklas said she doesn't leave the Inn at night—probably doesn't want to bring attention to herself." She shifted her eyes to the busy tavern room.

Vorkin followed Tigh's eyes and shrugged. "She has to eat."

Tigh led the way through the shadows to the front of the Inn. She took a quick peek into one of the windows and was surprised to see Ardhat seated at a table next to a woman.

"She's in there with Ardhat," Tigh said.

"What are we going to do?"

Tigh motioned for Vorkin to follow her until they were in a clump of trees next to the Inn. Tigh straightened and brushed off her leathers. "We're going to go in and say hello to our old comrade from the Wars."

"That'll make her night," Vorkin said as they stepped out of the trees and strode to the entrance of the Inn. Fortunately, the Inn was crowded with what looked like out-of-towners, most likely vendors for the festival.

They strode into the noisy tavern room. Tigh shook her head a bit as she observed Ardhat and the wizard were not seated so they could see the door. They were also deep in a conversation muttered between bites of their evening meal.

Tight was irritated at how such novices in the art of world conquest could cause such a threat to the safety of Jame and of Emoria. At least Misner had some military sense about her—not to mention recognizing the need for personal protection. Ardhat always gave off an aura of smug invincibility. Tigh knew arrogance and stupidity were ultimately a fatal combination.

They had no problem approaching the table in the noisy crowd without Ardhat or the wizard noticing them.

"Isn't it my old friend, Ardhat." Tigh placed a hand on Ardhat's shoulder and grabbed then released the wizard's shoulder. "You remember Ardhat, don't you?"

"Of course," Vorkin said. "We so looked forward to her visits. She always had interesting commands for us."

"Tigh." Ardhat made the effort to sound amiable and twisted as much as she could under Tigh's firm grasp on her shoulder to look at her. "I was hoping we'd have a chance to talk. Reminisce about old times and all that."

"We just came in to try the local ale," Tigh said.

She and Vorkin pulled out the other two chairs at the table and sat.

Tigh nodded at Vorkin. "This is Vorkin, regiment leader under Ienor Quet."

Ardhat tight face was a study in keeping her reaction under control. "This is Nantel, my arbiter."

Tigh nodded at the thin women with gray-streaked black hair.

"It's a great pleasure to meet the infamous Tigh the Terrible," Nantel purred, giving off a greater smug confidence than Ardhat used to, if that was possible.

A server put tankards of ale in front of Tigh and Vorkin. They took a sip and nodded in appreciation.

"As talkative as ever," Ardhat said.

Tigh shrugged. "Jame's the talker in the family."

"Family," Ardhat repeated carefully. "I have to admit, I was surprised to hear you becoming a part of that . . . society."

Tigh looked up, keeping her expression innocent. "Really? You of all people would understand how at home a former Guard would feel in Emoria."

"I can't imagine what you're talking about." Ardhat's nervous glance at Nantel and to the surrounding tables gave Tigh enough of a tidbit for Jame to make her happy.

"I feel very much at home in Emoria," Tigh said, noting Ardhat's relief that she didn't follow up on her comment. "The Archives there rival those in Ynit."

"I didn't realize you liked to read," Nantel said as she tore off a piece of flatbread and dipped it into her stew.

"I'm surprised Ardhat didn't tell you most of the Guards were scholars or aspired to be scholars before they were called upon to serve the state. Vorkin, here, was an archivist in the Maymi Archives before she started working for Cadryn and Rend Scroll Shops."

Nantel's eyes widened as she took in Vorkin's muscle definition beneath the black leather-armor.

"Haven't all of you been recleansed?" Ardhat asked. "So, you don't have the need to fight anymore?"

Vorkin eyed Ardhat. "The recleansing has restored to us our joy of battle."

"But with only ordinary skills." Ardhat's disgust at the idea was apparent through her voice and her expression.

Tigh puzzled about this until she remembered Ardhat had been against cleansing the Guards . . .

Shouts in the street were followed by pounding footfalls.

Nantel's expression turned to puzzlement and then to panic as she heard what was being shouted. "Death to Emorans! Death to their princess! Death to the unnatural creatures of Laur!"

Nantel stumbled to her feet. "No." The word caught in her throat as it tightened around her fear.

Ardhat stared up at her, fear and a growing anger warring on her face. "What happened? Do something," she hissed.

"This ale is really quite excellent," Tigh said to an equally casual Vorkin.

Ardhat turned to them and stared as if they had lost their minds.

By that time, the other patrons had pushed away from their tables and gathered at the windows. Curious and bewildered by the strange people running by and shouting even stranger words.

"This is impossible," Nantel muttered. She made no effort to pretend the object she pulled out her pocket was her amulet of magic.

"You only have yourself to blame," Tigh said as she stretched out her legs and folded her arms. "Never create a spell that is cast when magic fails. You never know when you suddenly can't wield magic, and spells like that are beyond your control once cast."

"Magic . . . fail?" Ardhat's chair fell back as she stood up, spun around, and faced Nantel, who was frantically clutching and speaking to her amulet.

"This isn't possible. Magic just can't disappear like that." Nantel was almost in tears from her frustration and loss of control.

Ardhat cast accusing eyes at a relaxed Tigh. "How did you do that?"

"You have your little secrets." Tigh shrugged. "I have mine."

"You still haven't won." Nantel shook a frustrated finger at Tigh. "They weren't just ordinary people . . ."

"I know, I know." Tigh waved a bored hand. "They think they're as invincible as an enhanced Guard."

Nantel looked thunderstruck. "How did you—?"

"There's more to being invincible than bashing in skulls," Tigh said. "I think Ardhat never really understood that part of who we were."

"You think you were so good at strategy, but you only followed our command." Ardhat's anger burned through. "You were brutish killing machines without us pointing you in the right direction and telling you what to do."

"You believe that because you refused to open your eyes to see anything other than what you wanted to see," Tigh said, quietly. "You appeared, gave commands, and left us to figure out how to carry them out. We were only killing machines when we were face to face with someone who wanted to do us physical harm. Just because we were treated like we were far worse than that doesn't mean we were."

Ardhat was so angry she could only sputter.

"Do you know why I can say this with such certainty?" Tigh asked.

Ardhat glared at Tigh. "Because you, like all the rest of the Guards are delusional. You were the ones hailed as the brilliant heroes. You, who would have been mousy bookish nobodies if it weren't for us. We were the ones who developed the enhancements. We were the ones who gave the commands. We were the heroes."

"You may have built the weapon that won the Wars." Tigh sat up and slowly rose to her full height, her black leather-armor doing a fine job of revealing her lean muscular body. "But we would have lost if we followed to the word the commands you gave us. We took the most important points of what we were supposed to do and devised our own strategies to make it happen. You are right. Weapons don't win a war— the minds behind the weapons do, and the weapons you created to win the Grappian Wars had minds of their own—brilliant scholarly minds because scholars happened to fit the meek profile you needed for optimum enhancement."

"I worked closer to you than anyone. I saw you on the battlefield." Ardhat spat the words. "Animals."

"Wrong." Tigh reached out her long arm and grasped Ardhat's chin, forcing her to look into her eyes. "The reason why I can say all this with such certainty is because I was never cleansed."

Ardhat stared into Tigh's eyes as she trembled, then struggled to break free of the tight grasp on her chin.

"Look at me," Tigh ordered. "Look into my eyes. Tigh the Terrible is still there. Completely there, once I got back my desire to fight. We were not ruthless fighting machines that couldn't be stopped from killing anyone unfortunate enough to cross our paths. That was not a part of the enhancements. That was simple mind manipulation—not only to us but to the rest of the world. Convincing them we were uncontrollable monsters."

"How do you explain the fact that Vorkin here was compelled to fight every few days or else slowly lose her sanity?"

Tigh released Ardhat's chin. "That was your contribution to the cleansing program. A little spell woven into one of the spells used to mentally prepare the Guards to return to society. You were against the cleansing, and you wanted the cleansing to fail, what better way than to prove Guards would always be a threat as long as they couldn't control the impulse to fight."

Ardhat straightened. "You're making this up."

"No," Tigh said. "I had a long conversation with one of the Wizards involved in wiping all traces of the enhancements from living memory. I didn't have the impulse to fight when I went through the cleansing because the healers discovered magic had stopped working on me, so they removed the mental manipulations the old-fashioned way, by hypnosis and conventional mind therapy. In other words, they couldn't cast the spell you hid in the magic used in the cleansing process."

Vorkin wrapped her fingers around Ardhat's neck. "I may not have the strength of an enhanced Guard anymore, but I have enough strength to crush your worthless neck."

Ardhat gasped and struggled against Vorkin's angry fingers.

Tigh put a hand on Vorkin's shoulder. "Let the Tribunal cast judgment on her. Give all the other Guards a chance to see the woman who wanted to ruin our lives because she needed revenge when her ideas about cleansing were ignored."

Vorkin slowly released Ardhat's throat. "Cadryn wouldn't be pleased if I choked the life out of her. No matter how deserving."

Tigh pulled her sword from its sheath and laid it casually on her shoulder. "Now you and Nantel are going with us to the local constabulary. You think this little encounter was unpleasant. Wait till you face Jame when she insists on bringing you to trial for the wrong you did to the Guards."

Chapter 18

MAURE STUDIED THE line of soldiers shuffling in the snow in front of the cliff face. "We don't get much chance to practice in winter conditions."

"We keep our sparring fields cleared of snow in the winter." Argis cocked her head at Maure. "We might be willing to share."

"We could offer you desert training in return," Maure said.

"What about us?" Kylara turned from her inspection of her troops lined up on the other side of the Emorans. "In the past, we had to join your army to get a well-rounded training."

"And we much appreciated your presence during the Wars," Maure said. "Except you failed to tell us you were the heir to Lukria's throne."

"We don't quite have the formality of Emoria," Kylara said. "And we've never tried to usurp our history by declaring a Queen of Lukria."

"Your split from Emoria must be an interesting story," Maure said.

Argis and Kylara exchanged enigmatic looks and then chuckled wryly.

"I'm sure it is," Kylara said. "But no one can remember why we split. That's why our current truce was a rather easy achievement."

"You mean nothing is known of it? Not even some kind of legend?" Maure asked.

"Not a thing," Kylara said. "And both our countries are meticulous in writing down our histories."

"Sounds almost like a conspiracy of silence," Maure said.

Argis and Kylara almost laughed at the simple explanation.

"You know, I don't think anyone has ever thought of that," Argis said. "Keeping things secret has never been something we're particularly inclined to do."

Maure grinned. "You see. Sometimes an outsider's point of view can be good."

Argis felt a warmth against her skin and pulled her wolf head amulet out from beneath her tunic and wrapped her hand around it. "Tigh has found the Wizard."

A huge blackness opened up on the cliff face. Warriors and soldiers reached for their weapons but none of the Wizard's army seemed to be near the cave's entrance.

Argis grinned. "Looks like Tigh took care of the Wizard."

"I bet that was fun to watch," Maure said.

"I'm sure Vorkin will tell us all the details," Kylara said.

Argis released the amulet. "As predicted, a group of crazy people thinking they're invincible are headed for the safe house. Goodemer has blocked their entrance, so any fighting will be done in the square in front. She has also blocked the back ways out of these caves. Now all we have to do is let that army know we want them to come out and play."

"Shall we send a sword engraved invitation?" Kylara asked.

"Would you like to do the honors?" Argis arched an eyebrow at her former enemy.

Kylara unsheathed her sword. "With pleasure."

"Probably about a dozen warriors should be enough to get their attention," Argis said. "Considering they're suddenly possessed with the urge to fight."

Kylara grinned and strode to her line of warriors and gathered a group of them. They lit several torches and disappeared into the blackness of the cave.

"Positions," Argis shouted and felt pride when lines of soldiers, former Guards, Lukrians, and Emorans snapped into a battle-ready stance. The odd idea that she, once again, had been chosen to lead combined armies filtered through her mind. Maure and Kylara and any of the former Elite Guards had much more experience, having all been commanders during the Wars and in peacetime. Yet all turned to her when Tigh asked who would be the leader of this campaign. No argument, no discussion. She'd have to remember to ask Tigh about that when they were celebrating their victory.

The clash of swords and shouts of surprise echoed from within the cave. Torchlight illuminated the inside of the cave as the Lukrians dashed ahead of the Wizard's army. The mercenaries ran into the snow-covered valley and stopped as if they slammed against an invisible wall.

"Attack at will," Argis commanded, taking advantage of the temporary confusion from the enemy army.

They certainly hadn't expected to be face to face with the best warriors in the Southern Territories, illuminated in a circle of torches. Looking like something from their worst nightmares—or about to become the subject of nightmares for years to come.

JAME AND OLET exchanged bewildered looks at the sound of shouts and taunts outside in the square. Jame stood and Olet shot up with her hand out.

"We don't know what's going on," Olet said as she went to the shuttered window.

Jame followed her and stayed to the side of the window as Olet listened and unhooked the shutters.

Olet pulled one shutter open enough for her to look out. "What the . . . ?"

Jame, losing patience, pulled open the other shutter and squinted through the thin glass of the Emoran-style window. People were gathered in illuminated windows and doorways around the square and on the rooftop, gawking at a commotion in the square.

Jame gazed at a group of soldiers in uniforms she didn't recognize. They were shaking their weapons and shouting . . . She looked at Olet. "Are they suicidal?"

Olet could only stare in stunned disbelief. "What are they calling us?"

Jame couldn't believe the awful words coming from their mouths. "They've been possessed by a spell. You couldn't pay mercenaries enough to hurl insults against Emorans in front of a safe house."

She looked down at the front of the safe house. A group of Lukrians lounged in a tough casual way, but she knew the mercenaries wouldn't know what hit them if they tried to get closer.

The citizens seemed to see something at the other end of the square and started chattering excitedly to each other. Jame pushed the window open and shook off the chill from the frozen air. A pair of black clad warriors were walking across the square to within twenty paces of the mercenaries. They crossed their arms and studied the shouting soldiers for several heartbeats.

"The Rihnon jail is getting rather full." Tigh's voice cut through the shouts.

The mercenaries spun around, swords ready.

"But I think there's room for the lot of you for disturbing the peace."

"Let's rid this city of those filthy Emorans, and we'll stop disturbing the peace," one of the mercenaries shouted.

"I have a better idea. Let's just rid this city of the puppets of a rogue Wizard." Tigh casually ducked the first sword thrust at her, and Vorkin's sword connected with the second.

Jame shook her head. "I'm glad Tigh gets a chance to have some fun."

The Lukrians joined in the melee, and the clash of swords and joyous battle yells echoed around the square. Jame had no double the citizens of Rihnon will be talking about the battle of the Emoran safe house for generations.

"I BET YOU HAVEN'T seen a party quite like this before in here," Jame said as Pranor watched with a bemused expression as more soldiers, Lukrians, and Guards entered the over-crowded common room.

"It's better than a hearing any day," Pranor said.

"Are you sure you don't want to press suit against Ardhat?" Jame asked.

"I know what she said is not a common sentiment among outsiders," Pranor said. "So it's best not to bring continual attention to it. She will get punishment enough at the hands of the Military Tribunal."

"That she will."

Everyone turned around at boisterous shouting from the narrow corridor leading to the front door. Several women rushed into the chamber, glancing behind them.

"That's it," came a voice. "I've had it with your challenges and your name calling. Let's have it out. Right here. Right now."

"You couldn't beat a drum." A young Emoran warrior strode into the common room, only to be tackled by a soldier. Women backed into the tables, leaving them plenty of room to work things out.

The soldier grabbed hands full of the warrior's leathers and hauled her to her feet and held her there. "You don't think I can beat you?" Her voice came out like a low growl. The Emoran stared wide-eyed at her and shook her head. The soldier pulled the warrior to her and pressed her lips against the shocked warrior's mouth. The soldier then released the warrior, turned, and strode out of the establishment.

The warrior took all of two heartbeats to come back to her senses. "Hey. Wait." She ran after the soldier.

"Laur's waterfalls," Argis grumbled and opened her belt pouch. "Remind me never to wager anything with you again."

Tigh grinned and sat back. The table against the back wall allowed them to watch the activities and stay safely removed from them at the same time.

Jame leaned in front of Tigh and put her hand out for the pieces of silver. "Let's start a new tradition, since our children, including yours, Tas, will all be growing up together. Every time you warriors make a silly wager, the winnings go into a shared pot that we split between each child every winter solstice."

Tigh and Argis and Tas looked at each other and grinned.

"Good idea," Tigh said.

"Who's going to keep the pot?" Tas asked.

Jame looked thoughtful for a heartbeat. "Mularke. At least, until she ever decides to settle down and have kids."

Tas laughed. "You won't see any of us placing a wager on that."

Jame took the silver and tied it in a rag and handed it over to a decidedly drunk Mularke. "When we get home, find a safe place to put this."

Mularke nodded solemnly. "On my oath as a master archer of the sovereign country of Emoria, I'll guard this silver until the next winter solstice."

They all laughed and settled back to enjoy the festivities.

"That reminds me." Argis bent her head low to Tigh's. "Something that's been bothering me."

Tigh raised an eyebrow.

"Why did everyone let me lead the army, without argument or even a discussion?"

Tigh took a sip of her ale. "Because you're the leader of the greatest army on the continent."

Argis thought about that for a heartbeat. "Kylara could have the same claim."

"The Emoran army is larger," Tigh said. "And, by tradition, Lukria still feels like Emoria's estranged relative."

"Emoria does have the greatest army in the world right now," Argis said, voice full of wonder.

"Yes," Tigh said. "It's strange, the reason Gindor didn't want Jame to bring me to Emoria all those years ago was because she was afraid I wanted the world's greatest army to conquer the world."

"You want it?" Argis cocked her head at Tigh.

"Nope. Didn't want it then and I certainly don't want it now," Tigh said. "It's all yours to enjoy."

"WHAT IS IT about getting joined that makes warriors turn into shaking bundles of nerves?" Mularke stood in the doorway, arms crossed.

"Fear of acknowledging who's really the boss," Jame said as she entered the chamber behind Mularke.

"Would you two stop teasing and help us get dressed?" Argis's voice was strained with nervousness.

With shaky hands, Tas gratefully handed her braids to Mularke.

"You shouldn't have promised Seeran you wouldn't drink last night," Mularke said.

"Her argument was very persuasive," Tas said.

Mularke snorted. "I bet it was something about your joining night."

"As I said, very persuasive," Tas said.

"Tas knows who the boss is," Jame said as she tied each of Argis's braids onto her belt and adjusted her shoulder sash.

Argis blinked up at her, and they gazed at each other for several heartbeats.

Argis lowered her eyes the polished floor. "Funny how things work out."

"Funny and sometimes wonderful." Jame captured Argis's hand. "I'm glad we're friends and will be spending a lifetime together. That our children will most surely be as close as sisters because of the bond we have."

Argis swallowed a few times. "I thank Laur every day for your friendship and for Tigh's."

Jame blinked away tears and wrapped her arms around Argis.

Argis straightened. "I'm not too happy your child will be older than mine."

"Only by a moon or so," Jame said. "It's only fitting don't you think. Since I'm just over a moon older than you."

Tas grinned. "Laur help us if history repeats itself."

"If your daughter is anything like you, my daughter won't have a chance against her charms," Argis said.

"It'll be fun seeing them grow up together whatever happens," Jame said.

Tigh entered the chamber. "It's time."

Argis and Tas sucked in nervous breaths.

Tigh grinned. "I'll let you in on a secret. It's much better than the Ingoran ceremony. At least you get to spill a little blood."

Argis and Tas took calming breaths and nodded. Jame and Mularke grabbed their arms and pulled them into the outer chamber of the Temple. They saw Goodemer and Seeran, surrounded by excited acolytes, and stopped and stared.

Goodemer and Seeran, dressed in Emoran leathers, turned to their warriors and smiled.

"And I'm the one who gets to escort those two beautiful women out," Tigh said.

"I'm never going to survive this," Tas muttered.

Jame and Tigh laughed and wrapped their arms around each other. Nothing was more perfect than the future they saw at that very moment.

Chapter 19

"TIGH."

Tigh's eyes popped open, and she propped up on her elbow.

"It's time," Jame said.

Tigh blinked and scrambled to her feet, amidst the large cushions on the floor of the Temple birthing chamber. She helped Jame to her feet and led her to the pool with gentle cascading waterfalls at each end. She reached for Jame's sleep shirt with hands that shook so hard she couldn't grasp the material.

Jame took Tigh's hands and kissed each one and held them until the trembling was under control. "There's nothing to it."

Jame's affection and joy was a soothing balm to Tigh. "I know. I can't wait to see our daughter."

She kissed Jame and then removed both their sleep shirts. She then helped Jame into the pool of wonderfully warm water.

Tigh slipped into the pool.

Panilope ghosted into the chamber and took her place beside one of the waterfalls.

"Laur's blessing upon you," she murmured.

Jame took in several breaths as she felt the child move within her. "She's coming."

Tigh got into position and didn't have time to think as a baby floated away from Jame. She slipped her hand beneath the babe and lifted her out of the water. Both she and Jame stared in wonderment at the miracle. Light-haired and beautiful like Jame . . .

"There's another one," Panilope murmured.

Tigh and Jame stared at her.

"Another . . ." Jame felt another soul move within her.

Tigh balanced the babe on her hand and scooped the second one out of the water with the other hand. Dark-haired and beautiful . . .

Jame knew she had found Laur's chamber of everlasting joy as she beheld the sight before her. Tigh, looking bemused, joyful, and close to fainting, holding their daughters.

"We did it," Jame whispered.

Tigh held the babies out to her, and she wrapped all three in her arms.

"Twins." Tigh grinned and slipped the babies into James arms.

Eyes full of tears, Jame looked down at what she and Tigh had produced together. Two perfect little girls, each a mirror of their mothers. She blinked away her tears. "We're never going to hear the end of this from Argis, you know."

Tigh pressed her lips to the foreheads of each of her babies and gave Jame a loving kiss. "I look forward to hearing about it until our great grandchild gets so sick of it she'll challenge Argis to a fight."

The babies gurgled and waved their little fists in the air. Jame and Tigh stared at them for a heartbeat. They looked at each other, and the chamber echoed with their laughter.

T.J. Mindancer may be a figment of someone's imagination or just someone who likes to imagine she's a figment while she creates worlds for her characters to inhabit. She has spent her life working with books as an academic librarian and as an editor for two publishing companies and has had some of her scribbled words published under a couple of pen names—at least one, not a figment. Her work includes the *Tales of Emoria* series of books and shorter tales set in the Emoria world. She also likes to make up places in the real world and write about them. She lives in her Tiny House of the Dragons in Northern California.

www.ingramcontent.com/pod-product-compliance
Lightning Source LLC
Chambersburg PA
CBHW050747250626
47155CB00005B/1954